I0715507

DESOLATE

BY KELLI STORM

A Tiny Fox Press Book

© 2025 Kelli Storm

All rights reserved. No part of this book may be reproduced, stored in a retrieval system, or transmitted in any form or by any means, electronic, mechanical, photocopying, recording, or otherwise, without the prior written permission of the publisher, except as provided by U.S.A. copyright law. For information address: Tiny Fox Press, Parrish, FL.

This is a work of fiction: Names, places, characters, and events are a product of the author's imagination or used fictitiously. Any resemblance to actual persons, living or dead, locales, or events is purely coincidental.

Cover art by Damonza

ISBN 978-1-946501-76-9

Library of Congress Control Number: 2025944569

Tiny Fox Press and the book fox logo are all registered trademarks of Tiny Fox Press LLC

Tiny Fox Press LLC
Parrish, FL

Dedicated to my mom and dad. And to my friend, Sarah. This book wouldn't have happened without you.

CHAPTER 1

For the record, Mia Walker didn't *mean* to poison Kurt.

The incident in question happened during their lunch break. Ella Stafford and Kurt Taulson were sucking each other's lips like they were going for some kind of Olympic medal. Mia kept her eyes focused on her veggie sandwich, shoving black olives back between the slices of bread before they could dribble onto the dirty cafeteria table. She did her best to ignore the saliva fest happening in the seats across from her.

Ella and Mia had agreed to meet during lunch to finalize their plans for the following weekend. Mia's favorite indie band, Hazy Dawn, was coming to town. For the past two months, they'd planned on going to the concert.

One month ago, the school's basketball star, Kurt, asked Ella out. Ever since, it'd been: *Sorry Mia, I can't hang out tonight, Kurt wants to go get dinner,* and *sorry Mia, I can't see that movie with you, Kurt said he might want to see it with me.*

The real irony was that it was Saturday, and she was at school. She was subjected to Kurt enough during the regular school week. But a bunch of her classmates had gathered to decorate the gym for prom, and she'd let Ella talk her into participating in school spirit.

Her friend let out a little giggle, drawing Mia's gaze. She regretted looking. Kurt was now nibbling on Ella's ear. Mia's eye twitched.

It was her fault really. Right around the time Kurt asked Ella out, Mia realized she'd stupidly fallen in love with her best friend. At first, she assumed her dislike for Kurt was because he was an obnoxious tool. He'd always been that way since elementary school.

Then she figured she was jealous of Kurt taking so much of Ella's time, because for so long, it had been just them and their friend, Colby Mond. Once they hit high school though, Colby started hanging out with people much cooler than them. It hurt to lose him. It was gut wrenching to watch Ella drift away. Mia didn't do well with losing people.

That still didn't pinpoint why she disliked Kurt so much, so she determined she was jealous that Ella had found someone to date and she hadn't. Granted, there weren't many openly queer people at school for her to choose from, but surely *someone* could see a little potential in her. She wasn't tall and slim like Ella was, with cheekbones that would make a model jealous and flowing brown hair that always smelled like honeysuckle. Mia was short and curvy, with black hair and deep brown eyes. She would never win any beauty contests, but she wasn't hideous.

But that still didn't give her a satisfying reason as to why she was so upset about Ella and Kurt, so she decided she was developing heartburn, and that was why she felt sick whenever they were together. But the truth was far more horrifying than something she could treat with one of her aunt's potions.

The simple fact was that she had fallen in love with Ella.

The couple had gone back to kissing again. Mia glanced impatiently at the clock in the cafeteria. Their break from smothering the gym in crepe paper was almost over, and they still hadn't discussed their plans. She pointedly cleared her throat loudly.

Kurt and Ella's mouths sounded like a pair of vacuums sucking in air as they broke apart.

Her best friend looked over at her in annoyance. "What?"

There was a smear of lipstick at the corner of her mouth. Kurt began to twist a strand of her long, brown hair between his fingers. When he moved his hand away to pick up his energy drink, her hair stuck out at a weird angle. She looked ridiculous and beautiful at the same time. Mia's heart *ached*.

"Sorry, a piece of olive went down wrong," she muttered. The pair started drifting toward one another again, so she quickly interjected, "El, are we going to talk about next weekend? When do you want to meet up? What are you going to wear?"

"Next weekend?" Ella looked at her like she didn't have a clue what she was talking about. Mia took a deep breath to control her temper.

"Yeah. The Hazy Dawn concert."

"Oh...that." She gave her boyfriend an unsure look.

"The thing is, Walker," Kurt said in that cocky, *I-think-I'm-the-shit*, tone. "My brother works at Salem Willows Park. He got us front row passes. You understand, right?"

Mia's fingertips began to warm, which was never a good sign. Her hands formed into fists. Her Aunt Tilly lectured her all the time about this very thing.

You're a powerful witch, Mia. You need to practice controlling your energy.

Powerful? Highly debatable.

Her aunt was powerful. Her grandma was a legend. Mia fumbled with her magical energy all the time—her A.D.H.D. making it nearly impossible to use it correctly.

But as she stared at the couple across from her—hurt and betrayal turning her stomach into acid—she did her best to control the power suddenly surging inside her.

Through gritted teeth, she said, "I thought we were going together."

Ella gave her a look that was a cross between begging and exasperation. "Come on, Mia. It's our five-week anniversary. You know that's important."

"No. What I understand is that we made plans to go together, and now you're canceling on me. Again!"

"Jesus, chill out." Kurt looked at Ella and rolled his eyes.

To Mia's fury, she giggled. Mia uncurled her fists and laid them flat on the table, glaring at Kurt.

The abandoned lunch bag on the table next to theirs began to vibrate.

"Let's get out of here," Kurt said.

He picked up Ella's hand and kissed it. She smiled back, a sweet blush appearing on her cheeks. And just like that, Mia knew her best friend forgot all about her.

Anger raced through her. Her fingers went from feeling warm to feeling like she'd touched a livewire. Her dark eyes blazed at Kurt.

You make me sick.

A bluish hue formed around her nailbeds. It lasted only a millisecond but that was all it took.

He smiled as he moved towards Ella again for one more kiss.

BELCH.

Ella pulled back with a look of disgust. "What the hell! Do you mind not burping in my face?"

"Sorry," he said. "I don't know what—"

Another loud rumble erupted from him. Some classmates from a few tables over started laughing. Kurt's face turned red. Mia stared at her fingers in shame, doing her best to ignore the erupting chaos around her.

"Kurt, stop!" Ella looked around in embarrassment. Her eyes narrowed as they landed on Mia, who quickly tried to look as innocent as possible.

"I ..." He slapped a hand over his mouth before turning swiftly in his chair. With another large belch, he threw up on the floor.

Ella shrieked, jumping out of her seat to avoid the projectile vomit. She landed on the table, sitting on her pudding cup. It splashed all over in a wave of chocolate congealed corn syrup.

Her hand flew to her mouth as she turned her head, making gagging noises like she was going to throw up, too. Everyone in the cafeteria was watching at this point, their faces varying between revulsion and laughter. A few phones popped out to record the scene.

"What is wrong with you?" Ella asked, her voice muffled by her hand.

"I don't know, I—" Kurt threw up again.

Mia's conscience reared its ugly head. She hadn't meant to make him sick, let alone this *sick*. The janitor shuffled over with a mop, looking disgruntled.

Keeping her head turned away from the mess, Ella wrapped her arm around Kurt's waist. "We need to get you some help. I think Mackenzie's mom is in the gym. She's a nurse."

They stumbled away from the table, but not before she shot Mia a look of pure venom. As they left, people noticed the big brown chocolate stain covering the backside of her jeans. Another loud wave of laughter echoed around the room as the pair hurried out the exit.

Mia's stomach stirred sickly and not just because of the smell of vomit. It wasn't common knowledge that she was a witch. Sure, when they were kids, Ella always made her be the witch when they reenacted the Salem Witch Trials. They lived in Salem,

Massachusetts. Playing "witch" was a part of their childhood, but she never told Ella she actually was one.

As much as she resented Kurt, Mia hadn't meant to hurt him. She didn't go around doing that to people, no matter how much of an ass they were. But as usual, she lost focus of her energy and things got out of hand. Her Aunt Tilly would kill her when she found out.

Though no matter how guilty she was currently feeling, she was still so unbelievably pissed at Ella. It had nothing to do with her heartache over loving someone who would never see her the same way. Ever since Kurt entered their lives, her best friend had turned into a complete pod person. He brought out a side to her that Mia didn't know existed. One that was selfish and inconsiderate and so unlike the girl she loved.

Mia looked at the faux wood table covered in pudding, the air thick with the stench of vomit, and decided she'd had enough of school spirit for the day. She got up from her chair on weakened limbs—hexes did that to witches her age—and left the cafeteria. The scent of the hallway's lemon polished floor made for a welcome change as she trekked her way toward her locker.

"Mia! Hey, Mia! Wait up."

She closed her eyes briefly but stopped walking as Colby caught up to her. Back when the three of them were close, Colby often acted as the voice of reason for their trio. But once they entered high school, he joined the soccer team and became their star player. With his newfound success came instant popularity and a new friend group. They were all still technically friends, but they didn't hang out like they used to.

It was really too bad. Considering that Salem was a hotbed for Others—creatures from the supernatural world—Mia and Colby were the only two Others at their school, though he was a werewolf.

"Hi," she said. She wished she could talk to him like they used to. Aside from Aunt Tilly, Colby was the only other person who knew she was a lesbian. She never told him about her crush on Ella though. She could just picture what he'd say.

Yeah, you have no shot there. You know that, right?

Ugh...she wanted to go home.

"I saw what happened in the cafeteria," he said.

Mia stared at a poster on the wall behind him featuring candidates for prom court. Of *course*, Ella and Kurt were on it. "Oh?"

"You need to be more careful," He pushed a wayward strand of his shoulder length, chestnut brown hair away from his face. "I don't want you to get in trouble with the Assembly," he continued, lowering his voice as he mentioned the government body who ruled over the Other world.

Mia lifted her chin, meeting his eyes—or what she could see of them anyway. Somewhere in Colby's family line, a werewolf mated with a human. He had inherited their colorblindness, and he wore dark shades designed to help him see color.

"I can take care of myself," she told him, her tone short.

"I'm just trying to help. You're one of my oldest friends—"

"Friends?" she said in a scathing tone. "Are we friends anymore, Colby?"

He blanched, his mouth twisting down. "How can you ask that?"

"When was the last time we actually hung out?"

"Hey Mond!"

A group of his friends were coming their way. As he turned to look over his shoulder, Mia took that as her cue to leave. She turned to walk away.

"Mia, wait—" Colby said. She paused and he continued, "Let's catch up soon, okay? We can meet at the doughnut shop tomorrow. What do you say?"

Her heart warmed slightly. The two of them used to take swimming lessons together when they were kids. They'd always go to the doughnut shop in town afterwards and get strawberry jelly doughnuts—their favorite.

She nodded. "Yeah, okay."

His face morphed into relief. "Great, because aside from hearing what's new with you, there's something I want to talk to you about. I've been getting this weird feeling lately that I'm being fol—"

His friends caught up to them, slapping him on the shoulder, ignoring Mia as they always did. She waved at him, but he didn't see, already too busy joking around with his fellow jocks.

When she finally reached her locker, she twisted the combination tiredly. She felt so drained, and not only because she accidentally used some of her magical energy to hex Kurt. All she needed was her jacket and she could get out of there. Mia started to open the door when someone came up and slammed it shut. She gave a startled jump and glanced to see who was next to her.

Ella glared back. "What did you do to Kurt?"

"What are you talking about?" she asked, playing dumb.

"He felt fine until he sat at the table with us. Now, he has food poisoning. People don't get food poisoning out of nowhere, Mia."

"Did he eat the mystery meat out of the vending machine?" She began working on her locker combination again.

Ella grabbed her hand in a grip that hurt. "He didn't eat anything today, not even breakfast. I know you did something."

"How the hell could I give Kurt food poisoning? You said it yourself, he didn't eat anything today."

"Are you seriously trying to play innocent with me?"

Mia yanked her hand free. "When did you get so paranoid?"

Her friend took a step toward her, invading her personal space. "You don't think I pay attention? I know you. You do things other people can't. Like make objects levitate—don't think I didn't see that at our sleepover in ninth grade. Or how about the time you couldn't find your car keys, and they magically appeared next to you."

"You're crazy," Mia whispered. She started to walk away—to hell with her jacket—when Ella grabbed her arm.

"I'm not done yet—"

"You've said enough." Mia pivoted to face her best friend. She looked pointedly down at where she still held onto her. "If I have powers like you're suggesting, you should let go of me before I do something you'll regret."

Ella dropped her arm like it burned, and Mia spun around, hurrying down the hallway and out of the school. Her eyes burned as she headed toward Gallows Hill Park. It was a little out of her way to get home, but less touristy than some of the other routes she had to choose from. She didn't want to see anyone right now. Her emotions were all over the place after her conversations with her friends.

How could Ella treat her like that? They'd been friends since kindergarten. How many times in the past two months had Ella canceled plans on her? It was like Mia didn't matter to her anymore. She felt as though she wasn't just losing the girl she loved. She was losing her best friend. It broke her heart in more ways than one.

A light breeze carrying the sea air from Salem Harbor helped return strength to Mia's limbs, still weak from the hex. Air was part of the five elements that young witches used to regain their energy after performing witchcraft. A nice blast of wind could go a long way in helping a witch regain power.

A crowd of tourists stepped in her way and Mia slowed down her pace. She really missed her car. It was a 1985 Ford Tempo handed down to her by her aunt. The car had continued on long past its prime. The transmission finally blew a couple of weekends ago and no amount of spell work could fix it. Her aunt had started mentioning the dreaded "B" word the other day. Mia argued that no self-respecting high school upperclassman rode the bus. Her aunt merely smiled before handing her the bus's schedule.

As she continued walking, she felt a familiar unease, one she always got whenever she went by the house near the corner of Cecilia Raillive Dr. Tourists didn't know the story about the teenage girl murdered there in the early 1990s, and locals didn't like to talk about it.

The girl was one of several killed in Salem around that time, though she'd been the only Common—*human*. The rest were Others, their murders covered up by the Assembly. No one had lived in the home for years.

Despite Mia's apprehension, she felt drawn to the house. She always had. It was as though an invisible string tied her to the structure, tugging her toward it when she tried to resist. Even now, she felt the bond, nagging at her spine.

With a weary sigh, she gave into the pull. She paused in front of the home, putting her hands on two of the worn wooden fence pickets that bordered the yard. The house had probably been pretty at one time. Most homes in Salem were, with that old New England charm. Now it was an eyesore that neighbors filed complaints against, but no one ever did anything about.

Weathered shutters hung crookedly from broken windows. Faded gray paint chipped away on the home's siding. The roof sagged in the center. It looked like one strong gale would bring the whole thing down. In the yard next to the house was a tall, oak tree. It looked sicker every time she saw it. A lopsided tire lay at its trunk, half of the rubber covered in weeds. A frayed rope that once supported the tire swing swayed back and forth in the breeze.

Mia's hands tightened on the fence. While the five elements gave witches their life-energy, there was also energy in the world that Others stayed away from. Dark energy created from all that was wrong with the world.

There was dark energy in this house. She could see it leaking through the broken windowpanes, crawling towards her as though intending to grab her and pull her inside. Every time she walked by the place, the darkness seemed to get worse.

The energy swirled across the lawn, turning the air visible and slightly blurry. It was hypnotizing to watch, but as it got closer, the smell of something rotten reached Mia's nose, like roadkill left out in the sun too long. It was the stench of death. She took a quick step back. It wasn't in time to stop the energy from brushing against her hand. Her fingers turned icy at the contact and her eyes closed against her will.

She could hear the girl's terrified screams. A hand shot through the darkness toward Mia, desperately seeking help.

"No! Please stop!" her voice cried out before it cut off with a wet whimper.

The squelching sound of a knife slicing through flesh burst inside Mia's ears, making her want to cover them to block out the sickening noise. She could see blood splattering over walls, body parts appearing inside a large pentagram. A finger...a toe...

The girl's body crystalized behind Mia's closed lids, her face turned away from her, her hair covering her lifeless features. She lay on a giant circular table. There was a bloody hole in her chest cavity. Her heart was missing. Nothing remained but bloody remnants.

A light gust of wind touched Mia's face, breaking the hold the house had on her. With a sharp gasp, her eyes flew open, and the image disappeared. The dark energy pulsed in front of her, pressing against the fence. Unable to get past the property's borderline, it slowly receded back into the house.

On shaking legs, Mia turned and hurried away without a backward glance.

CHAPTER 2

The scent of mixed herbs and spices greeted Mia as she entered her family's shop, *Fitzgerald's Tea & Gifts*. She headed toward Tilly's office, waving at Joe, her aunt's part-time employee, as she went.

She could hear her aunt speaking. "Try adding a dash of crushed mugwort to the pills, but if the signs are there, there's not a lot more you can do ..."

Tilly was sitting behind her antique, ash wood desk, her frizzy, reddish-brown hair piled into a messy bun on top of her head. There were dark circles under her eyes, like she hadn't slept well the night before, and tension lines around her mouth. She'd been looking like this for the past few weeks, but her aunt always brushed Mia off when she expressed concern, stating she was simply busy at the shop.

Tilly's phone rested between her shoulder and head as she drummed her fingers against the large calendar that lay across the flat surface of the desk. There were three large red circles around the day's date. Her aunt had written *lunar eclipse* inside the inner circle. She frowned when she noticed Mia standing there.

"Let me know if you need more ordered. It's not a problem," Tilly told her caller. Her chair creaked loudly as she leaned back. "Sounds good. Say hello to Henry for me." Her aunt disconnected the call and stared at Mia expectantly.

"Is that the tricky customer in Michigan again?" Mia asked, trying to avoid the awkward conversation she knew was coming.

Tilly didn't bother to respond. She crossed her arms over her chest and gave Mia an expectant look. "I thought you were helping out at school."

"Oh...that ..."

Her aunt let out a deep breath as though it came from the depths of her soul. "What happened?"

Mia put on her most angelic expression. "Why does anything have to have happened? Maybe I just missed you."

"Mia ..."

She knew that wouldn't work. Turning away from her aunt, she walked over to some shelves that contained supplies for Tilly's potions. One glassy blue jar read *mistletoe – don't consume.* Another smaller, clear jar contained the eyeballs of newts according to the label.

"I'm waiting," Aunt Tilly reminded her.

"What do you use eyeballs of newts for? That's disgusting."

"Mia!" The tone in her aunt's voice didn't allow for any more evasiveness.

"Fine." She threw her hands in the air in defeat. "I might have lost my temper and given Kurt Taulson food poisoning."

Her aunt's eyes narrowed. "Does this have something to do with Ella?"

Mia glared at the floor. "She backed out of seeing Hazy Dawn with me because Kurt got them front row tickets. She's going with him instead and acted like I should be fine with it. She doesn't even like Hazy Dawn!"

"That doesn't mean you go around poisoning classmates."

"I didn't mean to," Mia stated tightly. She already felt guilty enough without Tilly adding to her shame spiral.

"Did anyone see you?" her aunt asked, frustration making her tone sharp.

"Just Colby. It was a quick burst of energy. It happened before I knew what was going on."

"I've told you. You need to learn control, learn patience, bef—"

"Before I kill someone. I know," Mia muttered.

She scuffed her shoe across the willow design imbedded in the office's wood floor. Most witches had a willow tree carved onto some surface of their home. It was to honor Hecate. Commons thought Hecate was associated with Greek Mythology. They didn't know that the gods and goddesses were real. But they weren't gods. They were Originals—the founders of the supernatural world who ascended from an alternative earth that mirrored Mia's own. Hecate was the creator of the witch race, hence the reason witches honored her by placing her most sacred tree somewhere in their houses.

"Look." Aunt Tilly pinched the bridge of her nose with her fingers. "You and Ella are getting older. Things aren't always going to be the same between you. She has a boyfriend now. Someday you'll find a girl who'll return your feelings—"

"Stop, please." Like Mia needed it pointed out how hopeless her feelings for her friend were.

"I worry about you. You fall in love too hard and too fast. It's almost as though ..."

"What?" she asked when her aunt hesitated.

Tilly let out a quiet breath. "Sometimes I wonder if you fall headlong because you feel like something's missing in your life."

"Nothing is missing," Mia grumbled, hating where this conversation was going.

"I just mean because your parents aren't her—" she started to say.

The jar of newt eyes next to Mia started vibrating, shaking so hard it bounced off the shelf, heading straight for the floor. Her aunt waved her hand, and the jar froze in midair before floating slowly back to its spot.

"Mia, you *really* need to focus your energy." Her aunt didn't continue with her other train of thought. "What if you'd killed that boy today? We don't need the Assembly here. I doubt Parris will spare you even if we are related to him."

Doyle Parris was chancellor of the witch community and a distant cousin of theirs. He was also an incredible dickhead.

"But I can't focus. Remember?" Mia tapped on her temple for emphasis.

"Stop using your A.D.H.D. as an excuse," Aunt Tilly said, knowing exactly what Mia was getting at. "You're a bright, powerful witch. You don't know how powerful you ar—"

She scoffed. "Whatever."

"You know." Her aunt stared her down, which was impressive considering she was still sitting. "You've gotten really disrespectful lately. I never used to talk to my parents the way you talk to me."

"Well, you aren't my parent, are you?" Mia snapped her jaw shut, knowing she'd gone too far.

Tilly's body stiffened in hurt anger. Awkward silence filled the room for several painful seconds as Mia's hideous words hung between them. When she finally spoke, her voice was calm but cool. "Since you have some extra time on your hands, you can go ahead and run the register in the store until closing."

"Aunt Tilly, I'm sor—"

"Go!"

Her aunt got up from her desk chair and walked through the beaded curtains that hid her workshop. Mia watched the strands sway, the beads making clacking noises as they hit against each other. She wanted to try and apologize again, but she knew Tilly wouldn't be in the mood to hear it. She slowly moved toward the stairs leading to the living quarters above the store.

She shouldn't have said that. Tilly had raised Mia since her father died in a freak boating accident, and her mom left soon after to go "find herself." Whatever the hell that meant.

It's your fault he's dead.

Mia's shoulders hunched. For as long as she could remember, she'd been haunted by a memory. She didn't even know if it was real. It was stupid and irrational, but she sometimes felt as though she were to blame for her dad's death. She'd only been three when he died, too young to have been able to stop him from getting on that boat, but children coped with loss in different ways. For Mia, it was guilt over events she couldn't control.

Guilt was something she excelled at. She felt it heavily now. In the span of an hour, she'd made three of the most important people in her life upset with her, though at least she'd be able to make it up with Colby when they met the next day.

As she turned away from her aunt's workroom, Mia wondered what Tilly was working on. Probably some brilliant spell that she had no chance of copying. Her aunt's spell work was famous. Her tonics and charms were the main sources of revenue for their shop. Supernatural beings from across the world sought Tilly's help.

Mia was a realist. She was never going to be as good of a witch as the other members in her family. She couldn't follow the simplest of spells and constantly struggled to focus on anything. She was a mediocre witch at best.

When she reached the top of the stairs leading to their living area, she paused to pet her brindle pit bull, Winnie, who lay in the hallway. After giving her dog some love, she dragged herself down the hall, passing her grandma's closed bedroom door, the soft sounds of a Broadway musical playing from within.

Mia entered her own room. With a wave of her hand, her logoed work shirt and a pair of khakis flew from the closet and hit her in the chest. As soon as she'd come into her powers at thirteen, Tilly had shown her how to use her life energy to do several spells, including moving objects. Her aunt made her practice over and over again. While she'd hated the repetition at the time, she was grateful to her. Using her energy to move things was one of the few spells Mia mastered.

Grumbling to herself, she changed into her work clothes. Hating everything about the day, she accepted her fate and went down to the store with her head held high.

This was Mia's version of hell. The only people who shopped in this part of the store were Common tourists who wanted to have that authentic Salem gift—tarot cards (made in China) and crystal balls (made in Taiwan). It was the perfect punishment for Mia mouthing off. She poured a cup of lavender and orange tea from the store's French press and sat on the stool behind the counter, counting the minutes until closing. The shop's part time worker, Joe, ignored her as he studied his medical textbooks. Macklemore's "Thrift Shop" blasted from his iPhone 5, which sat on the counter next to him.

"Hey," she said. He grunted in return.

Joe was part gnome. He was tall for his kind at four feet four inches" and had lucked out by not inheriting his mother's pointy ears—he was able to blend in with Common society. Most Others avoided Commons, never quite sure how to act around them without revealing their powers or the supernatural world. There were some exceptions, families like Mia's and Colby's. The Monds made a living off Commons by selling recyclable items they found thrown in the woods.

Joe wanted to be a Common doctor. Mia wished him luck. Everyone should aspire to do something with their lives.

She wished she knew what she wanted to do, but she had no clue what would happen once she graduated high school. The luckiest Others were invited to intern at the Assembly, allowing them to start a career in the government, which opened a lot of doors. But she doubted they'd want her—not with her disability. The supernatural world expected perfection in their kind. Mia's learning disability was the opposite of that, which often led to Others like her being outcast.

"They're hypocrites," Aunt Tilly muttered more than once on the subject. "Too busy looking down on people to recognize what's right in front of them. Don't they know what makes people different is what makes them special? Your disability is a gift, Mia. Someday you'll realize that."

Mia always tuned her out at that point. Being stuck in the lowest reading groups at school and having to get tutors to help with basic math wasn't a gift. It was embarrassing. She'd probably end up exactly where she was. Serving tea and giving directions to lost Commons. With that depressing thought lingering in her head, she mentally began to prepare for a long afternoon in the shop.

Tourists came and went throughout the rest of the day, asking which talisman necklace would bring them better luck and why the crystal balls in the shop were so expensive. By the time five in the evening rolled around, Mia was ready to tear her hair out. The bell above the store door rang and a familiar girl entered. Mia's mood immediately brightened.

Ailsa Harper was a local who bought so much tea from their store, Mia often wondered if she was a caffeine addict. She was around her age but went to Cunningham, the fancy private school down the road. Despite the difference in schools, the two had become friendly over the past year. They weren't at the braiding each other's hair stage yet, but Mia wouldn't have minded if they became better friends. She just couldn't picture the other girl wanting the same thing.

Ailsa was everything Mia was not. She was tall, blonde, and so ridiculously beautiful, Mia often wondered if she might be fae.

"What smells so good?" Ailsa asked once she reached the counter.

Mia gestured toward her empty cup. "The flavor of the day is lavender and orange. Want some?"

The girl shook her head. "I can't. I just came here to buy some of the citrus mint."

That wasn't surprising. Ailsa had an aversion to any of their teas that had sugar in it—which was probably why she looked like a supermodel. The citrus mint was a safe option.

"Sure." Mia went over to the tea canisters and pulled down the pre-made blend.

"You, um, you look nice today," Ailsa said. "Is that a new shirt?"

She let out a snort, before looking down at her clean but worn work shirt. "What? This old thing? It's the same one I always wear."

She could feel Ailsa's eyes on her, watching her work. "Is everything okay?"

"Sure," Mia said. "Why?"

"You seem upset."

That was the other thing about her. Her uncanny way of always being able to read Mia. It was another reason she wondered if the girl had some Other blood in her.

Mia packaged the tea leaves and gave Ailsa her order. "It's been a long day."

She nodded and paid, but instead of leaving, she lingered, gnawing on her lip. Mia couldn't help but stare at her. For the hundredth time, she tried to figure out the color of Ailsa's eyes. Aquamarine? Ocean blue?

Remembering her job, she asked, "Was there something else you needed?"

The other girl clenched and unclenched her fingers around the paper bag storing her tea.

"No, I'm good." She started to turn away but stopped. Mia raised her eyebrows expectantly.

"So, uh ..." Ailsa said. "Did you hear Hazy Dawn is coming to town this weekend?"

"Yeah, I heard that." Her mood immediately soured.

"You like that band, right?"

"I did."

"I-I thought you still liked them." Ailsa's eyes traced the large Wiccan pentacle hanging on the wall behind Mia's shoulders. "I was wondering if you planned on going."

Mia frowned. She could just imagine running into Ella and Kurt. No freaking thank you. "I'd rather set myself on fire."

"Oh ..." The girl gave a smile that looked more like a grimace. Even with that uncommon expression popping on her face, it didn't detract from her beauty. She waved her crinkled paper bag. "Thanks for the tea."

With that, she turned and left the store, her long blonde hair swishing behind her.

"Hmph," Joe snarked from the corner where he was *still* reading.

"What?" Mia asked, feeling defensive for no reason.

"That's the thing about gnomes. Our eyes can see much more clearly than witches can apparently."

"What's that supposed to mean?"

He didn't answer her. He simply turned a page in his medical book instead of doing anything remotely work related.

Muttering to herself, Mia grabbed a cloth and began wiping down the countertops.

Honestly, sometimes Mia didn't understand why Tilly kept him around.

Chapter 3

After the store closed and Joe left for the evening, Mia restocked the shelves while keeping an ear out for her aunt. She hoped that if Tilly saw her hard at work, she might be able to get back into her aunt's good graces. It eventually got to the point, however, where she could no longer ignore the hunger pains in her stomach, and she strode to the backroom.

She could hear her aunt moving around in her workshop, the scent of chicory permeating the air. She was probably preparing a batch of her world-famous chicory cookies for the upcoming Wolf Trials, which was the Others' version of the Olympics. One bite could help Others travel great distances.

The one time Mia tried to help her make the cookies, she accidentally sent their stove to Antarctica. Thankfully, Tilly was able to track it down before the Assembly or any Commons noticed. She returned it to its spot, though it always felt a bit colder to the touch these days.

As Mia walked up the stairs to their living area, she felt a pang of remorse as she remembered her fight with Colby from earlier. She shouldn't have been so short with him. He didn't deserve it. Especially considering he was only looking out for her. She wondered what he was going to say before his friends interrupted them.

She wished they could get back to the way they used to be. Ella wouldn't forgive her for today, and Mia wasn't feeling too kindly toward her right then either. It'd be nice to have her other best friend back. Sometimes she felt so alone.

After finishing her extravagant meal consisting of nothing but instant Ramen noodles, Mia fed Winnie her evening meal before deciding to stop by her grandma's room. She knocked on the door as a courtesy, knowing there'd be no answer. When she entered the bedroom, she saw one of Tilly's spells in action as a bag of fluid flew through the air before hovering by an IV stand next to the bed. The empty bag of fluid currently in place disconnected from the IV and the fresh bag attached itself. The old bag fell into the waste bin below.

Mia walked over and patted her grandma's arm. The frail person lying in bed didn't acknowledge her. It was heartbreaking to see the once vibrant woman in a vegetative state, but no amount of Common medicine or witchcraft could slow down the cruel progression of Alzheimer's. And it wasn't for a lack of trying. Tilly had run herself ragged trying spell after spell to reverse the disease until Mia's grandma, in one of her more lucid moments, told her to stop. Mia would never forget that sad smile of acceptance on her face.

When her memory got too bad, the Assembly came to their door. A witch who struggled to recognize family from Commons was a danger, and they drained her grandma of the essence that made her a witch. It was one of the most depressing things Mia had ever witnessed.

She moved so that she could lay next to her grandma on the king size bed. She took in the familiar dark flowered wallpaper that her grandma had put on the walls before she was born. It matched the scratchy floral bedspread that covered her grandma. When her grandma was still healthy, Mia would snuggle up to her on the same comforter, listening to Grandma Eabha tell her the stories of their witch ancestors. She missed those times with her grandma so much.

West Side Story hummed from the TV in the corner of the room, the soft music of "Tonight" playing gently on the speakers. It was one of her grandma's favorite movies. Mia had seen it enough times over the years she could quote it by heart.

As she watched Maria and Tony sing sweet nothings to each other, she couldn't help but think cynically of the two. The pair had fallen instantly in love when their eyes met at a dance. And what did it get them in the end? Devastation and heartbreak.

Then again, maybe it was more realistic than Mia always thought. If the movie taught her anything, it was that love wasn't worth the heartache. Ella had shown her that.

Her eyes drifted over to the bedside table next to her grandma. A vase of aster flowers stood there. As part of her training, Tilly had made her practice protection spells on the blossoms. She had blown up multiple bundles of flowers before she finally mastered a small version of the spell. She had pushed her energy out and thought, *you'll never wilt.* Ten months later, and the flowers were still going strong.

Next to the vase was a picture of her grandparents with their two daughters, Tilly, and Mia's mom, Sadie. She reached over her grandma to grab the picture. As she lay back down, she stared at her mom.

Sadie had been beautiful back then with gorgeous red hair and light blue eyes. Her skin resembled porcelain. If Mia closed her eyes hard enough, she could almost hear the light lithe of her mom's voice, smell the scent of her perfume. But she didn't want to do that.

Because Sadie had been an awful parent, putting her own grief of losing her husband above the wellbeing of her daughter. She'd abandoned Mia without a second thought, leaving her sister to raise her only child. She hadn't tried to make contact since. So, to hell with her. Mia put the frame down on the table with a little more aggression than she should have, sending her grandma an apologetic look.

Lying back down, she grabbed Grandma Eabha's hand. "I really messed up with Aunt Tilly today. And Ella...and Colby."

She peered at her grandma, hoping for some sign of life. She could really use her advice right now. But there was no change. Mia didn't let go of her hand as she continued to watch the movie, pretending that for just a moment, everything was okay, and her grandma was alert and happy. As the melody drifted over her, she closed her eyes briefly. The strain of the day hit her before she knew it, and she tumbled into sleep as Maria and Tony exchanged their vows to each other.

The sound of loud sobbing jolted Mia awake. She looked over at the TV, where Maria was now crying over Tony. But that wasn't where the noise was coming from. With a wave of her hand, the TV muted itself. The sound of crying continued to echo through the room. She got up from the bed and hurried into the hallway. The crying only got worse.

Being as quiet as possible, Mia tiptoed over to the large air vent in the hallway, which ran from the floor to halfway up the wall. Their home was old and hardly soundproof, and the venting system did little to hide private conversations. Tilly always said she'd get around to casting a spell on them to block out noisy eavesdroppers—this, she said looking pointedly at Mia—but she never got around to it.

As she pressed her ear against the cold metal grate, she heard a familiar voice that made her heart speed up.

"He's gone, Tilly," Colby's mom cried. "His whole room reeks of dark energy, and we can't get a scent of him. Please, you have to help us."

"I will." Her aunt's normally calm voice showed a hint of worry. "I'll start working on a locator spell immediately and see if I have any luck."

"This is just like before when Others disappeared out of their homes in the middle of the night," his mom said, panicked. Their voices dimmed as they moved towards the home's side entrance. Mia strained to hear them. "And you know what happened to them. They were all found dead! I can't have that happen to my baby boy. I—"

Mia jerked her head away. A cold sweat broke over her body and she began to shiver. Something had happened to Colby. He was missing—kidnapped. She ran down the stairs to find her aunt shutting the door behind Colby's mom as the other woman left their shop. She turned to face Mia, her face grim.

"Colby's missing," Mia stated, knowing it was true by her aunt's expression.

"Yes," Aunt Tilly responded anyway.

"What can we do?"

Her aunt rushed over to her. "I need you to stay calm and do nothing."

"But's it's Colby!" she pleaded anxiously. "We got into a fight today, but he still asked to meet with me tomorrow. He had something he wanted to tell me. I need to find him! What if—"

She couldn't finish what she wanted to say. She didn't dare voice all the possibilities of what could happen to him.

"Mia." Aunt Tilly clasped her cheeks in her hands. "What I need is for you to go to your room and stay there. Don't do any magic. Don't try to help." Mia had never seen her aunt look so serious.

"But—" she tried anyway.

"No. If something or someone is going after Others, I need you to stay safe. Promise me you won't try anything."

Mia brushed away a tear that escaped from her eye. She didn't want to promise that. One of her friends was missing. How could she not help?

"I need to focus," Aunt Tilly insisted. "There's a lunar eclipse tonight, and you know how that can mess with a witch's energy. Please. Promise me."

"Fine," she finally muttered.

"Good." Her aunt's eyes were grave. "I'm sorry, sweetheart. I—"

She stopped speaking. Turning without finishing her sentence, she hurried back into her workshop, the beads that covered the entrance swaying dangerously behind her.

Mia went back upstairs and into her room. She changed out of her work clothes and put on her favorite vintage Led Zeppelin t-shirt that once belonged to her dad, pairing it with some sweatpants. The soft familiarity of the clothes did little to comfort her as they normally did. Usually putting on her dad's favorite shirt always calmed her, making her feel like he was close by. Now, all she could do was pace around her room, her stomach knotting with anxiety.

Where was Colby? Was he okay? Was he safe?

Mia kept seeing the hurt on his face when she asked if they were friends anymore, replaying it in her brain until she wanted to scream.

The sound of glass splintering broke the silence of the room. She looked around in confusion until she noticed the long mirror attached to her wall. A crack ran straight down the middle. Mia's gaze drifted to her hands where she saw the tips of her fingers glowing blue. She hadn't realized she released any energy.

As her aunt said, a lunar eclipse could mess with a witch's powers. Mia needed a distraction before she blew up the house. She looked at her phone where it rested on the table next to her bed, but she knew that wouldn't do. Common entertainment rarely kept her brain captive.

On legs that wobbled slightly from using her energy, she walked over to her bookshelf. Looking over the array of spell books, she grabbed a withered book that she'd found on her dresser a few weeks ago. It was one of several Tilly had given her for her seventeenth birthday. This one was old and covered in spilled potions and crusted herbs. Mia ran her hand over the title, *The Book of Aradia*. It responded to her touch, warming in her grasp.

Going over to her bed, she sat down and began flipping through the worn pages. Her eyes skimmed over the words and the handwritten notes on the side. Her brain didn't comprehend anything as her mind kept going back to Colby.

She remembered the first day she met him back in kindergarten. He'd marched right up to her, taken one long sniff of the air, and stuck out his hand. "I'm Colby. You smell like magic."

"I'm Mia," she'd replied. "You smell like a dog."

"You're both weird." A girl came up to them, her long brown hair tied back in a high ponytail with a bright yellow bow. *Ella.*

Mia glared at the spell book. She needed a better distraction if her brain went to Ella at a time like this. There was no point in trying to read anything. Her comprehension wasn't great on a good day. She was about to close the book when some words caught her eye.

Astral Projection

Astral Projection is the ability to separate the soul from the physical body to travel through the astral plane.

Underneath the description was some faded handwriting that looked as old as the book itself—easily two hundred years old, at least. It read, *offers perspective outside one's physical own.*

Hope flared inside Mia as she read and reread the note. Was she misunderstanding what it said? Or was it telling her she could use the spell to seek out Colby's perspective? Could she find him if she saw things from his point of view?

She read the words once more, *perspective outside of one's own.*

Energy spouted temptingly inside her.

Mia sucked at spell work. It would be stupid to attempt anything during an eclipse, *especially* after Aunt Tilly explicitly told her not to.

She glanced at her closed bedroom door. Her aunt hadn't wanted her to leave her room or try to help. But as Mia looked down at the spell, it seemed simple enough, and she wouldn't be leaving her room—at least her body wouldn't, so she wasn't breaking her word to Tilly. Technically, anyway.

She debated with herself for one more minute. She really shouldn't try it. If anyone could find Colby using magic, it was her aunt.

But he was *her* friend, not Tilly's. And he'd do the same for her, no matter what.

Decision made, Mia shoved the book to the side and stood up from her bed. Bending down, she rolled up the long, faded gray rug sprawled next to her bedframe, revealing a large pentagram carved into the wood floor. She reached under her bed and pulled out a box that contained different supplies she used for spell work. Inside were two brass bowls, measuring spoons, a bag of dirt from the Sacred Forest, a thermos of elves water, and her ceremonial candle. She placed the bowls and candle on three points of the pentagram.

Mia got up from the floor and opened her window so that fresh air could enter the room. Wind touched her face, recharging her. She grabbed the book off her mattress and sat down in the middle of the star. The floor warmed as the energy of the pentagram came alive.

While a witch's magical life energy came from inside them, spell books helped witches manipulate their power in different ways. The instructions for this spell seemed straight forward enough.

Tilly always cautioned her about astral projection spells—*they're more trouble than they're worth, Mia*—but she had to try. For Colby.

She began to read the directions.

1) Put a teaspoon of Sacred Earth into a bowl and place it on the point of the pentagram it represents. Turn it thrice counterclockwise.

Mia reached for the bag of dirt and measuring spoons. She grabbed the tablespoon and was about to dig out the dirt when she paused. Did the spell say a tablespoon or teaspoon? Letting out an aggravated breath, she went back and reread the spell, confirming she needed a teaspoon. She dug out the dirt and placed it in the bowl behind her and to her right. The energy coming from the floor pulsed briefly, making her legs vibrate as she read the next step.

2) Place fire on the point it represents.

Mia grabbed her candle. It was aqua blue, Ella's favorite color. A shot of pain whispered across her skin as she thought about their fight. But that didn't matter. Ella didn't love her like that. She never would. Mia needed to get over it. Especially when there were other, more pressing things to worry about.

Focus.

She turned to put the candle on the point behind her and to her right when she noticed the bowl of dirt was in that spot. That wasn't right. Earth was supposed to be on the point behind her and to her left. She read over the spell book and realized she mixed up the directions. Again.

Dammit!

With her frustration growing, she grabbed the bowl of earth, placing it in the correct spot. She put the candle on its proper point and waved her hand over it, feeling her fingers sizzle. The wick lit. Energy shook the floor inside the pentagram before it slowed to a steady buzz.

3) Pour elves water in the ceremonial bowl and place it on the water point. Turn it clockwise thrice.

Mia reread the instruction to make sure she didn't get it mixed up. She opened her thermos of water and placed it in the bowl on its designated place, turning it clockwise twice. Again, the pentagram flared.

4) Encounter the fourth element. Air. Make sure you have placed yourself in a position where you can feel the Mother's Breath.

Mother's Breath? What the hell did that mean? Did the book mean wind from Mother Nature? Mia had already opened her window. Was she supposed to wait until she reached this step in the spell *before* she opened it?

She closed her eyes and pressed her palms to her lids until she saw stars. Why couldn't she ever keep this stuff straight? Why was she *so* stupid when it came to spells, something that should have been so natural to her. She opened her eyes and read the last note.

5) Engage the fifth element, Spirit. Close your eyes. Concentrate on separating your spirit from your body. Focus your thoughts on your lit candle. Picture the flame, moving back and forth.

Mia did as instructed. Her mind wandered, though, to the Mother's Breath comment. Which made her think about Colby's mom and how worried she'd sounded. She wondered if her own mom, had ever cared about her like that. What was Sadie doing at this exact moment when she was Mia's age? Probably not worrying about spells to find her kidnapped friend. Mia bet Aunt Tilly would have been able to do this spell easily at seventeen, not that she could picture her aunt ever being young.

For the love of Hecate, would you focus!

Mia placed her hands on her knees and tried to picture the flame. She saw her aunt's face instead just as her equilibrium went off balance with nauseating speed. She tried to open her eyes, but they felt like they were glued shut. Her skin began to heat, warming so quickly, it consumed her. What the hell? Was her bedroom on fire?

Oh god. Something was wrong with the spell.

The magic pulled at her skin, seeping into her soul until she screamed.

No sound came out.

She went airborne. It felt like she was leaving a part of herself behind. The pressure on her eyelids lifted and she could finally see what was going on.

Mia floated above the floor. Her heart would be racing if she still had any connection to it, but it remained inside her unmoving body below, still inside the pentagram. She held out an arm and stared at it in shock. Her skin was translucent, outlined in pearly white. As she looked back down at herself, her body began to shake until it was a blur. Shimmery looking bubbles formed over her skin, completely covering her until her body evaporated into the floor with a loud pop.

The door to her room banged open and Aunt Tilly raced in. "Mia!"

Something wrapped around her celestial form before she could react, and she shot upwards through the ceiling of her room, the attic, the roof. Until there was nothing but emptiness. She flew through the air, going skyward until she was above the clouds, blasting through the atmosphere into outer space. There was no time to react. There was only a moment to look around and see the vast darkness before Mia hurtled back toward Earth, speeding to the ground with horrifying quickness.

She saw the roof of her house growing larger with alarming speed. She passed through it. Her body lay inside the pentagram. Her only thought was, *oh, my body's back*, when she slammed into it. Hard.

And then, everything went black.

CHAPTER 4

Mia came to with a groan. Every muscle in her body ached. She opened her eyes but flinched at the brightness from the overhead light. Her forehead wrinkled in confusion.

She never turned on her overhead, preferring the soft warm light of her bedside lamp. Music played from somewhere in the room and Mia recognized it with a start.

"Rhinoceros."

It was a song from her aunt's favorite band, Smashing Pumpkins. Tilly had played their music so much when she was growing up that it had become an integral part of her childhood.

Mia didn't have a radio in her room. She broke hers months ago when she'd lost control attempting a spell.

What the...

She jerked into a sitting position. Her stomach rolled queasily in protest. As the room began to spin, she shut her eyes, hoping that would help her get her bearings.

What was happening?

Don't freak out. The spell went wrong, that's all. You probably just knocked yourself out and now you have a concussion.

She tilted her still whirling head toward the open bedroom window in search of a fresh breeze.

Mia frowned when she felt nothing.

Her eyes cracked back open.

Disbelief made her jaw drop as she took in her room. At least, she thought it was her room. The bed was in the same spot, though the comforter was black instead of the bright blue one she used. Posters of *really* old bands covered the walls. Nirvana, Pearl Jam, Soundgarden.

"The hell?" Mia rubbed the side of her head, which pounded with the aftereffects of her spell. Was it making her hallucinate? She looked back over toward the window.

It was shut.

She may have messed up her spell, but she was *positive* she hadn't closed it before everything went to shit.

Mia stood on legs that shook, taking in everything. All of her stuff was gone. A Hazy Dawn poster normally hung on the wall behind her bed's headboard, but now there was a poster of some band named Jane's Addiction. Her dad's record collection that she kept in a crate next to her desk was missing. A pair of worn combat boots lay on the floor underneath her bookshelf instead of her beat-up black Vans. On top of the shelf was a clunky black radio, which blasted the music she heard. The space beside the radio was crammed with make-up and bottles of dark nail polish she didn't recognize. Mia walked over to it and picked up a golden tube of lipstick with trembling hands. Who put that there? Mia didn't wear any, hating the feel of it caking her lips.

Trying not to panic, she hurried over to her closet and threw open the folding doors. Dark t-shirts with thermal underwear poking out of the sleeves fought for space with an array of flannel button-down shirts. She jerked away.

Holy hell, she had to get out of there. She obviously wasn't in the right house, despite how familiar the room felt. Mia ran out the bedroom door on teetering legs and into the hall. Everything looked like her house, but nothing was the same. A moss green runner went down the middle of the hallway, covering most of the wood flooring that Aunt Tilly loved so much. A lace doily lay over a thin table situated between the rooms of her aunt and grandma. Her aunt hated those kinds of things.

Mia couldn't breathe as panic tightened the muscles of her throat. Putting a hand against the wall, she tried to find a focal point to concentrate on as she pulled short breaths of air into her lungs. Only one thought screamed through her brain loud and clear.

Get out. Get out. GET OUT!

Forcing her feet to move, she rushed toward the stairs only to halt upon hearing heated voices coming from the workshop below—a man and two women. Trying her best not to hyperventilate, Mia tiptoed down the stairway, making as little noise as possible as she entered the office. Again, everything was familiar yet different. There were even more jars of different ingredients for spells and charms than normal, filling every nook and cranny of the room. Not letting it distract her, Mia bypassed Aunt Tilly's workshop as quietly as she could. Not that the occupants inside would have noticed her with how loudly they were arguing.

Entering the store, Mia noticed that it was the same set up of what she knew, but the souvenirs were tackier than the ones they normally sold. Dolls dressed up as witches and plastic witch hats lined the shelves. Her aunt would never allow something so stupid to be in their store.

Fear almost cut off her airway as she unlocked the shop door and stumbled outside. Her Ford Tempo sat along the curb. It still had that same tired look, but it was missing its normal rust as well as the large dent from her aunt's accident a few years back.

Mia turned to look back at the shop. The sign on the store read, *Fitzgerald's Gifts*. The "Tea" part on the sign was missing but...this was her home, though something was seriously off. She needed to find her aunt.

A light wind from the nearby harbor touched her skin. Some much needed energy pinged through her body. She took a deep breath in as her head steadied and the shakiness left her limbs. She wasn't a hundred percent—not by a long shot after such a huge spell—but she did feel slightly better. Physically anyway.

Mia snuck back into the store and made her way past the people still arguing in the workshop.

"I don't see why I can't study at the Assembly now that I'm done with high school," the one woman yelled.

"And who will take over the shop one day?" the man said. "We need you here, learning the business."

"This is crap!"

"Is this about that boy?" the other woman said.

"Oh my god, not everything is about him."

Mia crept up the stairs and went back into her room. Eventually Tilly would have to come check on her. She sat on the bed, feeling weak and nauseated, her unease increasing.

She didn't have to wait too long. Tilly backed into her room, screaming down the hall, "I hate you. You're just trying to stifle my creativity!"

Her aunt slammed the door before spinning to face Mia. They both froze as they stared at each other. Mia wasn't sure if this *was* Tilly or not. The girl looked like her aunt, but if it was her, it was a much younger version. She lacked the strain lines that normally etched across her face, and her long, reddish-brown hair didn't have any gray strands running through it.

"Tilly?" Mia asked, her voice unsure.

She stiffened before she threw her hand out so fast it was a blur. Mia flew backwards, hitting the wall hard enough that her breath knocked out of her. She tried to move but could barely bat an eyelash thanks to her aunt's hex.

"Who are you and what are you doing in my room?" Tilly's face was a mix of rage and fear as she approached Mia, her fingertips pulsing blue.

Mia closed her eyes as she thought of the counter spell. Ironically, this was something Aunt Tilly had made her practice repeatedly ever since she developed her powers. She wondered briefly if her aunt knew she would get herself in this situation one day.

As she pushed her energy into her eyes, Tilly's hex formed behind her eyelids. She could see the electric blue ropes wrapped around her torso, arms, and legs. It was all that held her against the wall. Her fingers began to warm, and she pushed her own energy outward. The power burst cut through the invisible cords holding her in place and she fell to the ground in a heap.

"How the ...?" Tilly's hands began to glow even brighter as she lifted them to place another hex on her.

"I'm your niece," Mia shouted before Tilly could try anything else.

She laughed. "Yeah, right."

"I'm serious."

"Sure, fine. This has been fun and all, but I think it's time you leave my parents' house before I call the police."

"I'm not lying to you. I am your niece. You taught me the counter spell."

"I don't have a niece!" Tilly did a circular motion with her hands and Mia found herself hanging upside down. She was getting seriously annoyed despite how upset she was about everything. Her head and body ached from her spell, her magical energy was running on fumes, *and* she was going to have several bruises from being thrown against the wall.

Mia's hands formed a bluish hue and with the flick of her finger, her aunt went flying back, hitting the nearby dresser with a pained whimper. The distraction was enough to break the hold on

Mia and she fell to the floor again, adding more bruises to her body. She was lucky she didn't land on her head. Before Tilly could react, she threw out another hex, freezing her aunt's hands at her sides. Tilly's eyes widened when she realized she couldn't move her arms. She'd have to thank the older version of her aunt for teaching her that move too...if she ever saw her again.

"I need you to listen to me," she said. "I *am* your niece. My name is Mia. I'm Sadie's daughter. I did an astral projection spell from a book *you* gave me, and I ended up here. I...I think I might be in the wrong timeline."

Tilly's face paled as her eyes ran over her face. "You're Sadie's daughter?"

She nodded. "If I release you, will you promise not to put a hex on me?"

Her aunt was silent for a moment before nodding. She released her and the other girl stumbled forward.

Mia walked over to the bedroom window on quivering legs and opened it, letting the fresh air give her another energy boost.

"What year is it?" she asked. She turned to face Tilly who still stood with her back against her dresser.

"1992."

"Shit." She swayed on her feet. She grabbed the edge of the windowsill for support.

"Are you...uh...are you supposed to swear in front of me?" Tilly asked. Mia smiled despite her predicament. Aunt Tilly was constantly after her about using bad language. It was reassuring to see some things never changed.

"I learned from the best." She tried to make her voice light and her aunt gave her a tentative smile, which Mia was sure was just to pacify her. She wouldn't put it past her to put another hex on her.

"You...you look like her," Tilly whispered.

She frowned. "Who?"

"Sadie. I mean, you don't have her hair color or her pale-as-a-corpse skin tone, but now that I really look at you, your face is the spitting image of her."

Mia didn't say anything. She already knew that. People who'd known her mom always told Mia how much she looked like her. It felt like a curse given what a jerk Sadie was.

"What year are you from?" Tilly asked. She continued to stand in one spot as if she were too nervous to make any sudden moves.

"2013."

"Shit."

"Exactly."

"Look," Tilly said, finally moving until she was in front of her. "I'm not sure what to believe. The idea is crazy. There are plenty of spells that can let you see glimpses of the past, relive moments of history. There are even some that can take you to another dimension, but it's more of a mental state." Tilly reached out and poked her in the arm. "It's extraordinarily rare for people to physically enter other timelines. What book did you use?"

"The Book of..." Mia stiffened as she tried to remember which book she'd grabbed. She was pretty sure it started with an A. Alice? Agnes?

Tilly's eyebrows rose. "You don't know the book? What was the spell?"

Her cheeks burned with embarrassment. "I don't know. I was trying to help locate a friend." Worry for Colby crashed over her as she remembered the whole reason she'd gotten into this situation. "It was supposed give me a glimpse of another person's perspective or something like that."

"You don't know what the spell does, and you did it anyway." Tilly scoffed. "Are you stupid?"

Anger rippled through Mia. A glass of water that rested on her—Tilly's—bedside table exploded.

"Don't call me stupid," she snapped.

It was fine if she believed she was dumb. She'd called herself that enough over the years before her A.D.H.D. diagnosis. But her aunt had always been her biggest cheerleader, encouraging Mia and telling her how brilliant she was. It hurt her more than she would ever admit to hear her aunt call her that, even if it was coming from the teenage version.

Tilly looked over at the broken glass and turned back to glower at her. "You're cleaning that up. But right now, we need to figure out how to return you to your timeline."

She exited the room. Mia followed her on weakened limbs, the little energy she'd be able to recuperate, lost with the unexpected power surge that broke the glass. Once she got back to her timeline and found Colby, she'd work on that with her aunt. She couldn't keep going around breaking things (or poisoning people) whenever she lost her temper.

They headed down the hallway, but Mia stopped, noticing something on the doily covered table that she'd missed earlier.

Underneath the painting of Hecate that hung in the same spot as it did in her timeline was a black framed picture. She knew the photo well. It was the one from her grandma's room. They must have taken it recently in this timeline given that Tilly's hair and dress style matched the girl a few feet away from her.

Her grandparents looked so happy in the picture, like the prosperous middle-aged couple they were. When they married, they'd had to get special permission from the Assembly first because her grandpa was a Common and Commons weren't supposed to know about Others. They were the love story Mia always hoped to have.

Her grandpa had been a loud and energetic man who offered his blunt opinion, whether people wanted it or not. His sudden death from a heart attack when Mia was eleven ripped a hole through her family that never quite healed.

She looked at the final person in the photo. Her mother. Sadie Fitzgerald. She must have been sixteen in this picture.

Her stomach twisted as she realized something. She might actually get to meet her mom. She barely remembered her and now she was going to see her again—granted a teenage version of her—but maybe it would help Mia understand why Sadie abandoned her.

"What are you staring at?" Tilly asked as she came back to stand beside her.

"Is …" She swallowed over the painful lump that had formed in her throat. "Is your sister here?"

"Sadie?" Tilly took the picture from her and put it face down on the table. "No. The Wolf Trial Semifinals are this week. She's in Wyoming watching the game with her friends." Her aunt's lips pursed as she stared at the back of the picture frame with disgust. "Her highness gets away with everything. I don't care if the Wolf Trials is the biggest sporting event of our kind, there is no way Mom and Dad would have *ever* let me go when I was her age. Hell, they would have thrown a fit if I tried to go now and I'm eighteen. But whatever the princess wants, the princess gets."

Mia felt the breath catch in her lungs. She hadn't realized how much she wanted to see her mom until that moment. Tears spilled down her cheeks before she could stop them.

"What?" Tilly asked, staring at her in bewilderment. When she didn't say anything, her aunt's face turned to slight shame. "Sorry. It's hard for me to visualize Sadie as your mom. She's—don't get me wrong, I love my sister—but she's a bit of a spoiled brat."

"I know," Mia said, and the other girl frowned at her. "My mom, she—"

"Wait," Tilly interrupted. "Are you going to tell me something about the future? Don't do it. Haven't you ever heard of the Butterfly Effect theory? Seen *Back to the Future*?"

"Frequently. You make me watch it every year." She gave her a watery smile as she wiped her cheeks.

"Then you should know better. Time travel is dangerous. The Assembly outlawed it centuries ago when some psycho warlock traveled back in time and gifted Jack the Ripper a knife set. It's never a good idea for someone to know about the future because one small change can mess with the timeline, causing catastrophic events."

Mia nodded. "Sorry."

"Come on."

They headed downstairs and entered the store's office. Mia could hear a couple speaking in her aunt's workshop, the same people she'd overheard earlier. Tilly walked through the beaded curtains.

"Mom. Dad. We have a problem."

Mia stopped, her eyes widening. She was going to see her grandpa for the first time in six years. Her grandma—her amazing, strong grandma—wouldn't have her disease at this point.

Tilly poked her head back out when she took too long. "Are you coming?"

She nodded. Mia parted the beaded strands with hands that shook and entered the workshop. The occupants in the room froze as they stared at each other.

Mia couldn't believe what she was seeing as she took in the occupants. Grandma Eabha stood in front of her, healthy and vibrant, with her reddish-brown hair in a twist. She wore a white blouse and pale pink slacks. Slacks were a part of her signature look. Her grandma used to say jeans were unladylike, though she never tried to prevent Tilly or Mia from wearing them.

Grandpa Ray stood behind his wife. He was tall with crinkle lines beside his eyes. It looked like he had just gotten back from his nightly walk, the Vietnam Vet hat he'd always worn sitting proudly on his head. Oh god, her grandpa was *alive*. A sob escaped from her mouth, and she ran over to him, hugging him close.

"Grandpa!" Her voice broke as she buried her face against his shirt.

Her grandpa always smelled like oranges. The familiar scent made Mia want to hold him tighter so she would never lose him again. He went stiff in her embrace, patting her awkwardly on the shoulder.

"Uh…there, there."

"Grandpa?" Grandma Eabha sounded shocked.

"So …" Tilly said. "This girl says she's Sadie's daughter from the future."

Mia let go of her grandpa and turned to face her grandma. Grandma Eabha stared at her warily. At least she was registering her presence. It was such a different expression from her normal blankness, Mia's heart started to hurt.

"I am …" She cleared her throat of the emotion choking her. "I am your granddaughter. My name is Mia. I did a spell on the pentagram in Tilly's room and ended up here."

When her grandparents looked at their daughter, her aunt shrugged. "I never told her about the pentagram."

"It's my room now," Mia said. "I use the pentagram when I'm trying to do spell work."

"Mia." Grandma Eabha took a cautious step forward, lifting a hand and running it over her face. Though she didn't make contact, Mia felt the warmth of her grandma's palm as though she were physically touching her. It was a spell. Tilly used to perform it on her when she was little whenever she thought Mia was lying. Nine times out of ten, she ended up grounded.

Her grandma frowned as she took a step back. "She's telling the truth."

"Of course she is," Grandpa Ray said, his own eyes becoming misty. "She looks just like Sadie."

"How...how did you end up here?" Grandma Eabha asked.

"I'm not sure." Mia looked down. A bruise had formed on her arm. She wondered where it came from—her time travel or Tilly's hex. "I tried doing an astral projection spell during a lunar eclipse and something got messed up. I...I left my body briefly and when I returned, I blacked out. When I came to, I was in this timeline."

"I didn't know witches could time travel," her grandpa said.

Grandma Eabha continued to stare at her, her expression thoughtful. "They don't. The Assembly made time travel illegal. There are wards all over the planet blocking people from doing that very thing. Yet, Mia managed it. You must be quite powerful."

"I'm really not. I just happen to have a gift for messing things up." She looked at her relatives, feeling desperation setting in. "Can you help me?"

Her grandma touched her face, making contact this time with fingers that trembled. Mia grabbed her wrist, holding onto it like a lifeline.

"We'll figure it out." She gave her a reassuring smile. "Tilly and I will put our heads together and see what we can come up with to get you home. There's a black moon in a week. If an eclipse got you here, a black moon should help send you back. It's a night of high energy. Perfect for doing powerful magic. In the meantime, we're going to need you to stay indoors and out of sight. Catastrophe happens to those who mess with time."

Mia nodded, taking in a relieved breath. It felt like her first real breath since waking up in 1992.

CHAPTER 5

Mia's family gave her Sadie's room to use since her mom was at the Wolf Trials. When she first entered it, she could only stand and stare. For her, it was Tilly's room, not her mother's. She was used to seeing it a certain way; walls painted a warm rich khaki color, the vibrant maple wood floors polished to perfection.

In 1992, white chair railing split the room's walls in half. On the bottom portion was cream-colored wallpaper covered in large pinkish chrysanthemums intertwined with green leafy vines. Forest green paint coated the area above the railing. Plushy green carpet ran rampant underneath her feet, hiding the beloved wood flooring beneath. Sadie had smothered the bedside table in a ruffled tree skirt which bore the same flowers as the wallpaper. She apparently had inherited her mother's taste in floral patterns.

On top of the table was a single picture frame. Mia's lips curved cynically as she looked at the photo inside. It wasn't one of Sadie with her friends. It wasn't a picture of her with her family. It was only Sadie in the photo. She wore a beautiful white dress, and her long, red hair flowed down her shoulders as she hugged the trunk of a tree. Apparently, she didn't care about anyone else enough to pose with them. Unlike the family photo in the hallway that Mia viewed earlier, her mom looked happy in this picture, her eyes beaming with delight. Typical. She was happiest when she didn't have family around.

Aside from the terrible decorating and stupid picture, her room was sparse. Unlike Tilly's room, no posters hung on the walls. The clothes in her closet were boring and unassuming.

Nothing in the room gave Mia an idea of who her mother was. She hadn't put a personal touch on anything. It made Mia wonder again if Sadie ever intended to stay in Salem. As she lay in bed for the night, the general emptiness of the room started to get to her after a few hours.

Around one in the morning, she gave up on sleep and climbed out of bed. Throwing on her sweats and a V-neck pink t-shirt she found at the back of her mother's closet, she got dressed and went out into the hall. Mia paused as she passed her aunt's room. The quiet hum of Nirvana's *Lithium* played softly on Tilly's radio. She took a few more steps, but froze when she heard her grandpa's familiar snore coming from her grandparents' room. Closing her eyes for a minute, she listened to the sounds of the house and the people in it.

She held her hand tightly to her mouth as grief hit her. It wasn't fair what happened to her grandparents, and she couldn't give them a warning. Her family made it clear to her earlier that they shouldn't know anything about the future. Despite knowing her grandpa had heart problems when she was little, it had still been a shock when he died from a massive heart attack. He'd always taken care of himself, exercising regularly and eating well. And there wasn't a cure for Alzheimer's so it wasn't like she could say anything to her grandma about what was coming her way. She felt helpless.

There was nothing Mia could do to change their fate. Not when it was the result of natural causes. With that depressing thought weighing heavily on her shoulders, she hurried past the bedrooms and made her way down to the main floor.

Her grandma's warning whispered inside her head: *Stay indoors and out of sight. Catastrophe happens to those who mess with time.*

Mia had no intention of messing with the timeline. She just needed some fresh air. Besides, it was a little after one in the morning. No one would be out this late on a weekday. She opened the shop's front door and stepped outside.

The store overlooked the Salem Harbor. The water seemed particularly loud as she walked away from it, heading toward the center of the tourist district. She could hear the waves crashing unrelentingly against the shoreline, urged on by a howling wind. It was as if the harbor was preparing for an upcoming storm. There was nothing forecasted in Mia's timeline, but who knew what they were expecting in 1992.

Then again, maybe the mermaids who guarded the harbor were having a party. It wouldn't be the first time they celebrated something and created a problem so huge that Commons noticed. They had once caused a tsunami to hit the Alaskan coast in the 1950s when they were celebrating their queen's coronation. The Assembly had worked overtime convincing people that it had been caused by an earthquake.

It didn't matter if it was mermaid related or not. When the harbor was turbulent like this, it reminded her too much of when her father died. She didn't remember much about that day. All she remembered was that it had been really dark and rainy.

It's your fault he's dead.

Mia pushed away that unrelenting inner voice from her head. She glanced up at the night sky and saw the moon peek out before clouds covered it.

"They say Selene lives on the moon," Colby had told her once, mentioning the Original who created the werewolf species. They'd gotten to sleep in his backyard that night. Ella had already gone to bed in her tent, but Mia and Colby had laid outside for hours. As

they'd stared at the starry sky, he told her the sad story of Selene, who was cast to the moon by her lover to protect her from a jealous rival. The story had fascinated her. She'd always loved learning about the origins of Others.

Her heart plummeted now as she thought about her friend. He must be so scared. She wondered if Aunt Tilly had any success in finding him, or if she was too worried about her idiot niece to focus on him.

She stared at the faint light of the moon seeping through the clouds. *Selene, if you're up there, please watch out for Colby. Keep him safe.*

Mia continued walking along the sidewalk lit by the streetlights above. Too many thoughts raced through her mind. Aside from Colby, her most concerning worry was how the hell was she going to get back to her timeline. Her grandma and aunt were powerful, but they both said it was rare for witches to time travel. What if they couldn't figure out how to help her? What if she never got home?

A brightly lit storefront distracted her from her inner panic, and she stopped to look inside the window. A mannequin stood wearing a short, loose, floral dress paired with combat boots. The store had a sign which said, *All Babydoll Dresses On Sale, This Week Only!* Next to that was a male mannequin wearing something called a Hypercolor shirt. Another sign read, *Watch Your Shirt Change Colors While You Wear It.*

Man, the nineties *were weird.*

A muffled scream broke the silence, making Mia jump. She whirled around and noticed an alley nearby. Was that where the sound came from? Another noise—this one more of a pained whimper—shot through the air. It sounded like a woman. On instinct, she reached for her phone before remembering she didn't have it. It wouldn't have worked in 1992 anyway. She chewed on her inner cheek as she internally debated.

Grandma told you not to mess with time.

On the other hand, she couldn't leave someone hurt when she could do something about it. How would she be able to live with that? Her family wouldn't be happy with her, but she crept forward anyway.

The alleyway was narrow, running between a block of stores. People used it as a shortcut to Derby St. in Mia's time. From what she could see from the dim lights shining above the stores' back exits, people threw their garbage in the space now. It was dirty and smelled rotten, like death and suffering. The stench saturated her skin, leaving behind a film that made her want to take a shower.

Her unease spiked when she realized what she was sensing. There was dark energy in this alleyway. She hesitated, not wanting to be anywhere near that stuff.

Another pained groan resonated through the air. The sound of something crashing to the ground soon followed. Despite her trepidation, Mia tiptoed toward the noise. Her hands balled into fists at her sides, her power ready to be unleashed if needed. She hadn't gone more than twenty feet when she stepped around a dumpster and saw the backs of two people, standing over a girl slumped on the ground. The girl wasn't moving. Was she dead? Or were they about to kill her?

"No," Mia whispered before she could stop herself.

Both people turned around. She wanted to scream when she saw their faces. Their eyes glowed red and their noses were beak-like. Red shimmering feathers covered their skin. They were possibly Other, but she didn't recognize the species.

That meant they were most likely Originals. They didn't usually travel to this realm anymore. They had a long history of causing issues whenever they were here for too long, which was why they normally only came for special events.

Like the Wolf Trials. Which were currently taking place in the United States.

Damn!

The Originals took a step toward her in eerie unison, raising clawed hands as if they planned to reach out and grab her. Mia lifted her own fists and focused her energy at them.

As soon as she did, something in the atmosphere changed. The dark energy in the alley rushed toward her. It pooled around her feet, seeping into the bottom of her shoes. Mia sucked in a breath as it touched her heels. She wanted to step back in terror, to run away from the evil. But she couldn't move as the dark energy pushed through her body.

An incredible rush began pulsing through her system. It was as if a switch flipped on, and power suddenly roared inside her. But with the power also came the inexplicable feeling of being pissed. The more the darkness took over, the angrier she became. The emotion felt almost foreign to her, like it wasn't coming from her but from the energy itself.

The darkness reached her eyes, making her vision go black, and yet, everything became crystal clear. She saw a centipede crawling across a crumpled, empty bag of potato chips. She could see the label of the shoes one of the creatures wore—Nike. In Mia's mind, she saw the Originals getting far away from her, disappearing from this world.

They moved closer.

She unfurled her hands and unleashed everything she had.

Power erupted from her. She staggered as a brilliant bluish-black hue filled the alley. It surrounded the creatures in so much light, Mia closed her eyes against the brightness. When she opened them, the Originals were gone and the alley was in darkness, only lit by a single flickering bulb above one of the store's exits. On the ground where the Originals once stood were two large piles of dust.

"What the hell," she muttered. She stared at the dust with dawning horror. Her hand flew to her mouth, and she barely made it to the dumpster before throwing up.

She hadn't meant to kill them. She just wanted them away from her and the girl. Aunt Tilly's voice echoed loudly in her head, *learn control, learn patience...before you kill someone, please.* What would her aunt say when she found out what she had done?

And, oh God...what if she messed up the timeline? What if she just killed an Original who was meant to shape the future? What was she going to do?

Mia struggled to breathe. She was in the middle of a full-blown freak out when the girl on the ground moaned. It brought her to another problem. Had the girl seen her use magic? She didn't know how to do a memory wipe, though she had a shocking amount of strength left. Usually when she performed a hex, it left her feeling weak and she'd have to encounter one of the five elements to regain some power. With the dark energy polluting the earth and air in the alley, she was having trouble finding something to center herself.

The darkness was still inside Mia, slowly escaping through the pores of her skin, leaving a sweaty, grimy coating. The anger drained with it, leaving her feeling horribly off—depressed even. As if the emotions from whatever terrible event created the dark energy to begin what was inside her—a murder victim right before their life was taken, a child's tears after being kidnapped.

With the depression, came confusion. What just happened? She'd never felt so powerful before. Was the dark energy what gave her that raw strength? The thought was too horrifying to think of, so she made herself focus on the girl. Trying to shake off the lingering sadness and worry, Mia walked over to her.

"Hey," she said but froze as she stared at her.

She wasn't able to see the girl's face because her hair had fallen across it, but there was something very familiar about her. If she didn't know any better, she would have thought she was looking at Ella. From what she could see in the dim light, the girl's hair was the same length and sugary brown color as her friend's, and their bodies were about the same slim shape.

Mia's panic increased. What if she had brought Ella into this timeline with her? She'd been thinking about her when she performed the spell that sent her back in time.

With shaking fingers, she bent down and pushed the girl's hair back. She let out a sigh of relief when she saw her face. Not Ella, though she reminded her so much of her best friend, even with her features being slightly different. Her cheekbones were more prominent, her chin a little more pointed.

The girl's long eyelashes fluttered open, and Mia's heart lurched. Even in the darkness of the alley, she could see the rich chocolate brown color of her eyes. She was beautiful. Somewhere in the back of Mia's mind, "Tonight" from *West Side Story* began to play. It was odd, but she felt more drawn to this stranger than she'd ever felt to anyone before, even Ella.

Maybe Tony and Maria weren't complete morons after all.

The magical moment was ruined when the girl took one look at her and screamed. Mia took a hurried step back and raised her hands in front of her.

"I'm not going to hurt you," she said.

"W-who are you?" the girl's soft, musical voice stammered.

"I'm Mia." There was no point in not telling the truth. It wasn't like she was going to see her again. That thought made her sad even without the dark energy affecting her. "Are you okay?"

The girl flinched as if only just remembering her situation before she glanced frantically around the alley.

"They're gone." Her stomach reeled with guilt at that reminder. "Did they hurt you?"

The girl shifted, her face wincing. "Aside from a couple of bruises, I think I should be okay."

"Why don't we get you out of here?" She held out her hand.

The girl looked at it hesitantly before placing her hand in Mia's. The assurance of her touch, steadied Mia, and the rest of the darkness left her, replaced with a warmth she didn't want to analyze. She gave the girl's hand a comforting squeeze and helped her up.

"Let's go," she said. They continued to hold hands until they reached the safety of the well-lit sidewalk. Once they were several feet away from the alley, Mia reluctantly let her go. She breathed in the fresh, clean air, feeling comforted by the element.

"Where are you headed?" She looked over at the girl, mystified all over again by how much she looked like Ella. Maybe she was some relative of her best friend, though Ella's immediate family wouldn't move to Salem until the summer before they entered kindergarten.

"I guess I'll go home," the girl said.

Mia scanned the area to make sure no other creatures were lurking around. After everything that had just happened, she would never forgive herself if something else went after her. "I'll walk with you."

"That's okay." She gave her a weak smile. "There seems to be some bad elements out tonight. I wouldn't want to cause you any problems."

Mia snorted. "Trust me, I can take care of myself."

"You don't have to bother. I'll be okay." The girl lifted a trembling hand and clutched at something around her neck. The street lighting made it difficult to see what it was, but Mia guessed it was a necklace.

"I'd still feel better if you'd let me walk you home," she insisted. The other girl bit her lip, looking conflicted so Mia added, "Seriously, I'll be fine."

She slowly nodded. "Okay."

As they began walking, Mia asked, "Do you know the, uh, people who attacked you or what they wanted?"

The girl looked over her shoulder as if to reassure herself that the creatures weren't following. "No, I don't know who they are. I was walking by the alley and the next thing I knew, I was being pulled behind a dumpster and pushed against the wall."

She shivered and Mia decided not to push her for more details, despite being super curious as to why two Originals would attack a Common. A boat horn went off in the distance and the girl almost jumped out of her skin. Mia gave her arm a comforting pat. The girl startled at the contact before giving another slight smile.

Mia's heart sped up at the sight of it. *Get a grip!*

"What were you doing out so late?" she asked.

The girl tensed briefly before lifting her chin. "What were *you*?"

Mia's lips turned up at her defensive tone, but she smothered the expression. She had spirit even after what she'd gone through.

"That's fair." Mia shrugged. "I'm visiting some relatives and couldn't sleep. Strange bed and all." She shoved her hands into her pockets. "I don't know...I had some things on my mind and figured some fresh air would help."

"What kind of things?"

Mia looked at her in confusion. Why would a stranger want to know?

"Sorry if that was rude," the girl said. "I think I might be a little more freaked out by everything than I realized and talking to you...it's keeping my mind off my problems."

"What kind of problems?" Mia winced. Talk about being rude, but she couldn't help wonder about her. Why had those Originals attacked her? "I mean...besides the obvious."

The girl let out a forced laugh, clutching her necklace again. "You tell me your problems, and I'll tell you mine."

The scent of honeysuckle reached Mia's nose. She looked past the girl and saw a flowering plant climbing up a trellis attached to someone's porch. Honeysuckle was Ella's favorite scent, and Mia felt some of her tension leave as a sense of home washed over her.

Maybe it was because the girl reminded her so much of her best friend that she blurted, "I was thinking about my mom. She, um, she left when I was a kid and my family has me using her childhood bedroom. It's weird."

The girl nudged her with her shoulder. "I'm sorry. I shouldn't have asked."

She felt the remnants of the contact even after she moved away. "It's okay."

They both walked in relative silence before the other girl said, "I have my own mom problems. That's why I was out. She...she's an alcoholic. She came home trashed tonight, and I just...I had enough, you know?"

"Yeah, I get it," Mia said. And she did. They both had the bad luck of having really crappy mothers.

They turned onto a quiet street and approached a gray house near the corner. The girl stopped in front of its wood picket fence.

"This is me."

After what they'd just been through, Mia wasn't quite ready to leave her. "Well...it was nice meeting you. Stay out of dark alleyways."

She nodded. "Thanks for walking me home."

"Sure." Mia looked around before glancing at the house.

She frowned as she stared at it. The home was familiar to her, and not in the it-wasn't-too-far-from-her-house kind of way. Goosebumps broke out on her skin, and she shivered.

Pushing away her apprehension, she said, "I guess I should get going. Goodnight."

She turned and had only taken a few steps when the girl said, "Hey, Mia?"

She looked back at her. "Yeah?"

"Would you like to meet me for coffee tomorrow morning? My treat. It's the least I could do for all your help tonight."

The answer should have been an automatic no. Mia needed to work with her family on finding a way home. She needed to get back so she could help find Colby. She only hoped her family didn't find out what she'd done tonight. "I...I can't. I need to spend time with my family."

"Please? I won't feel right until I repay you."

It was wrong and stupid to consider it, but she was seriously curious about this girl. She wanted to know why the Originals targeted her. If spending time with her needed to happen to figure that out, then so be it. The fact that she looked so much like Ella had nothing to do with it.

"Okay," she finally said.

The girl's smile was visible in the shadow of the night. "Great. Let's meet at Pickney's, around ten?"

"Sounds good." Mia turned away again before she thought of something. Whirling around, she said, "Hey."

She still stood there. "Yeah?"

"I don't know your name."

She laughed, the sound making Mia want to grin in return despite everything going on. "Oh yeah. It's Cecilia. Cecilia Raillive."

Mia nodded and Cecilia waved at her before going inside. Lines formed on her forehead as she began to walk. Cecilia Raillive. She knew that name.

Glancing over at the street sign to see where she was, Mia noticed she was standing at the corner of Proctor and Pope. She'd never heard of Pope before. With a frown, she looked at the surrounding buildings and finally recognized where she was. Her high school wasn't too far from here. Pope wasn't the right street name though. It should be—

She swung back to look at the house as realization hit her. She didn't recognize the home in its present state because she was used to seeing it as a disaster area. It was somewhat kept up in 1992. The roof wasn't sagging in the middle and the windows weren't broken.

This was the home Mia always felt drawn to. The one saturated in dark energy. The girl who'd lived there in the early nineties had been murdered in the basement, the killer never found. They'd named the street after her.

Cecilia Raillive Dr.

Chapter 6

Mia tossed and turned for what remained of the night, dreaming of creatures turning into dust and bloody body parts appearing in a basement. Someone in her dream kept yelling over and over, *It's your fault he's dead.* Finally giving up on sleep around eight in the morning, she threw back the sheets. She could hear someone whistling outside, and she stumbled her way to the window to see who it was. She felt a pain as she watched her grandpa head down the sidewalk for his morning walk.

Rubbing at her face, Mia made her way into the hallway bathroom. She brushed her teeth before hopping into the shower. As she stood underneath the warm water, she tried not to freak out over the murder she'd committed the night before. By Assembly law, she hadn't done anything illegal. The Originals had attacked an innocent before coming after her. She had every right to defend herself. That didn't make their deaths any easier. Similar to when she poisoned Kurt, Mia had lost control and it resulted in two lives extinguished, just as her aunt always warned would happen.

Scrubbing at the tears streaming down her cheeks, she forced herself to think about Aunt Tilly. She hoped she wasn't worrying too much. Her terrified face right before Mia jet-setted herself into the unknown flashed through Mia's mind. Her heart sunk as she realized how scared her aunt must be. She only hoped Tilly was spending time on Colby's locator spell. His parents had to be going out of their minds. They needed her aunt's full focus to help find their son. Mia would never forgive herself if she caused her aunt to be too distracted and something happened to him.

"I don't understand the problem," ten-year-old Mia muttered before shoving her math book away. "I should drop out of school. I'm never going to get this. I'm too dumb."

"You're not dumb at all," Colby encouraged before grabbing her book. "You just learn differently. Let me show you another way to look at it."

He grabbed a plate of homemade cookies his mom brought to the table in his kitchen. "If you have two cookies and you times them by..."

Growing up, Colby's house had been a second home to her, his parents similar to a loveable aunt and uncle who always overfed them with snacks.

Mia rubbed at her face with her hands, trying to rein back her worry. More than anything, she wished she could hug his parents. She should have listened to her aunt and not tried an astral projection spell. Had she listened, she could be home right now, searching for Colby.

Stepping out of the shower tiredly, Mia dried off and dressed in stonewash jeans and a red sweatshirt that she'd taken from her mom's closet. Her mom was one jean size smaller than her. The pants were snug but doable. As she finished drying her hair, she heard a loud knock downstairs. It sounded like it was coming from the side door that the family used instead of the front shop entrance. Confused as to who would be at the private door, Mia stepped into the hallway.

She hadn't walked more than two steps before the teenaged version of her aunt was there, grabbing her arm. Tilly lifted a finger to her mouth, indicating for her to keep quiet. She pulled her toward the nineteenth century cast iron grate in the hallway's wall that Mia always went to when she wanted to eavesdrop.

Her mouth dropped open in indignation. How many times had her aunt lectured her about doing this very thing? She was about to say something, but Tilly motioned for her to keep her mouth shut, so Mia held back her retort.

"Doyle, it's good to see you," Her grandma said from the floor below.

Tilly whispered, "The Assembly's here."

Mia's stomach coiled. They'd found out what she'd done. They were there to haul her away from her family, and she would never get home. Aunt Tilly would die alone all because of her stupidity. Even if she did get back to her own timeline, the Assembly could still go after her. They didn't set time limits on crimes against Originals. In one tiny blip, she'd ruined her life!

"Hello Eabha, it's good to see you again."

Mia barely held back a groan. She recognized the voice of Chancellor Parris. In her time, Doyle Parris was in charge of all the witches around the world. No witch ranked higher than him.

"Have you met my associate, Gavin Alexander?" Parris asked. Tilly sucked in an audible breath.

"Yes, I believe you went to the same school as my daughter." Grandma Eabha's tone was slightly cooler. "I've met your uncle before. He's a good man."

"Thank you," another man said, his voice deep and strong. Tilly's cheeks turned red upon hearing him.

"What?" Mia whispered as she took in her aunt's expression. "You have a thing for Gavin Alexander?"

"Shut up." She looked mortified.

Mia turned back to the vent, her tone still hushed. "Why would the chancellor come here?"

"The chancellor? Gavin and Parris are Examiners. Oh God, please tell me you mean Gavin might be chancellor someday. Parris is such a douche." Mia opened her mouth, but Tilly glared at her. "I didn't mean it. Don't tell me about the future. Butterfly Effect, remember?"

"*Okay.*"

She leaned in closer to the vent as she heard the group walk down the hallway and enter the store's office. Examiners were detectives and enforcers all rolled into one. If anyone broke any laws or revealed themselves to a Common, Examiners took care of the situation. Witches usually ended up excommunicated and labeled warlocks...or much worse. Her grandma came to mind, and the day they drained her of her powers. Though, thankfully, the Assembly usually only reserved that course of action for medical situations and not as a punishment since most Others considered it to be inhumane.

"Are you all right?" Tilly asked. "You've gone really pale."

She swallowed the bile that rose in her throat. "I'm fine."

"How's your apprenticeship going with the Examiner's office, Gavin?" The sound of Grandma Eabha's chair squeaking loudly indicated she was now sitting behind her desk.

"Fine, thank you," he answered. "I really enjoy the challenge the work gives me. If they offer me a position after my apprenticeship, I'll most likely pursue it."

Mia couldn't help but snort despite her nerves. Gavin definitely pursued it. He was the Lead Examiner in her time. He was extremely powerful and not someone Others messed with.

"Eabha," Parris said, "we're here to look into a complaint we received from two Originals who were in the area last night."

"There were Originals in Salem?"

"They said they were out enjoying an evening stroll when they were hexed by a young woman."

Her grandma's tone turned hard. "Really?"

"Yes." Parris sounded more pompous in real life than he did on Witch TV.

"Do they know who the girl is?"

"If they did, do you think she would be aliv—"

"What Doyle is trying to say," Gavin interrupted, his shoes heavy as he walked across the office floor, "is that the alleyway was dark, and they don't have the best eyesight on a good day. Thankfully, they were of Phoenix ancestry. They turned to ash and spent the rest of the night re-growing their bodies."

Relief rushed over Mia. She hadn't killed them. Her aunt stared at her suspiciously. Her guilt must have read clearly on her face because Tilly's mouth tightened.

"The Originals have filed charges and would like the girl prosecuted," Parris said. Did he have to sound so gleeful? "We were wondering if you could verify your daughter's whereabouts last night."

Mia looked at her aunt in horror. Did they think Tilly did it?

"Why do want to know?" Grandma Eabha asked.

"Your coven is the closest to the scene of the crime," Parris replied. "And let's face it, the Fitzgeralds are well known for being powerful. An ordinary witch couldn't have eviscerated two Originals. We need to rule out your family."

"*Our* family. Or are you forgetting that we're related, dear cousin?" Her grandma sounded annoyed. "What a scandal it would be for you and your political aspirations if our family was involved."

"No one is accusing anyone." Gavin's voice was calm. "We just need to do our due diligence, ma'am."

"I'm surprised they sent you, Doyle," her grandma continued, "especially with the Wolf Trials going on. A lot of important people are there who could use your protection. Isn't investigating a young person performing hexes a little below your pay grade?"

"The hex *was* against Originals," Parris said, his voice offended. "Besides, I'm in town investigating the disappearance of an Other. Gavin was assigned the hex case and I offered to assist him."

"A disappearance? Who?"

"Well, we can't really disclose—" Gavin started to say.

"Susan Flightfast." Parris didn't seem to have any problem dishing out information.

"The harpy?" Her grandma sounded shocked.

"You know her?"

"We've both lived in Salem a long time. We have friends in the same circles. When did she disappear?"

"Her family said she went missing last night. Now, if we could return to the matter at hand. Where is your daughter?"

Mia felt sick. She wouldn't let Tilly take the fall for the hex. "I...I need to talk to them."

"No," her aunt argued, "you need to stay out of sight."

Mia shook her head and started to walk toward the stairs. She didn't get very far. Her legs lost all strength and she fell soundlessly to the ground, rolling just in time so that she was on her back. Tilly stood over her with glowing hands.

Mia went to get up, but her flesh rippled with every motion. The hell? Tilly turned her into the equivalent of human Jell-O. She tried to think of the counter spell to undo the hex, but her aunt never showed her that one.

"Be quiet," Tilly whispered before making her way down the stairs.

"Ah, there's the girl of the hour," Parris said when her aunt's footsteps indicated she'd entered the office. "So good to see you, cousin."

"Hello, Tilly." Gavin's voice didn't sound as grave as it had when he'd been speaking to Grandma Eabha.

"Hello, Gavin." Even though Mia wasn't in the same room as the others, she could picture her aunt staring awkwardly at the ground.

"Now then," Parris continued, "where were you last night at approximately one a.m.?"

"In my room."

"Were there any witnesses?"

"It wasn't like I was having an orgy."

"Tilly!" Grandma Eabha said as one of the men let out a snort. Mia bet it wasn't Parris.

"Look." Tilly's tone was bored. "Do a truth spell on me if you don't believe me."

There was some shuffling from below and then Gavin said, "She's telling the truth."

"We'll be in touch if we have any further questions," Parris said, his disappointment clear.

"Always good seeing you, Parris." Her aunt's voice dripped with sarcasm. It was much softer as she said, "Goodbye, Gavin."

"You take care," he replied.

Mia heard the Examiners walk down the hallway before exiting the building. Her family moved up the stairs, the noise of their steps echoing in the hallway before two sets of shoes appeared next to Mia's head.

She tried to act casual. "So, Parris. What a jerk, huh? I swear, he was probably looking forward to turning Tilly in just so he could brag about solving the case quickly. He'd do anything to boost his own image, including sacrificing family. Am I right?"

"Just stop." Her aunt waved her hand at Mia and the feeling of being a restrained puddle of goo ended.

"And on another note, what the hell was that?" Mia rubbed at her arm as a pins-and-needles sensation spread over her whole body.

"Never mind that," Tilly said. "Did you, by chance, leave the house last night?"

Her face burned. "I couldn't sleep."

"Oh, Mia." Her grandma's disappointment was clear on her face.

"I'm sorry, okay." She got off the floor, her legs wobbling for a moment before they righted themselves.

"Tell us what happened with the Originals," Grandma Eabha said.

"I took a walk downtown." She didn't meet their eyes. "I heard someone scream and I went to see what was going on. I saw two creatures standing over a Common girl about my age. They weren't out walking like they told the Examiners. They were trying to kill her. So, I helped."

"By reducing them to dust." Mia flinched at Tilly's angry tone. "Not to mention using magic in front of a Common. What hex did you do?"

"I don't know. It just happened."

"You don't even know the hex?" Tilly looked at her in disbelief before turning toward Mia's grandma. "Mom ..."

Grandma Eabha held up her hand for silence. "I've never heard of an Original attacking a Common. They've always thought of Commons as something similar to a beloved pet. Why would they try to hurt one?"

Mia continued to eye the floor. "I'm just telling you what I saw."

Her grandma looked thoughtful. "You must have used quite a bit of your energy to be able to turn them into ash. I'm surprised you're able to move around today, especially after time traveling. You said you aren't that powerful, and yet here you are, standing in front of me looking perfectly alert."

She could only shrug. She didn't know how she managed to absorb the dark energy in the alley and use it against the Originals. She certainly couldn't explain it.

"First a harpy disappears," Tilly said, "then two Originals try to kill a Common. It doesn't make sense."

"No, it doesn't," Grandma Eabha agreed. A worry line formed between her eyes. "Who was the girl?"

Mia paused. She wanted to tell her family the truth, but she could just picture how they'd react if they found out she had agreed to meet up with Cecilia that morning.

Don't mess with the timeline, Mia. Keep out of sight, Mia. You're going to cause a catastrophe, Mia.

If Cecilia was destined to die, she knew she couldn't and *shouldn't* do anything about it. But *why* had the Originals attacked her? Were they the ones who would eventually murder her, or were they working with someone else? Someone who might also kidnap a harpy.

And what ironic timing that Colby's kidnapping sent her back to a time where there was another Other kidnapping in Salem.

Mia froze. She'd overheard Mrs. Mond mention that Colby's kidnapping was just like before. Was it possible she ended up in the same time period Mrs. Mond had been referring to? And if it was like before…was it possible that the kidnappings were connected?

"It does seem weird," she finally said, echoing Tilly, "That Originals would attack a Common on the same night a harpy disappears."

"Yes, it's quite the coincidence." Her grandma's eyes narrowed on her. "Are the two related?"

"Mom—" Tilly cautioned but Grandma Eabha held up a hand again as she continued to stare Mia down.

"I don't know," she admitted, knowing it was the first truth she could tell them without having to be evasive.

If it was all related—the attack on Cecilia, Susan's disappearance, maybe even Colby's kidnapping—Mia knew she couldn't do anything to change Cecilia's fate. If she saved her, who was to say the murderer wouldn't turn around and go after someone else. Perhaps a whole family. She had no idea how her actions could influence the coming days and weeks. She couldn't step in. She couldn't play Hecate like that.

But if she could figure out who was behind the disappearances and Cecilia's murder, maybe she could find a way to help Colby once she returned home. She needed to figure out if there was a pattern.

"Mia." Grandma Eabha's voice was soft and encouraging. "Who was the girl?"

She peered up at her grandma—her amazing, powerful grandma—before looking at her aunt. She wanted to tell them so much about what was going to happen. She wanted—*needed*—their guidance.

They couldn't help her.

If Mia told them the truth, she knew what they would do. They'd try and stop Cecilia's murder. As much as it went against their own principles of not messing with the timeline, they wouldn't be able to turn their backs on someone in danger. Who knew what kind of ripple effect that would cause?

Feeling suddenly exhausted, she said, "I...I don't know."

Her grandma looked disappointed. She looked at her daughter. "Tilly, would you go downstairs and start working on the order for that Cleveland ghoul? He wants it completed before next month's eclipse. You know the dough has to sit at room temperature for several weeks."

Tilly gave Mia a questioning look before she nodded. "Yeah, fine."

Grandma Eabha waited until she left before she turned back to Mia. She motioned for her to follow, and they headed toward Sadie's room.

"Mia, are you sure you didn't catch a name?" she asked.

"I...I'm sorry, I didn't."

"Very well." Grandma Eabha said as they entered the bedroom. "I need you to understand that it's not just you we need to worry about. If you do something that's out of the norm in this timeline, it could have dire consequences down the road."

"I know that." More than anything.

"Do you?" Her grandma gave her a steady stare. "Because most witches understand you don't use magic in front of Commons unless you want to summon the Assembly. Make sure that doesn't happen again."

"I promise."

Grandma Eabha nodded. "I think it'll be best if you stay in here for the rest of the day."

Mia's jaw dropped. "Are you grounding me?"

"Of course not. I need you to review these books and see if you recognize the spell you used to get here."

Her grandma snapped her fingers, and three books flew into the room, landing gently on the bed.

Giving them a glance, Mia shook her head. "None of those are the book I used."

"Sometimes if it's by the same author, they put the same spells in different books. Look over them and let me know if you find the spell." Her grandma walked out of the room, closing the door quietly behind her.

Mia moved her jaw from side to side to release some tension and heard a satisfying crack. The radio clock on the bedside table showed she had a half hour before she was supposed to meet Cecilia. She bit her lip as she walked over to the window. As she leaned against the windowsill, she thought about Colby.

"What do you want to be when you grow up?" Mia asked him once when they were younger.

"I'm going to take over my family's recycling business someday," he replied without hesitation. "I want to make it a chain. Something so big that we clean up all the pollution in our forests. What about you?"

"I don't know," she replied dourly.

"Well, whatever you end up doing, you'll be brilliant." He looked thoughtful for a minute before excitement lit his face. "I

know! You can be my vice-president. We'll clean up the world together. What do you say?"

He stuck his hand out for her to shake.

She laughed as she took it. "Deal!"

Mia swallowed over the painful lump now in her throat. Colby used to believe in her so much, even when she didn't believe in herself. She had to find a way to help him. Even though the idea of hanging out with Cecilia, knowing she was about to die a gruesome death, made Mia queasy, she had to do it. Cecilia might be the key to saving him.

As Mia stared out the window, she absently took in the familiar view of the Derby Wharf inside the Salem Maritime National Park. The wharf looked the same, a path mixed of stone and grass that led out to a small pier, which housed a white lighthouse, but the Pedrick Store House was missing. If she remembered her Salem history—and history was one of the few classes in school she was good at—the National Park Service wouldn't acquire the 1700s building and move it to its location in Salem until the twenty-first century.

A familiar figure caught her attention as he headed toward the pier. The man glanced around, and Mia backed away, so she wasn't as visible in the window. Even from a distance, she knew that profile anywhere. The chancellor's image was imprinted on Other money in Mia's timeline, like all five representatives of the Assembly were. What was Parris doing though?

Once he seemed to assure himself that no one was watching, he threw out his hand. A white bright circle encompassed him before both it and the chancellor disappeared. It was a glamor. If anyone looked in his direction, they wouldn't see him. But Mia knew he was there. She pushed her energy into her eyes as Aunt Tilly taught her to do so she could see through the illusion. It wasn't easy. Parris's glamor was powerful, but she was able to make out enough, even if everything was slightly blurry.

He crouched down and dropped several gold coins into the water. The surface began to bubble before a man's head popped out. Mia sucked in a breath. She'd never seen a mermaid before. They usually didn't come to the surface unless there was a good reason. The man's hair looked like it was made of seaweed, and he had skin the color of the deepest part of the ocean. What was he doing speaking with Parris? Did this have to do with the investigation of the missing harpy?

The mermaid threw his head back and laughed at something Parris said. Mia wished she could divert her energy to her ears so she could hear what they were saying, but she hadn't mastered the trick of pushing her energy to multiple senses yet. It was something she and Tilly were working on as part of her training.

The mermaid held out his hand. Parris frowned before pulling several more coins from his pocket and tossing them. The mermaid caught the money in his palm, running a finger over them as if to assure himself they were genuine. Seeming satisfied, the man dropped the money into the water before reaching down below the surface. He pulled out a small shell and gave it to Parris. It grew larger until it was about the size of his hand. Even with all that she had seen in terms of magic in her life, this was new for Mia. Mermaids didn't typically give up their treasures. Not without a fight anyway.

And given the greedy smile on Parris's face, that shell was a treasure. He waved his hand, and it disappeared. The mermaid nodded to him before sinking underneath the surface of the harbor. Parris stood up and scanned around. Looking satisfied, his glamor disappeared. Thrusting his hands into his pockets, he began walking casually back toward the street.

Mia continued to stare at the water.

What was that about?

Parris said he was in town because of Susan Flightfast's disappearance. But was that the actual reason he was here?

If not... What was he really doing in Salem?

CHAPTER 7

Mia was not proud of what she'd just done. After putting the strange occurrence with Parris on her mental back burner, her mind returned to Colby. Out of desperation to leave the house to go speak with Cecilia—and inspired somewhat by Parris—she put a glamor on Sadie's room.

It took a few tries.

The curtain caught fire at one point. She doused the flames with a quick stamping of her foot before there was major damage, but one corner of the fabric was singed.

She hoped Sadie noticed and it pissed her off.

Maybe if you'd stuck around instead of abandoning me, you could have taught me better.

When Mia finished, the glamor created the illusion someone was in the room. If her grandma or Tilly used their magic to sense if she'd stayed put, they wouldn't know she was missing unless they actually entered the room. Mia ran to the bedroom window on weakened legs and looked outside. It was too far to jump, and she wasn't feeling too confident in using her energy to float down, especially after using it to create the glamor. Knowing her luck and lack of Adderall, she would try and end up in Timbuktu.

She was going to have to aim for the rickety portico attached to the side entrance of their house. Shimmying out the window, she hung on the edge of the sill before swinging her body toward the covering a couple of feet away. She landed on it with a thud, banging her leg on the surface. It creaked in protest. She prayed to

Hecate that no one heard her. As carefully as she could, Mia bent over the side and swung down to the ground. She landed with a hard thunk, jarring every muscle in her body. Giving a quick look around for any family members, she took off running. She wasn't a hundred percent sure how she was going to get back into the house, but she'd worry about that later.

She passed a house renovating their yard. There was a pile of dirt near the sidewalk, and she dragged her fingers through it, letting the fresh earth restore some of her magical energy.

Once she got to the hub of town, she relaxed for a half a second before she realized she had another problem. The coffee shop where Mia was supposed to meet Cecilia didn't exist in her timeline. She had no idea where she was going.

She walked further into town and stopped at a gas station for directions. Once she was pointed in the right way, she used their bathroom to freshen up. As she washed her hands, she took in her wide-eyed dark eyes and black hair. She was a bit of a mess, but she couldn't do anything about it.

Mia kept her eyes down as she headed toward the coffee shop. Who knew if the Assembly still had any Examiners in the area or if Parris was lurking around. All she'd have to do was give off a suspicious vibe for them to use a truth spell on her. It would prove she was the one who'd hexed the Originals. Out of sight and out of mind was her best option.

When she arrived at the coffee shop, Mia couldn't help but smirk. This was a tourist shop in her time, selling even dumber souvenirs than what her aunt sold in theirs. Fake wands that did nothing and love potions that gave Commons diarrhea. When she and Ella had decided to go as witches one year for Halloween—it had been a funny idea at the time—they'd gone to this shop to buy cheap costume accessories. The shop would seriously give her family business a run for their money, except most of the money her aunt made wasn't from tourist sales, but from the services she provided to the Other community.

Her aunt hoped that Mia would take over the shop one day, but she couldn't see that future for herself. Business was not her strong suit, not to mention she had too much trouble doing spells. In the last ten hours, she'd accidentally sent herself back in time, blew up two Originals, and almost set her mother's room on fire.

There was no way Others would be knocking on her door asking for help like they did her aunt's.

Mia thought back to the conversation she'd overheard between her grandparents and Tilly right after arriving in 1992. Her aunt had been arguing with them about wanting to study at the Assembly, but her parents had pressed her to learn how to run the shop.

It was weird. Aunt Tilly always seemed so proud of their business. Why hadn't she pursued her dream if she wanted to do something else?

Her mind drifted back to Ella. Had she made it to prom the previous night with Kurt? Mia already knew she would've looked beautiful. They'd gone dress shopping together and the red one Ella picked out looked like it had been designed specifically for her. Had she given Mia a second thought last night? The three of them were supposed to go to prom together, but after their fight, it wouldn't have surprised her if her best friend ditched her.

A tired sigh escaped her lips, her mood souring, as she reached for the door handle of the shop. As she entered, the scent of coffee, mocha, and wood polish surrounded her. In one corner of the building was a dark oak counter. A drip coffee maker sat on top of it while a harried looking barista put the nearby brass espresso machine to work. The sound of a coffee grinder running competed with the loud alternative music blaring from the overhead speakers.

Mia's gaze landed on Cecilia who waved from where she sat near the window. Some of her spirit lifted. It was a risk coming here, but seeing her safe and alive, made it worth it. She maneuvered around several tables situated close to each other before sitting in a chair opposite the other girl.

"I'm so glad you could make it," Cecilia said. She was even prettier in the daylight. Her long, caramel colored hair shimmered in the light of the window. Warmth shone from her chocolate eyes, despite everything she'd been through in the last twenty-four hours.

"Hi," Mia said, running her fingers nervously along the edge of the deep brown table.

"Is everything okay?" she asked.

She was smiling and seemed so happy that she even showed up, Mia couldn't help but stare. Who would want to hurt this girl?

"I'm fine," she replied. "I got busted for being out so late last night and I think I'm grounded."

"Well, I'm glad you were able to make it." Cecilia reached over and gently squeezed her hand before letting go. The brief contact made Mia's skin break out into goosebumps.

A waitress came over. "Hi, I'm Gertie. Our special today is the cheese Danish with a raspberry mocha latte."

"That sounds delicious," Cecilia said. "I'll take that."

"And you?" Gertie gave Mia an expectant look.

"What do you have that doesn't have dairy products in it?"

Gertie frowned. "Uh... black coffee?"

She nodded, figuring as much. Few coffee shops carried vegan options even in her timeline. "I'll take that."

"Are you sure?" Cecilia said. "It's my treat."

"Nah, I'm good. I can't have dairy."

"Allergies?" she asked.

"Vegan."

Gertie gave her a strange look but said, "I'll be right back with your order."

After the waitress left, Mia examined Cecilia's features more closely. In the daylight, she didn't look as much like Ella as she originally thought. Her hair was lighter. Softer looking. She wore a light yellow sundress that appeared to be one size too big and had definitely seen better days. She still managed to wear it with more grace than Mia could ever pull off.

"Cecilia ..."

"Yeah?"

She didn't know how to phrase what she needed to know. It wasn't like she could say, why is someone going to kill you? Did you steal something from a supernatural gangster? Is your future murder connected to the Originals who attacked you last night? Were you just in the wrong place at the wrong time?

A beeping sound rang out from across the shop distracting her. Glancing over, she watched a man pull a small black device out of his brown leather jacket.

"Don't you hate beepers?" Cecilia said. "People bring them into the store I work at all the time."

Mia nodded, having no clue what she was talking about. She took in how relaxed Cecilia looked compared to the night before.

She forced herself to stop staring as she remembered why she was there. To help Colby.

Never being known for having a filter, Mia blurted, "Are you sure you don't know why those people attacked you last night?"

Cecilia's face instantly dimmed. "I wish I did, but...I'm sorry, I don't."

"I know, but I'm trying to figure out why they went after you. Salem isn't exactly a hot bed of criminal activity."

"I don't know." She looked uncomfortable. She grabbed the necklace that hung around her neck, rubbing the pendant. "Can we talk about something else?"

"Sure," Mia said, her mouth firming into a thin line.

She leaned back in her chair, taking in the different patrons in the shop. A woman sat a couple of tables away from the guy with the beeper, reading a romance novel featuring a shirtless guy with long blond hair. She wore a boxy gray business suit that looked like it had football padding stuffed underneath the shoulders. Her bangs were raised high toward the ceiling. Mia hoped no one lit a match around her. The woman had so much product in her hair, she'd probably go up in flames.

She turned her head to find Cecilia staring at her. Unable to help herself, she asked, "Why you, though? I was near the alley, too. Why didn't they grab me?"

The other girl began to fidget with the saltshaker on the table. "Well...you managed to scare them off. Maybe they knew you weren't someone they could mess with."

"Let's face it though." Mia waved her hand at Cecilia, taking in the other girl's lithe frame. "Look at you compared to me. You're taller and look like you could run a marathon. I, on the other hand, am short and way out of shape."

"I think you have a nice body." Cecilia's mouth closed with an audible snap. Her cheeks turned a delicate red and she looked like she hoped the floor would open up and swallow her whole.

Mia's own face flushed. Was...Cecilia flirting with her? This was new territory. She had focused so much on Ella that if someone *had* flirted with her, she probably wouldn't have noticed.

"I, um ..." Mia said. "I'm trying to make sense of it. You don't owe anyone money or anything, do you?"

"What? Of course not."

"And you're not a secret master thief or anything?"

Cecilia leaned back in her chair. "Do you ask every girl these kinds of questions?"

"No, of course no—"

"Do I need a lawyer present before we continue?"

Gertie set a mug down in front of Mia, oblivious to the sudden tension between the two girls. "Here's your black coffee." She took another mug and a small plate off the tray she held and placed them in front of Cecilia. "And here's your latte and Danish. Can I get you anything else?"

"No, we're all set." Cecilia's tone was short. The waitress nodded and walked away. Mia opened and closed her mouth, trying to figure out how to ease the atmosphere.

"I'm sorry. I'm not...very good at talking to people," she admitted. "I have a very small circle of friends at school. As in two people. And I don't think one of them is speaking to me right now." Ella was most likely a lost cause. Colby was just lost. Her heart panged at the thought. "People aren't really my thing."

"It's fine," she said, but Mia could tell she was still upset.

"Seriously, I'd rather hang out with my dog than hang out with people."

That made the other girl laugh a little. "I don't blame you there. What kind of dog do you have?"

"She's a pit bull. Her name is Winnie and she's perfect."

"Maybe I could meet her."

For the first time since arriving in 1992, Mia felt a twinge of disappointment at the idea of returning to her own timeline. Winnie loved meeting people. She'd adore Cecilia. "I didn't bring her with me. She's back home."

Cecilia's expression turned sad. "I always wanted a dog, but my mother never wanted the upkeep that came with a pet."

Given what Cecilia mentioned about her mother arriving home drunk the night before, Mia bet there wasn't a lot her mom did for her. It was her turn to give the other girl's fingers a squeeze.

Cecilia turned her hand so that the girls were touching palm to palm. Almost like they were holding hands. Mia couldn't be misunderstanding the signals here.

"I wish I could make things better for you." Mia meant that in more ways than Cecilia would ever know.

"I appreciate that, I do," she responded. "But please don't worry about me. I genuinely think that last night was a one-time thing. As for my mom, it is what it is. She's always been that way. She's a toxic person and tries to make everyone around her as miserable as she is. But I'm fine. I've got a plan."

"Yeah, what's that?" Mia moved her fingertips to Cecilia's wrist and held back a grin when she felt the other girl's pulse speed up.

"I'm going to leave Salem as soon as I turn eighteen."

Knowing that was never going to happen, she forced herself to nod. "And go where?"

"Out west. I heard that's where my dad is. He lives in Seattle, I think."

"You don't know him?"

She gave a little shrug. "Like you, I had a parent abandon me when I was little. At least, that's what my mom told me."

Cecilia let go of her hand to grab a bite of her Danish. Mia sighed inwardly at the loss of contact as she reached for her black coffee and took a sip. It was bitter and delicious.

"Do you believe your mom?" she asked after a moment. "About your dad, I mean."

"Who knows." she shrugged. "She's an evil liar on a good day. I wouldn't blame my dad if he couldn't take it anymore and decided to split. I also wouldn't put it past my mom to lie about him."

She grabbed her necklace again, moving the pendant back and forth on its chain.

"You do that a lot," Mia said. When Cecilia looked at her in confusion, she nodded toward the necklace.

"Oh." She showed it to her. It was beautiful. The pendant was made of crushed pearl encased in a bed of silver. "It was my grandma's. She died shortly after I was born. My family doesn't have very much in the way of money, but this has been in our family for generations." She smiled as she looked at it. "Apparently some relative of mine got it by less than honorable means." The humor left her face. "It's worth a lot, which is why my grandma didn't leave it to my mom—she was probably afraid my mother would drink it away. I inherited it when I turned sixteen. It probably sounds silly and stupid, but I like to think she left it to me because she loved me. It's nice to think someone in my family gave a damn about me, you know?"

Despite growing up knowing that Tilly loved her, a part of Mia still felt lonely. Like something was missing. She could sympathize with the other girl.

"I get it," she said.

Cecilia continued to touch the pendant before letting it go so that it gently swayed beneath her collarbone. "I guess I've gotten in the habit of grabbing for it whenever I get upset."

The girls were silent for a moment before Cecilia gave a nervous laugh. "Sorry for bringing down the mood."

"You didn't." Mia gave her an encouraging smile which she returned. The sight of it warmed her before grief wiped the feeling away. Cecilia was in front of her, her cheeks flushed with life, looking carefree despite the hand life dealt her. It was hard to believe that in a short time, someone would take her away from the world. It wasn't fair!

"What about you?" Cecilia asked. "I know your mom isn't in the picture anymore. What about your dad?"

Mia felt the same sadness she always did when she thought about her father. "My dad died in a boating accident shortly before my mom left. I was three. He was a fisherman and was out in the harbor when a bad storm came through. Parts of the boat washed up on shore a few days after it happened. They found his body a week later. At least, that's what I was told."

"I'm so sorry. I shouldn't have brought it up."

"It's fine. My mom's sister raised me. She's awesome." Mia's mouth briefly turned down as she thought back to her fight with her aunt before she accidentally time traveled. "I haven't always made it easy on her. She didn't have to take me in. I must feel like a burden to her sometimes. But my aunt's never treated me like one. She's always shown me nothing but kindness and love."

Cecilia took a sip of her latte. "Do you remember your dad?"

She shook her head. "No, I wish I did. I was told he was handsome and kind and that he had amazing taste in music. But I don't remember a single thing about him. It makes me sad when I really think about that, but maybe it's self-preservation, like if I don't remember him, it won't make his loss hurt as bad."

Cecilia gave her an empathetic look. "What about your dad's family? Are you close to them?"

Mia swallowed. "I've never met them. They didn't approve of my mom and disowned my dad once he told them he was going to marry her."

"That's too bad."

She turned her coffee cup in her hand, watching the liquid swish back and forth. "It's fine. Like I said, my mom's family took care of me."

"It's not the same though."

Mia nodded. Cecilia probably understood the feeling of loneliness better than most people. As Mia's mind went back to her dad, she realized something that almost made her jump out of her chair.

Her dad was alive in this timeline.

She could see him. Maybe get to know him a little.

Not going to happen.

Mia was playing Russian Roulette with the timeline as it was by hanging out with Cecilia. There was no way she could *or should* meet her dad. Besides, she'd mourned him her entire life. She didn't think she'd recover if she met him now, knowing she would have to lose him all over again. She was already dealing with the emotional rollercoaster of seeing her grandpa alive, her grandma healthy...not to mention Cecilia. The longer Mia talked to her, the worse she felt about her impending death.

She didn't want her to die. The thought of it—of someone tearing her apart, piece by piece—made it hard for Mia to breathe. She was so alive. It wasn't right!

Maybe Mia needed to get some space from the other girl before her...concern deepened any further. She shouldn't have agreed to meet her in the first place. She wasn't supposed to save her. That wasn't how this worked.

Yet looking at Cecilia, every instinct inside her told Mia that she could protect her. She'd had such a crappy life so far. Why shouldn't she get her dream of running the hell away from Salem and finding some happiness? Why couldn't something positive happen to her?

Mia could make that happen. All she needed to do was find out who was behind her murder. But how would she even begin to figure that out? She wished she could talk to Tilly—the Tilly who'd raised her. Her aunt always helped her see the details that she sometimes missed.

If she asked the younger Tilly for advice, she knew immediately what her aunt would say.

Don't mess with the timeline.

Mia's shoulders drooped. Her aunt would be right, too. She couldn't do anything for Cecilia. It was foolish to think otherwise.

"Why do you look sad all of a sudden?" the other girl asked.

"I have a tendency to worry about a lot of things."

"I'm sorry if our conversation triggered something for you."

Mia shook her head. "I know you don't want to talk about it, but I'm worried about you."

"Hey." She reached over and full on grabbed Mia's hand, lacing their fingers together. "I told you, you don't have to worry about me. I'll be fine."

Mia stared at their hands as heat rushed through her. She bit her bottom lip nervously.

Cecilia looked at her before lowering her eyes shyly. "Does this make you uncomfortable?"

Her hand tightened slightly, her thumb going back and forth across Mia's skin. Her flesh tingled where they touched.

"No," she choked.

Mia had never encountered a situation like this. The ability to openly hold a girl's hand was entirely foreign to her. She had never mustered the courage to confide in Ella about her feelings. And aside from her aunt and Colby, no one else knew about her sexuality. She was proud of who she was. She just wasn't ready to announce it to the world yet. Perhaps it stemmed from a fear of rejection, rooted in the childhood trauma of her mother's abandonment, but she'd never wanted to risk the dynamics of her relationship with people changing—especially Ella.

But sitting in the coffee shop, she felt a surge of courage as she held the hand of the beautiful girl across from her. Regardless of what lay ahead for both of them, she would cherish this moment forever.

Her heart raced as she met Cecilia's dark brown eyes. "So ..."

"So ..." Cecilia responded. "Can I see you again?"

"Yes." Mia didn't hesitate. It was going to be a problem for her family, but in that moment, with her hand wrapped firmly in the other girl's, she didn't care.

"Do you like live theatre?" Cecilia asked. "The Salem Actors Group is doing Macbeth at the park in a couple of days. We could meet here at seven. Maybe get some dinner?"

Cecilia didn't know anything about her attackers. That should be the end of their contact. Mia needed to look into other ways to help Colby.

That didn't stop her from saying, "Sounds like a date." It'd be her first one ever, but she tried not to get excited about it. She shouldn't be going out with her again at all given the circumstances. She reluctantly pulled her hand back. "I, um, I should probably get going. My family and all."

"Yeah, okay," Cecilia beamed at her.

Mia waved at the other girl and walked out of the coffee shop. She continued until she was out of Cecilia's sight. Mia's steps slowed and she briefly closed her eyes.

Stupid, stupid, stupid.

Cecilia was going to die no matter how many dates they went on. Mia needed to stay focused, otherwise, she was going to end up heartbroken—even more so than she'd been with Ella. She and her best friend might have had the mother of all fights, but at least she knew she was safe and sound.

The same couldn't be said for Colby.

Even if Cecilia didn't know why the Originals went after her, they'd still done it for some reason. And that reason could very well be related to his disappearance.

Mia didn't have a choice. She *had* to spend time with the girl. It would be the perfect way to see who was after her. If that person was somehow also connected to Colby's kidnapping, then Mia could track them down once she returned to her timeline.

It was only to help Colby.

With that reassurance, she tried to come up with a game plan. She thought back to the previous night. The first step she needed to do was figure out why the Originals went after Cecilia. Maybe there'd be some clues in the alley where she was attacked.

She hurried toward the scene of the crime but came to a halt when she saw two men standing at the entrance, surrounded in a blue hue.

Examiners.

Mia avoided looking at them as she walked into the store across the street. If a Common glanced their way, they would probably see the men standing in waste management uniforms or something. The Assembly liked to use glamors to hide in plain sight.

The men didn't seem to notice her as she stood near the window. Mia shoved her hands in her pockets to hide the blue hue forming on her fingers. Focusing her energy toward her ears, her hearing slowly enhanced. She stared at a shirt on the wall that had characters from *The Simpsons* on it as she listened in on the Examiners' conversation.

"What's the chief make of it?" the one man said.

"There was an upside down pentagram etched into one of the bricks on the wall. What do you think?"

Mia tried to keep her face blank even as her breath quickened. An upside down pentagram could only mean one thing ...

"Warlocks?" the first man asked. "In Salem? I didn't think any of them dared come here because of the Fitzgerald coven."

She felt a slice of pride shoot through her. She always knew her family was famous for being powerful witches. She hadn't known they were such a force that they scared off warlocks.

Warlocks were bad news. Once upon a time, they were witches, but they'd committed a crime so hideous that they were excommunicated. Being excommunicated was worse than death. They were outcasts, unwelcome in any society. It wasn't just witches either. Vampires, werewolves, mermaids, faes... any member of the supernatural world that was excommunicated became an Unmentionable. And Unmentionables loved to create chaos because they had nothing to lose.

Their crimes were legendary from the Hindenburg explosion to Amelia Earhart "disappearing" to *much* worse. Behind some of the most horrific crimes in human history was an Unmentionable. They kept the Assembly busy.

"If it is a warlock," the second man said, "they failed to register that they're in town. Gavin will go after them, you know he will."

"The kid's off to a good start with the chief."

"Hold up," the second Examiner said. Mia could feel him gazing at her through the window.

She hurried out of the store but stumbled from a combination of weakness from the spell and shock from what she'd overheard. She braced her arm against the window until she regained her balance.

"Excuse me, miss," the second Examiner called out, his voice thick with suspicion. "Are you all right?"

She didn't dare face them in case one of the Originals remembered any details about her that the Examiners could use to identify her.

"I'm fine," she yelled back. "Just cramps from my period."

The man coughed in an attempt to mask his discomfort. Mia would have laughed if she wasn't so terrified. She walked away on steadier feet as she let the element of fresh air give her a boost.

A warlock was in the area.

That was bad news. *Really* bad.

It also gave her a suspect. Warlocks specialized in dark magic. They had no qualms about practicing hexes on unsuspecting Others...like the harpy who disappeared. The warlock could very well be the one behind Cecilia's murder.

But why? That's what Mia couldn't figure out. Cecilia was a Common. What the hell would a warlock want with her?

She soon reached her house. Knowing there was no way she'd be able to climb back in through her window, she entered the side door and hoped she wouldn't run into anyone. Luck was on her side because she didn't see any family, even once she reached Sadie's bedroom door. With a quick glance down the hall, she backed into the room.

"Hello Mia. We're so glad you're back."

She swung around. Her grandma sat on the bed, her face a mix of disappointment and fury. Tilly stood behind her with her arms crossed, looking seriously pissed. Her grandpa leaned against the closed closet door, staring at her with one eyebrow raised.

Well...shit.

CHAPTER 8

"Did I or did I not tell you to stay indoors and out of sight?"

Mia had never seen a person actually seethe before, but her grandma was doing it now. A vein popped out on her forehead as if to emphasize the point.

"You did." She looked down at the floor and tried to make herself appear as small as possible.

"And why was that?"

"Because nothing ever good happens when timelines get messed up."

"Then explain to me why you put a glamor on this room and left anyway."

"If you ladies will excuse me," Grandpa Ray said. "I need to get back to the store. Mia, glad you're back safe."

She moved out of his way, so she wasn't blocking his exit. She averted her eyes, so she didn't have to look at him. It was a stupid reaction, but Mia needed to avoid him. She didn't want to let anything about his fate slip. And a part of it was her stupid self-preservation. Maybe avoiding him would help her heart ache less when she lost him all over again.

"Wimp," Tilly muttered at her father's retreating form before shaking her head at Mia. "I could've told you glamors don't work on Mom. She knows all. I've been grounded more times than I can count because…" Grandma Eabha glared at Tilly and she stopped talking, muttering a quiet, "Sorry."

Mia continued to keep her mouth shut. Something invisible wrapped around her waist, and before she knew what was happening, she found herself dragged across the room, the sound of her toes scrapping across the carpet jarring to her ears. She stopped when she was in front of her grandma.

"We need some answers."

"No."

"What do you mean no?" her grandma asked, indignant.

"You don't want answers." Mia pointed at Tilly who hadn't dared speak again. "You've made it clear that you don't want to know anything about the future so I can't tell you why I left today."

"Mia." Her grandma attempted to sound a bit calmer, but given the pinched expression on her face, she was struggling. "I need you to explain this to me. Explain why you're acting so carelessly. Because for the life of me, I can't understand what's motivating you right now."

"Mom …" Tilly started to say but Grandma Eabha held up her hand.

"Mia hasn't been here twelve hours, and she's already snuck out of the house twice and has a warrant out for her arrest for attacking those Originals. That alone should be incentive enough for her to *stay inside!* Parris probably has Assembly members still investigating the area. So, I'm going to need her to explain what's going on."

Mia chewed on the inside of her cheek as she tried to think of the best way to answer without telling them too much about the future…or the fact that she already almost ran into two Examiners a short while ago. Then there was what she'd witnessed between Parris and the mermaid.

"I'm waiting."

"Okay," she said. "I...it has to do with my timeline. Something happens here—and I think it's going to happen soon—I mean, it's already starting, but it gets worse. It creates problems down the road. So, I'm going to fix it. Later."

Mia felt pretty proud of herself. She managed to explain everything while giving nothing away. She let out a relieved breath.

"What?" Tilly and her grandma asked in unison, confusion etched in their faces.

Okay, so maybe she hadn't done such a good job explaining. Mia shook her head. To hell with it. "Someone in Salem is going to be killed very soon. There was already one attempt on her life."

"The girl from last night." Grandma Eabha had always been quick at putting puzzles together. It made Mia angry all over again about what Alzheimer's would do to her. Her grandma gave her a steady look. "I thought you said you didn't know her."

"I don't, but everyone in my timeline knows about her. Her death is pretty infamous." Kids told the story of Cecilia's murder at slumber parties to scare their friends. People claimed that they could hear her screams coming from her house at night, demanding for her killer to be found. "She and I agreed to meet today. She wanted to repay me for the help last night."

"Who is she?" Tilly asked.

Mia shrugged. "Does it matter?"

"No." Tilly looked sad. "I know you don't want to hear this, but if this girl is meant to die...you can't stop what's supposed to take place. I mean, how do you know you didn't stop her killer when you hexed the Originals? What if you've already altered the future?"

Mia walked over to Sadie's closet. She opened the door and kicked off the white Keds she'd borrowed so they landed inside with a thump. If this was going to be an interrogation, she might as well get comfortable.

"I don't think I've stopped anything," she said as she turned back to face her relatives. "Like you both said this morning,

Originals don't kill Commons. It's not their style. I think someone else might be behind the killing."

"You still can't stop her death." Tilly said gently.

Mia flinched. She knew that. It didn't mean she wasn't pissed off all over again about the situation. "I'm not trying to stop anything."

"Then what are you doing?" her grandma asked.

"I ..." Mia felt tears well up in her eyes. She wanted so badly to tell them everything, but she couldn't. From what she knew of their town's history, and what she overheard Colby's mom say, Others would start disappearing soon, and her family couldn't do anything about it. Mia wouldn't put that burden on them.

Grandma Eabha stared at her, her lips turning down. "You carry the weight of the world on your shoulders, little one."

She walked over and touched her face. Mia felt the telling warmth of a truth spell wash over her.

"No!" She jerked away, but it was too late.

Grandma Eabha's eyes widened as she realized what Mia just revealed. "I see."

She glared at her grandma. "Why did you do that?"

"Because this isn't your burden to carry alone. That's what family's for."

"You shouldn't have to carry this burden either."

"Oh, Mia." Grandma Eabha wrapped her in a brief hug. "You're a good girl."

She shook her head before whispering, "You won't be able to save them."

Her grandma stepped away from her, looking like she'd aged ten years in the span of a few seconds. It made Mia's heart ache. "I know."

"Okay," Tilly said. "Since everyone else is in the loop, does someone want to fill me in on what's going on?"

"A friend at Mia's school disappeared in the middle of the night. It's very similar to how the harpy, Susan Flightfast, vanished. More in our timeline will disappear and die before they find the girl murdered. Mia's trying to figure out if the person behind Susan's disappearance is connected to her friend."

"Then...what are we going to do?" Tilly asked. "I could call Gavin. Give him a head's up."

"No." Grandma Eabha didn't take her eyes off her granddaughter. "We can't stop this from happening, Tilly."

"But—"

"As you just told Mia, it could alter the future. That's why she didn't want us to know. We can't change things that are meant to happen."

"But the next victim could be any of us," Tilly argued. "One of my friends."

"We can't *change* anything," Grandma Eabha repeated firmly. Tilly walked over to the bed, sat down, and covered her face with her hands.

"I'm sorry," Mia whispered.

"You didn't disobey anyone by telling us about the future," her grandma said, the corner of her mouth ticking up. "I cheated."

It was selfish of Mia, but she already felt like some of the pressure she'd been carrying was gone. She gave her grandma a watery smile before turning away. She moved over to the bedroom window, which was still open from her escape earlier. As she looked out onto the harbor, she saw the quick flash of a mermaid's tail before it disappeared under the water. She wondered if it was the same mermaid Parris had spoken to earlier.

"Just be careful." Her grandma came up behind her. "Don't let your feelings for this girl get in the way of what's supposed to happen."

She said it quietly, but Mia could see in the reflection of the window that Tilly heard her anyway. "Feelings? You're gay?"

Mia stiffened. Her aunt never had a problem with her being a lesbian. Tilly was always so accepting of her. Then again, apparently she'd known Mia was queer before she was even born, thanks to this conversation. She just hoped her aunt wasn't a bigot in her youth.

She turned to face her aunt, her chin high. "Do you have a problem with that?"

Tilly looked offended that she asked. "Of course not."

Her defensiveness instantly left, and she gave her aunt a tentative smile which Tilly returned.

"So, who's the girl?" Tilly asked her mom.

"I don't know her," Grandma Eabha said. "She looks to be about your age, but she's not anyone I recognize from your school."

Tilly got off the bed and started pacing around the room. "Well, if she's a Common, she wouldn't go to Cunningham."

"Hold up." Mia scowled at her aunt. "You go to Cunningham? Why do I go to public school, and you go to Cunningham?"

"Cunningham is full of pretentious Others," Tilly said. "Sadie probably didn't want you exposed to that."

Mia was about to open her mouth and remind them that Sadie abandoned her long before she entered school, but her family didn't know that tidbit yet. Then her head comprehended Tilly's full statement.

"Wait a second. There's a school for Others?" She started getting angry. "You were the one who suggested I go to public school."

Tilly crossed her arms over her chest. "Well, then I was being smart."

She was about to argue this further when she thought of something else. "Ailsa goes to Cunningham." Her mind drifted to the gorgeous blonde who always came to their shop for tea. "I knew she was too pretty to be human."

"Let's focus here," her grandma said. "You didn't tell us about the dark energy."

"Dark energy?" Tilly moved over to her mom. "What about it?"

"I don't know," Grandma Eabha said. "Mia pulled away before I could see the full picture, but I did get a glimpse. Mia, care to explain why you have a connection to it?"

"I …" Her stomach tensed. How could she explain what happened last night? What always happened when she encountered the darkness. "Okay, I promise I'm not a warlock."

"Promising start," Tilly muttered.

"Shh," Grandma Eabha told her daughter before looking at Mia. "What were you going to say?"

She stared at a snag in the green carpet as though it was the most fascinating thing she'd ever witnessed. "When the girl was being attacked last night, I felt dark energy in the alley."

"What?" Her aunt took a step toward her, tilting her head as she examined Mia. "How did you manage to get near it without going insane? Didn't it affect you?"

"No, it…" They were going to hate her so much.

"It's okay." Her grandma's voice was comforting. "What happened?"

"I can't really explain it." Mia looked at Tilly—her one constant—silently pleading for her understanding. She didn't know what she'd do if her aunt ever turned her back on her. She was the only mother she had. "I swear. I seriously don't know what happened."

"Walk us through it," Grandma Eabha encouraged.

"I was standing in the alley when I felt the darkness surround me. It…it seemed to enter me—"

"What? How?" Tilly interrupted.

"Like I said, I don't know what happened. All I know is that I felt the most incredible boost of energy, like I'd slammed a hundred energy drinks, you know?"

"What's an energy drink?" her aunt asked.

"Tilly, shush." Grandma Eabha gave Mia a nod. "Go on."

Mia lifted a shoulder. "The rest you know. I disintegrated those Originals."

"And you didn't feel tired after? Young witches are usually exhausted after doing a hex."

"No, I felt fine. Stronger even."

Her grandma walked over to Sadie's dresser. She picked up a perfume bottle and stared at it, lost in thought, before she turned back to her. "Most Others are sensitive to dark energy of the magnitude you experienced last night. It can have a tremendously negative effect on someone. Depression. Even death. That's why we avoid it and why it's so popular with Unmentionables. Over the years, they've figured out how to harness it. They usually absorb it inside them and then unleash it on their enemies like a weapon. But it eats away at their soul until it consumes them, turning them into mindless nothings."

"That didn't happen to me," Mia said. "I mean, I felt anger when it was inside me, but the feeling went away after the darkness left."

"It left?" Tilly asked. "When an Unmentionable releases it, some of it still remains inside them, becoming a part of who they are. It doesn't ever leave them."

"It did with me. It poured out of my skin like sweat. And then I only felt depressed, but that feeling didn't last too long." Mia frowned as she tried to gather her thoughts. "It... I know this is going to sound weird, but sometimes I feel like I can sense it, even when I don't want to."

"How so?" Grandma Eabha asked, walking over to her.

"The girl who I met with today—the girl who dies—she gets murdered in her basement, and her death triggers dark energy in her house. It seems to be dormant in this timeline, but in my time, it's very alive. I...I don't know why, but I always feel drawn to the house. And it's getting worse. Last time I went by that place, the darkness reached out and touched my skin. It showed me ..."

Grandma Eabha's face never looked so serious. "Honey, what did you see?"

Mia's mind flashed back to what the dark energy revealed. She could see the body parts on the table. The blood splattering the walls. She could hear the sound of Cecilia's screams. She swallowed over the painful lump in her throat. "It showed me her murder."

Her grandma placed a hand against her cheek. "I'm so sorry."

"I wish I could stop the darkness. I don't want it anywhere near me. But...it calls to me."

Tilly and her grandma exchanged glances.

"What? What was that look?" Mia said before pleading, "I swear I'm not bad."

"Of course you're not," Grandma Eabha said. She grabbed her hand and led her over to the bed. They sat down and Tilly joined them, sitting on her other side.

"Mia." Her grandma tucked a strand of her loose, raven black hair behind her ear. "You're a Desolate."

"I'm a what?"

"A Desolate."

"I don't know what that means."

Tilly gave her a light punch on the arm. She looked almost proud of her. "Desolates are extremely rare and very cool. You can manipulate dark energy."

Mia looked between her relatives. "I'm still really confused."

"What do you know of our family history?" Grandma Eabha asked. When Mia stared at her blankly, she said, "Are you aware that we're descendants of Samuel Parris?"

She nodded. "Yeah. You used to read stories to me from some diaries of our ancestors when I was little. He was mentioned a few times."

"Do you know who he is?"

"Every kid who grows up in Salem knows who he is. His family started the Salem Witch Trial massacre. His daughter and some friends accused Commons of being witches."

"Her name was Betty, a spoiled girl with too much time on her hands and a streak of jealousy that poisoned her." Grandma Eabha's gaze went to the picture of Sadie hugging the tree. "Her mother, sister, and brother were witches, but she didn't have any abilities. She grew resentful and acted out, thrashing around in public and yelling gibberish. She told the town that a bunch of Commons cast spells on her. Many innocents lost their lives because of her antics."

"Okay, but what does this have to do with me being a Desolate?"

Her grandma smiled though it was more of a grimace. "Samuel Parris hated witches almost as much as Betty did. It was a nasty shock for him when he found out his wife, Elizabeth, was one, but he couldn't do anything about it. Divorce was scandalous back then and completely unheard of for puritans. Elizabeth, for her part, was a good person and an even better witch. To see people she cared about in the community getting hung because of her daughter and husband...well, it was incredibly shocking and stressful to her. When a witch is surrounded by so much death, one of two things can happen. They either go dark and most likely end up a warlock or they evolve."

"Evolve how?"

"Do you know how dark energy forms?"

Mia nodded. "It comes from death."

"Not just any death. Murder. Pain. Suffering. Elizabeth saw twenty of her friends and neighbors die at the hands of her family. The town hung nineteen of them. One had rocks piled on top of him until he was crushed to death. Their suffering caused dark energy to form, and Elizabeth absorbed all of it into her system. Only a very strong witch could have survived. She couldn't stop her family from what they were doin—"

"But why?" Mia interrupted. She knew this part of her family's history well thanks to the stories her grandma told her when she was a kid. It didn't make her want to shout about it from the rooftops. She carried a sense of guilt whenever she thought back to her ancestors and their actions. "Innocent people died because of our family. If Elizabeth was such a strong witch, why couldn't she have done something?"

"She eventually did," her grandma assured her. "Before she became a Desolate, she couldn't do much without exposing herself. Pandemonium would have broken out if they'd caught her and confirmed witches were real." Her grandma seemed sad for a moment before looking at Mia. "Once she became a Desolate, Elizabeth was able to take the dark energy and turn it into something positive. She could sense when darkness was forming, when whispers were starting to turn into accusations. She pioneered spells that protected more innocents from dying. Many of her spells are still used by the witch community today. Thanks to her, the Salem Witch Trials came to an end. She *sensed* dark energy. Sound familiar?"

"Yes," Mia whispered.

"It's rumored she could even see an Unmentionable's brand on their skin."

"It looks like an upside-down pentagram," Tilly added.

"Yes, exactly," Grandma Eabha said. "It's usually invisible to most Others' eyes because Unmentionables have found ways to conceal the mark over the years, but Elizabeth supposedly was able to take one look at a warlock and see it. Thanks to her gifts, she protected people from coming into any further harm. Commons adored her, despite what her husband and daughter did. She was greatly mourned when she died." Grandma Eabha glanced over at

Mia, a grim smile on her face. "The Desolate gene has passed down through our family ever since."

Tilly gave Mia a sympathetic look. "Someone has to go through major trauma for the gene to activate."

Mia looked between her relatives before it dawned on her what they were saying. Mia experienced death in her life: her father, her grandpa. She experienced suffering: her mother, her grandma. If trauma was what someone needed to gain the power of a Desolate, Mia certainly fit the bill.

She frowned, looking at Tilly. Her aunt had gone through just as much as Mia. Her brother-in-law and father died, her sister ran away leaving Tilly to raise her child, and her mom developed Alzheimer's. As far as Mia knew, Tilly wasn't a Desolate.

"But..." she said. "I can't believe I'm the only witch out there who's gone through stuff. Why isn't the world full of Desolates? Why aren't there more in our family?"

"We've had some in the past, and there are other Desolates out there now. The problem is that there aren't enough of you for the Assembly to determine why some people get the power and others don't."

Mia still didn't understand why Tilly hadn't become one. She glanced at her grandma. "Do you have a theory?"

"It could be a number of things. Our family line is extremely old and powerful. That could have something to do with it." Her grandma shrugged. "Another theory is that Elizabeth lost many people within the span of a few months. Perhaps she felt so guilty, she wanted to right the wrong, and that's what triggered the gene. Maybe you're a Desolate because you're young and you've obviously gone through some kind of trauma at a vulnerable age. There are many things to consider."

Mia got up from the bed and walked back to the window. She watched a yacht cut through the waters of the harbor as she tried to process everything. She didn't know what this meant for her or how it was going to affect her life. What if she couldn't handle it? She struggled with so many things, simple math and reading comprehension. She messed up spells right and left. Now they were telling her she had powers that even the Assembly didn't understand. She was terrified, but she put on a brave face as she turned to face her grandma and Tilly.

"Okay, so I'm a Desolate." Mia leaned against the windowsill. "What now?"

"Now..." her grandma said. "We teach you how to use your power."

Chapter 9

Mia stood inside the pentagram in her bedroom. Everything past the border of the star was in shadow and out of focus. A pulsing blue hue lit the space she was in, the color a vivid contrast against the wood floor. Burn marks scorched one point of the star, a spell gone wrong. Not one of Mia's for once. Tilly had done it when she was younger.

As Mia tried to see beyond the star's boundaries, she saw the shadows of two figures on either side of her. They were speaking to each other, unaware *she was* standing between them. Their voices were frantic, but the words sounded muffled, like someone trying to speak underwater. Stepping closer to one of the shapes, the figure came slightly into focus. The person's blonde head seemed familiar to Mia. The face lifted and looked right at her.

She gasped. The girl's eyes glowed a brilliant white, the pupils gone, but Mia knew that face.

"Ailsa?"

"Tilly, I see her," Ailsa yelled.

She turned to look at the other figure. The person said something that still sounded unclear, but Mia could see the woman had long hair and her aunt's stature.

She ran toward Tilly with her hand out. Relief washed over her at seeing the aunt she knew. All she wanted was to hug Aunt Tilly tight. But before she could reach her, her arm slammed into something hard. She staggered back as pain shot through her. Mia tried to assess the situation as she shook off the lingering ache. She slowly lifted her hand to press it against whatever blocked her. An invisible barrier met her fingertips. It felt like she was touching ice. Balling her hands into fists, she banged against it.

"Tilly," she yelled, frantic to get to her aunt. When she received no response, she ran back to Ailsa. "Can you hear me?"

Her luminous eyes locked on her. "Mia..."

The sound of her soft voice made Mia homesick, her heart swelling with longing. She whispered, "Please help me."

The other girl lifted her hand and pressed it against the barrier. Mia slowly lifted her own and tried to make contact, but the wall stopped her. As she stared powerlessly at Ailsa—for just a second—it felt like the spot where they were almost touching grew warmer.

"Mia..." She looked heartbroken. "Mia!"

"Mia?"

She shot up in bed, her heart racing.

"Are you awake?" Tilly asked from the other side of the bedroom door.

Mia looked around. She was in her mom's room, still safe and sound in 1992. With a trembling hand, she rubbed at her eyes. Did she just have a crazy dream or was that real? Was her aunt trying to find her? Why was Ailsa there?

"Mia?" Tilly called again.

"I'm awake," she said, her voice groggy from sleep.

"We're leaving in a half hour. You better get dressed if you aren't already."

"Okay."

She tried to shake off the dream. After taking a quick shower and dressing, she made her way to the kitchen, her hair still damp and leaving wet marks on her borrowed clothes. Her grandpa greeted her from the table, causing Mia to misstep. She reluctantly entered the room.

A part of her hated herself for how she was acting. She knew she should be cherishing every second she could spend with him. A bigger part of her was still clinging to that reliable self-protection she enjoyed so much. She'd already mourned her grandpa once. The idea of losing him a second time and experiencing that crippling grief all over was too much for her to handle. At least with her grandma, she could still talk to her and touch her hand. It hurt so much to know she wouldn't be able to do any of that with her grandpa when she returned home.

"Where are you off to this early?" Grandpa Ray asked as he picked up a newspaper and began to read. Mia stared at it. She couldn't remember the last time she'd seen a newspaper. Maybe since before her grandpa passed away.

"Uh, to the cemetery." She grabbed a bowl out of the cupboard and a box of cereal before hesitating. "I don't suppose you have any almond milk?"

"Almond what now?"

"I'm vegan. I don't eat dairy."

Her grandpa stared at her for a moment like she'd spoken a foreign language before he nodded toward a basket on the counter. "There's some fruit in there. You can have that."

She nodded and put the cereal box back before grabbing a banana and sitting at the table. Her knee bounced up and down as she ate, reminding her that she was going on a second day without taking her A.D.H.D. medication. Whatever experiment her grandma had cooked up for her was sure to fail. Mia wasn't going to be able to concentrate long enough to do anything.

As she began to eat her banana, her mind switched to Ailsa. For just a second in that dream, she really thought they were going to make physical contact. Had she slept for a few more minutes, would Ailsa have been able to break through the barrier with those strange, glowing eyes?

And Tilly...how was she handling this? Mia hadn't had time to ask. Had she had any luck finding Colby? Were his kidnappers feeding him? He always used to get so hangry when he didn't eat regularly—the problem of being a growing werewolf. They always ate everything. And she meant everything. It wasn't unusual for him and his family to go hunting at night in the woods near their house, stalking and eating whatever prey they could find. Usually eating it raw.

"Here," Colby said, proudly tossing a dead rabbit at her feet once when they were twelve. They were out camping in the woods with his parents for the weekend.

Mia swallowed down the bile rising in her throat as she looked at the poor, mangled animal.

"What am I supposed to do with that?" she asked.

"Duh, we're going to eat it," he said. "Raw rabbit is good for a werewolf."

"I don't think I'm ever going to eat meat again," she replied queasily as she watched his claw pop out so he could skin his prey.

And she never had.

There were so many of these little moments with Ella and Colby throughout her years. After that particular vacation, she'd come home and done a deep dive on veganism. Ella had been staunchly supportive of her and had tried it for a short time herself. Colby thought they were both ridiculous, teasing them like the loveable brother from another mother that he was.

She rubbed at her forehead. She hoped he was okay.

Grandma Eabha came into the room, pulling her attention. She grabbed a pill bottle off the counter and waved it at her husband. "Did you take your vitamins?"

When her husband shook his head, she walked over and placed the bottle next to him, kissing his temple as she did. Mia found it hard to swallow the bite she'd just taken. She *missed* these two like this. It wasn't freaking fair.

"Are you ready for our day?" her grandma asked her.

Mia focused on peeling more of her banana. "Yeah... Sure."

Grandpa Ray took a pill out of its container. "Why are you taking her to the cemetery?"

"It's the perfect place for her to tap into dark energy."

Nerves made the acid in her stomach roll, and she put down the remainder of her fruit, unable to eat anymore.

Grandma Eabha reached over and lifted her chin, frowning at whatever she saw. "Did you sleep last night?"

Mia shrugged. "Just some weird dreams."

"About what?" Her grandma took a seat in the chair next to her, grabbing the orange juice and a glass her husband left her on the table.

"I... I had a dream that Aunt Tilly from my time and a girl I know were trying to find me. I was trapped in the pentagram inside my—Tilly's room."

Grandma Eabha smiled, a look of satisfaction on her face. "That's encouraging. Dreams like that are often born in reality. In Ancient Greece, Commons saw dreams as messages from Originals. It's said that the fae could even use dreams to open portals to other dimensions."

Mia perked up at that. "Fae? I have a theory that Ailsa—the girl in my dream—is at least part fae. She's inhumanly beautiful."

"She probably is then," her grandma said before taking a sip of her juice. "It sounds like Tilly and your friend are looking for you. Both my daughters must be frantic that you're here. I'd be going out of my mind if I were in Sadie's shoes."

Mia pressed her lips together to hold back any negative comments about her mom. A spoon on the table began to vibrate before falling off and hitting the floor with a loud clank. Her grandma raised an eyebrow.

Mia bent down to pick it up, her face flushing. "Sorry. Still a bit out of it from the dream, I guess."

Grandma Eabha didn't give her a lecture about losing control like she half expected. Instead, she asked, "How do you know this Ailsa?"

Mia placed the spoon carefully back on the table. "She's a customer from the shop. She's the one I mentioned who goes to Cunningham. I'm surprised she's helping. I don't know her that well."

Though, that wasn't entirely true. She and Ailsa had made small talk with each other over the past year since Ailsa first started coming to the store. She knew, aside from Ailsa's weird aversion to sugar, she spent her summers traveling the world with her aunt who was some type of politician or diplomat. Her mom was in the same line of work and had set up an office in Massachusetts last year, which was when her family moved to the area.

And Ailsa knew about her quirks, too—her love for indie bands and Reese's Peanut Butter Eggs. Mia started eagerly looking forward to her visits, her days a little bit dimmer when the other girl didn't appear.. It was nice to expand her social circle. A part of Mia always hoped they would grow close someday. But Mia tended to avoid putting herself out there, her fear of rejection and abandonment too strong.

"It makes sense if this girl is a fae and she's trying to help find you," Grandma Eabha said. "Seeing as they've mastered connecting interdimensional worlds better than any Other. It was a smart move that Sadie asked one to help look for you."

Mia snorted. "I'm going to go out on a limb and say all the credit goes to Aunt Tilly."

Her grandma's eyebrows lifted. "Don't be so quick to dismiss Sadie. I'm sure she's very worried."

She didn't say anything else. Her grandparents seemed to be blind when it came to their youngest daughter's true nature, and Mia didn't have the heart to tell them the truth. After she found out she was a Desolate, she'd spent the afternoon with her grandma and Tilly, going through different books that might contain the spell she messed up. The entire time Grandma Eabha talked nonstop about Sadie this and Sadie that. The longer she spoke, the tenser Tilly got, and the more upset Mia felt. It was no wonder her mother turned out the way she did. She could do no wrong in Grandma Eabha's eyes. She was spoiled to the core.

"Morning," Tilly said as she walked into the room. She wore dark red lipstick, a red and black flannel shirt, frayed bootcut jeans, and black combat boots.

"Always flannel," Grandma Eabha muttered.

Mia hated the way her grandma put Sadie on a pedestal, and yet seemed to criticize Tilly all the time. And Grandpa Ray didn't say anything about it. It saddened her to admit it, but her grandparents weren't the best parents, even if they'd been awesome grandparents. They weren't the perfect people that she had built up in her mind. She loved them, but maybe when she got back to her own timeline, she wouldn't give Tilly such a hard time. Her aunt didn't deserve it.

Mia gave her an encouraging smile. "I like her shirt."

Tilly rolled her eyes, though she had a pleased expression on her face.

"So," her grandpa said. "Mia says you're going to the cemetery this morning."

Tilly grabbed an apple from the basket on the counter and took a bite before answering, "Yeah, Wadsworth."

Grandpa Ray whistled. "There are some bad elements buried there."

"Exactly," her aunt responded, her mouth full of apple after taking another bite. "It's the perfect place for her to experiment with her Desolate powers."

"Finish your breakfast, Mia." Grandma Eabha got up from the table to put her glass in the dishwasher.

Mia shoved the remainder of the banana in her mouth before also standing up.

"Good luck," her grandpa said.

She smiled vaguely in his direction before following her grandma and Tilly out of the room. They headed outside and got into her aunt's Ford Tempo. Mia sat in the backseat and lovingly caressed the armrest, wishing all over again that the car was still working in her timeline.

When they arrived at Wadsworth, they made their way to one of the oldest graves in the cemetery. Mia tried not to look over at one of the newer sections they passed. They'd eventually bury her father and grandpa there.

Her grandma and Tilly came to a stop in front of a headstone. They put their hands over their hearts before lowering their heads respectfully. Mia knew the headstone well. When her grandma was still somewhat coherent in her timeline, she would bring Mia to this spot. Mia knew whose grave it was, though Grandma Eabha had neglected to tell her at the time the significance of this particular ancestor.

She looked at the brittle stone, the writing on it faded and barely legible. Elizabeth Parris. One of the most powerful witches in known history, and from what Mia learned the day before, the first Desolate in her family.

"This way," her grandma said as they moved onto another section.

They finally stopped under an old tree. There were no headstones in the area. Mia shifted on her feet, a sense of unease making her skin start to crawl. She looked upward and took in the tree's branches.

The tree was beautiful in her timeline. Pink flowers bloomed on it around this time of year. In 1992, the tree looked dead. There were no leaves, the branches sparse. Scanning the cemetery, she noticed all the trees appeared to be dead.

"What happened to the trees?"

"What do you mean?" Tilly asked.

"Why don't they have leaves on them?" She touched the tree closest to them. "This one is usually covered in flowers. Pink ones that bumble bees love to swarm. It's beautiful. Are the trees sick?"

Her relatives exchanged glances. Mia was getting a little sick of those.

"It's been like this for years," Tilly finally said.

"Weird." Mia observed the bare branches. "Have you tried Googling this area? Maybe it has something to do with climate change."

"What's Google?" Tilly asked. "Is that some kind of new spell?"

Her jaw dropped in dismay. "Wait? You have Google, right? Explorer, at least?"

Her aunt looked even more confused. "Is that code for a glamor?"

"Holy sh—how do you people survive?"

"Ladies, let's focus." Her grandma turned to Mia. "Do you know who's buried here?"

She glanced at the ground. The grass was dry and patchy. There was nothing to indicate there was a grave below. "Uh...no one?"

"Sarah Good. Do you know who that is?"

Mia nodded. "She was accused of being a witch during the Salem Witch Trials."

Grandma Eabha's face turned somber. "The town targeted her because she was different. Sarah spent her days going to her neighbors' homes, begging for handouts. She was one of the first people they accused. They were only too happy to get rid of her."

Mia thought back to the history she knew of Sarah. "Was she the one that was pregnant when they arrested her?"

Her grandma nodded. "She's the one. They threw both her and her four-year-old daughter in prison." Her face turned sorrowful. "That poor little girl. They eventually let her out, but being in that setting at such a young age damaged the child. They'd kept her in unsanitary conditions in a cell barely big enough for a growing girl to move. She died when she was sixteen. Sarah's baby was stillborn—too much stress on the mother. Sarah was hung shortly thereafter."

Mia thought of a story Aunt Tilly once told her. "She was a real witch, wasn't she?"

Her grandma smiled roughly. "She was, though not very powerful. She hexed the reverend who ordered her execution—a truly vile man. She told him he would die choking on his own blood, and twenty years later that's exactly what happened." Grandma Eabha looked approvingly at the spot on the ground before her face lost its humor. "After Sarah was hung, her family stole her body from the crevice the town left her in and buried her here. They couldn't give her a proper burial because she'd been labeled a witch, hence the lack of a tombstone."

Mia's eyes widened as she realized what her grandma was saying. It was beginning to make sense why she felt uneasy since arriving at this spot. She held her hand out over the ground. She couldn't see it, but she sensed something beneath her feet, trying to claw its way toward her.

"There's dark energy here," she said. She looked up at her family for confirmation.

Her grandma inclined her head.

"But why?" Mia asked. "Sarah was just as much of a victim as the rest of the people killed."

Grandma Eabha lifted a shoulder. "Sarah accused a Common of being a witch during the trials. She knew it wasn't true, but because of her confession, they hung the woman. Sarah's actions led to the direct death of an innocent and that created the dark energy you sense."

Mia frowned. She crouched low and placed her hand on the ground. "How come it isn't affecting me like it did in the alley? How come it's not affecting you?"

"It's dormant," her grandma explained. "It's attached to Sarah's body, though, as you can see, there's enough dark energy throughout the cemetery to drain the life out of the trees. The Commons called in tree specialists, but every time they tried to plant something new, it died." She touched the top of Mia's head briefly. "We'll teach you how to pull the darkness from Sarah and cleanse the area."

Mia stood back up. "I can do that?"

"You can manipulate dark energy to use for defense or you can cleanse it. That's part of the Desolate's gift and responsibility."

Her nerves started to act up as she took an unsteady breath. How on earth was she going to manage this? She put on a brave face as she said to her grandma, "What do I need to do?"

"First, you need to learn how to control your energy. Tilly said you broke a glass in her room when you lost your temper, plus there was that display with the spoon earlier."

Mia *knew* she wasn't lucky enough to avoid a lecture about that, not to mention feeling slightly betrayed by her aunt. She gave her a dirty look. "Thanks, narc."

Tilly rolled her eyes in response—a gesture her teenaged aunt specialized in. "Mature much?"

"Girls." Grandma Eabha's tone was stern before she looked at her granddaughter. "Close your eyes."

Mia did as instructed.

"Witches come into their power the same time as most Others do. When puberty hits."

Mia's face reddened. Oh god, she really hoped her grandma wasn't going to start talking about pimples and periods.

"When a witch does a spell," Grandma Eabha continued, "particularly when a teenage witch does a spell, it has a tendency to drain you. And what gives you your strength back?"

"The five elements," she answered.

"Yes. Air, fire, water, and earth are all things you can feel and touch. But the fifth element, spirit, that's internal. That's an element you can tap into no matter where you are, no matter what the situation. Sure, air and earth are around you at any given time, but they can be soiled. Your spirit is the purest element and the very core of your power. Your spirit gives you control, and in turn, it can give you a never-ending source of strength. You just need to know how to use it."

"But how?"

"Let me tell you some things I've noticed about you in the short time I've known you. You carry too much on your shoulders for such a young age. You also seem easily distracted."

"I have A.D.H.D.," Mia admitted.

"Oh!" Tilly said. Mia cracked an eye at her, but her aunt glared at her so she closed it again. "I do after school tutoring for the kids at the public school. A few of them have A.D.H.D. and do something called hyperfocus. That's where they get so locked in on a task they're doing, they block out everything else around them."

"Yes, that's perfect," Grandma Eabha said.

Huh. She never thought her disability could have an advantage. It had always seemed to be more of a burden.

"Mia," her grandma said. "Being a Desolate isn't easy. You take on the pain of the murdered, the suffering of the oppressed. If you're not careful, you can become addicted to the dark energy until it consumes you. You won't lose your mind like others who encounter it, but it can weigh you down and leave you severely depressed. Or worse. You need to be able to balance it."

"How do I do that?"

"You do that by focusing on your spirit," her grandma replied. "Tell me about something that makes you happy."

Mia's face scrunched. "What?"

"What makes you happy?"

Mia's mouth turned down. They stood in silence for several moments as she tried to rack her brain for something positive. At one time, she would have said Ella. Their friendship meant the world to her, even before Mia realized she had feelings for her best friend. Now when she thought of Ella, she felt nothing but heartache.

Her thoughts shifted to Colby.

"Mia, look what I got for the winter solstice!" he told her excitedly as he pulled five action figures out of his backpack when they were nine. They were miniatures of the representatives of the Assembly—the five who ruled the Other world. The Wolf King, the Queen Vampire, the Chancellor Witch, the Queen of the Merfolk, and the Faerie Queen. Mia had only collected three so far. She still needed the Faerie Queen and the Chancellor.

"Here," Colby said, handing her the tiny figure of Parris wearing a witch's hat, "You can have the Chancellor."

"I can't take this," Mia said, trying to give it back to him.

"I want you to have it," he insisted. "I'll ask for him for my birthday."

"Why would you want to break up your set?"

"Cause you're my best friend and that's what friends do."

Her throat ached as she tried to hold back her tears at that particular memory.

"Surely, there's something positive in your life," her grandma said. She sounded worried.

"What about that girl you mentioned who comes to the shop? The pretty one," Tilly added, mentioning Ailsa.

Mia's brain flashed briefly to Ailsa, before it switched to Cecilia. Cecilia with her hypnotic, brown eyes and long, gorgeous hair that Mia wanted to touch to see if it was as silky as it looked. But then, a core memory settled in her mind.

Mia thought back to a conversation that took place between her and her aunt a couple of years ago. She had been so nervous to tell her aunt that she was a lesbian. When she finally told her the truth, Aunt Tilly had gotten up from her office chair and hugged her, telling her she loved her. She also said that if anyone ever gave Mia a hard time or hurt her in anyway, she'd hex them into the next century. Love settled over her, calming her nerves and trepidation.

"I thought of something," she said.

"And how does it make you feel?" Grandma Eabha asked.

"Safe." A smile formed on her face. "Protected."

"Good. Concentrate on that feeling while breathing in and out."

Mia did as instructed until her shoulders relaxed, the lines of strain on her face smoothing away. She clung to the feeling of security her aunt gave her that day—the feeling of acceptance she always gave her—when her mind unexpectedly shifted back to Ailsa.

She saw the girl coming into the shop, making a point to talk exclusively to her. Mia thought about her dream the night before, of Ailsa searching for her. She could hear the relief in her voice when she realized she'd made contact with Mia. The feeling that she was cared for by both her aunt and Ailsa made her heart warm.

"Yes, that's it," her grandma said. "Open your eyes."

Mia's lids slowly lifted. She sucked in a breath when she saw a bright bluish hue surrounding her skin. It wasn't the first time she'd seen it. Usually the hue only showed up on her hands and was typically a deeper shade. She felt strong as she stood there, much stronger than when the dark energy had touched her the previous night.

"You're ready," Grandma Eabha said. She nodded at Tilly who stood on the other side of Mia. Together they raised their hands. A white line encircled her, flaring brightly.

"A ward," her grandma explained, "to keep you protected while you draw out the darkness. We can show you how to create these wards yourself. You should use them whenever you practice with dark energy so that it doesn't overwhelm you too much. Have you ever pushed your energy into your eyes to advance your sight?"

"Yes," Mia murmured, still in awe of the power coursing through her.

"Good. Creating these wards are the same concept, except you're pushing your magical energy outward instead of inward. As you continue to practice tapping into your spirit, you won't need this extra protection. You'll be able to find the balance you need to keep your emotions intact and not lose control of your energy. More importantly, as you hold onto the happiness your spirit creates, it'll stop the dark energy from consuming you." Grandma Eabha looked at her encouragingly. "Now, reach out with your senses and lock onto the darkness beneath your feet."

Mia dropped her gaze to the grass. She blinked and when she focused her eyes again, the ground became translucent, as though she was looking at the bottom of a clear lake. As she stared, something white started to form in her vision until the image crystallized and the skeletal remains of Sarah Good appeared.

Mia skimmed over Sarah's neck, noticing the break in the bone most likely caused from the rope they'd hung her with. Her hand was missing, probably carried away by some underground rodent. Mia swallowed hard when she noticed the black hue swirling around the body. She latched onto it until the dark energy was all she could see.

It rose from the skeleton as if sensing she was there to challenge it. The darkness oozed through the ground and entered her just like the other night. The stench of death filled her nose. Maybe it was because she'd been so worried about protecting Cecilia at the time that she hadn't felt the full force of the dark energy. She felt it now.

Strength flew through her, making her feel invincible. But as her strength increased, the darkness taunted her mind, preying on her weaknesses.

You're so stupid.

It's your fault he's dead.

You're a terrible friend.

Sadie abandoned you for a reason.

Across the entire cemetery, the dark energy woke, making a beeline straight for Mia under the surface of the ground, too far below to affect her family.

"Mom," Tilly whispered. "Her eyes...they're completely black."

"Don't break the barrier!"

The darkness roared loudly in Mia's ears. It sped toward her like an out-of-control freight train, hitting her all at once. Her knees buckled as everything that created the dark energy in the first place assaulted her.

She could feel the terror people experienced right before they were murdered.

She could feel their heartbreak as their lives drained from their bodies.

Pain ripped through her body as she endured the suffering of the abused.

There was *so much suffering.*

She couldn't take it anymore. It was too much.

Mia threw her head back and screamed.

"Stay strong!" her grandma yelled.

She could barely hear her over the buzzing in her ears. There were too many sounds. Crickets chirping. Someone mowing their lawn five miles away. Her eardrums felt like they were going to explode.

"Think of your happy memory," her grandma shouted.

Mia looked at Tilly standing beside her, her face worried, her hands still raised as her ward surrounded Mia. Protecting her as she always did. The warmth returned, a beacon through the darkness. It spread through her, making her feel safe and loved.

Bright blue light shot out of Mia. It slammed into the dark energy, brightening Mia's vision with a flash of white that momentarily blinded her.

She fell to her knees, gulping in several breaths of fresh air as she tried to regain her bearings.

Her body was shaking so hard it took her a minute to realize the screeching noise in her head was gone. So was the darkness. It had disintegrated upon impact of whatever energy Mia had just emitted.

Tears pooled in her eyes as her emotions ricocheted between extreme happiness and crushing depression—the despair of the suffering still lingering inside.

"You're okay," Tilly said, crouching down so she could wrap an arm around her shoulder. Mia buried her face in her aunt's neck and cried, the aftershocks of what she'd done turning her into an emotional mess.

"Mia," Grandma Eabha said, her voice awed as she stared up at the tree above them.

Mia followed her grandma's gaze and gasped. The tree next to Sarah's grave no longer looked dead. Flowers bloomed on it, bright and pink. She scanned the cemetery. The grass was bright and green. Every tree had come back to life. Flowers blossomed and birds chirped brightly from the various branches. Where the cemetery had appeared like it was in a state of forever mourning before, it now looked like a place of honor and fond remembrance for the dead buried below.

"You did it," Tilly said. "The dark energy's gone."

"Awesome," Mia said, her voice unsteady. Pulling away from her aunt, she got back to her feet on legs that shook. "I never want to do that again."

It had been too much. Without her family's steady presence by her side, protecting Mia with their ward, she wasn't sure if she could have managed what she'd done. Would she have been able to defeat the darkness on her own? Or would it have consumed her?

"Oh child." Her grandma patted her cheek. "This is only the beginning."

Chapter 10

Mia sat on a bench beside the Salem Harbor Walk. A couple of kayakers floated by on the South River. The sound of their paddles rhythmically hit the water, distracting Mia as she tried to focus. She promised her grandma she'd work on getting in touch with her inner spirit since it was the key to fighting off the darkness.

"It's about finding harmony, Mia," Grandma Eabha said as they drove back from the cemetery. "Always keep a collection of positive thoughts in your head, ready to be recalled at any given moment. Then you'll be able to balance your emotions when you encounter dark energy. Your spirit will remain strong if you focus on the positive."

Mia shifted in her seat as her mind tried to pull up a running list of happy memories.

Thwack, thwack, thwack.

She glared at the kayakers as they continued to beat the paddles against the water's surface.

Mia was on day three without her Adderall, and she was feeling it.

After her success at the cemetery yesterday, Grandma Eabha insisted she rest for the remainder of the day. She'd gladly accepted her grandma's offer. Mia had felt mentally drained upon their return, her emotions on the brink of spiraling out of control, and she'd sat in their family room for most of the evening. Tilly had kept her entertained by educating her on the best bands that were currently out while they continued to look through spell books for the one she'd used to time travel

"You haven't lived until you've seen The Pixies live," Tilly insisted.

Seeing her aunt's enthusiasm lifted Mia's spirit, creating another happy memory to file away.

When she woke up that morning, her grandma told her to practice hyperfocusing on positive thoughts. Mia started her training in her mom's room first, but that stupid picture Sadie had hugging the tree distracted her, making her angry. She then moved to the living room settling on the couch, but her grandpa soon came in to watch the Price is Right. The familiar scene made Mia emotional, and with a tense smile sent his way, she abruptly got to her feet and walked out of the room. She found her grandma in the store and asked if she could go outside. Much to her surprise, Grandma Eabha relented.

"Keep your head down," her grandma told her before walking away, muttering, *"Been out too many times already anyway. What's one more?"*

As the sea air riffled through her hair, she closed her eyes, whispering, "Balance. Harmony."

Easier said than done. Tourists went by, their shopping bags crinkling with every step. Mia's shoulders tensed as she tried to block out the noise.

Focus.

She did her best to get in touch with a happy feeling, but without her grandma and Tilly's presence, her mind kept wandering. She wondered how Ailsa and her aunt were coming along with finding a way to bring Mia home. Lightness trickled through her at the thought of the other girl working to help her. It was very sweet of her. She just hoped it wasn't in vain.

Mia had to return to her timeline soon. She wished she could find out if there were any updates on Colby. She wanted to use a memory of him to help guide her, but any thoughts of her friend made her sad.

What had he wanted to tell her the day he disappeared? She wished she would have stayed instead of using his friends' interruption as an excuse to walk away.

Mia pressed the heel of her hand against her forehead, trying to push back the sickening guilt and worry she had over her friend.

She couldn't focus for anything.

Taking a deep breath, she thought back to the night before. She'd sat around the kitchen, eating dinner with her perfectly healthy family. Her heart filled with the love of being with them. It left her longing for something she couldn't have. She'd been feeling so lonely over the past few weeks, ever since Ella began dating Kurt. And she thought...what if?

What if she stayed just a little bit longer? She could have her grandpa again. She could learn more from her grandma before her illness overtook her. Maybe Mia could even meet her dad.

Her heart did a funny little thump at that thought.

And then there was Sadie.

What would she say if she got to meet her mom, the person who was supposed to love her above everything else but still left her?

You're being stupid. You don't belong here.

She frowned.

Happy memories. Focus on happy memories.

The last true time she felt happy was when she'd held Cecilia's hand in the coffee shop. They were supposed to go on their date soon—Mia's first—but even that happy thought was tainted.

Cecilia's life was currently on a countdown and then her time would be up.

The sound of a ball bouncing on pavement had Mia cracking an eye open. Two young girls stood nearby wearing soccer uniforms. One was bouncing the black and white ball from her knee to the ground. The sight of it reminded Mia of Colby again.

He'd been so excited to share his news with her when he made the varsity team.

"The Others might not want me," he told her in the school cafeteria, back when they still sat together, "but I bet the Commons will give me a scholarship somewhere. Maybe I'll become a huge soccer star."

"I thought you planned on taking over your parents' business," Mia told him, not really paying attention because Ella just walked in the room.

"I'll take over that after my soccer career," he replied before taking a huge bite out of his venison sandwich. "There's plenty of time."

Mia's stomach clenched. She should have given him more of her attention. Maybe they wouldn't have drifted apart if she had. Even now, with her friend in serious danger, she was being terrible, thinking only of her selfish desire to stay with the healthy version of her family.

She didn't deserve Colby, but she'd make it up to him. And the best way to do that was by focusing on if there was any connection between the murders in 1992 and his disappearance.

She tilted her head from side to side, trying to relieve the tension she felt. This was not what her grandma had in mind when she told her to focus on the positive.

Happy thoughts, happy thoughts, happy—

"My purse!" someone shouted.

Mia's eyes flew open. A Common across the road was looking frantically around, trying to see past a large crowd of tourists who'd just stepped off a bus. Mia's gaze centered on one of them. A tall man who looked to be in his twenties despite his thinning hair, kept looking around nervously while clutching his stomach. The sweater he wore did little to hide the abnormal purse-shaped bump under his clothing. A blackish hue surrounded his body. Dark energy didn't form over petty theft. He had to be a repeat offender for there to be a little darkness visible on him.

It's a Common problem. Don't get involved.

The woman started sobbing hysterically, her voice carrying over the crowd. "My rent money! I'm going to b-be evicted now."

Releasing an annoyed sigh, Mia got up from the bench. The man was moving quickly toward her, away from the crowd. As he got closer, the darkness on him was unmistakable.

There was the familiar smell of something gone bad that always accompanied dark energy. Usually when the supernatural created it, the stench smelled like death decaying. On a Common, the smell was a combination of B.O. and someone who hadn't showered in a few days. With that pleasant thought in her head, Mia grabbed the man by the wrist.

"What the—" he started to say.

She moved her energy to her hand as he began to struggle, using her power so that he couldn't escape her grip. The guy easily outweighed her by a hundred pounds. It was going to take nothing short of witchcraft to control the situation.

She glared at him. "Do you always steal from women? Do you know how much you're about to screw up her life?"

"Screw you, bitch," the guy said through gritted teeth.

"Sorry, you're not my type." Mia twisted her hand and with the tiniest flash of blue hue, drained the dark energy from him. He fell to the ground, unconscious, the purse he'd stuffed under his sweater falling on the cement beside him. People around them began to clap. The woman ran up to them, out of breath.

"Thank you so much," she said as she bent down to retrieve her purse.

"Sure." Mia took several deep breaths as the darkness coursed through her. She felt strong. She felt furious. Now would have been a good time to think of a happy memory, but she was drawing a blank.

Mia stared at the guy, focusing on him instead of the turmoil inside her. He was still lying motionless. Maybe she'd taken too much energy out of him, and she briefly wondered if she'd killed him. When his chest moved up and down, she let out a breath. She hadn't killed him; just made him pass out.

It was a dumb move on her end, doing that to a Common, but what an interesting turn of events. Now that she was aware of dark energy and why it sought her, Mia was more aware of it. More importantly, she could do something about it.

A large group of Commons started forming around them, discussing what they'd witnessed. Mia glanced at them nervously, half expecting a hundred cell phones to be on her, recording what she'd done. Her shoulders relaxed when she remembered that kind of technology wasn't around yet. She turned to leave.

"What did you do to make him faint?" the woman asked before she could walk away.

"Karate move. Lots of training," Mia replied over her shoulder as she hurried through the crowd. She ran into someone and ricocheted back, barely managing to steady herself.

"I'm sor—" The words froze in her mouth as she stared up into the face of Doyle Parris. She'd never been this close to the future chancellor, not even in her own timeline. He was shorter than she expected and had perfectly cropped, bland brown hair that matched the color of his equally dull blue eyes.

"That was quite impressive," he said as he scanned her features. "You must be quite the expert in...what did you say it was? Karate?"

"Uh...yeah."

"Amazing that you were able to hold onto a man twice your size like that. I'd say it was almost magical."

Mia's heart sped up. "Excuse me." She tried to step out of his way, but he moved with her, continuing to block her path.

"You look familiar. Do you have family in the area?" Parris asked.

She lifted her chin defensively. "Why do you want to know?"

He gave her a thin smile. "I have family here myself. Perhaps they know each other."

"I don't have family here. I... I'm a tourist."

"Really?" Parris said, stepping closer. He lifted his hand and Mia's stomach sank. He was going to use a truth spell on her.

"Hey, sorry I'm late."

She turned and saw Cecilia coming toward them. She wore a blue slip dress that's neckline was so worn out it looked transparent along with the necklace she always had on. Large, clunky white sunglasses hid her eyes. She walked right up to Mia and kissed her on her cheek. Mia stilled in surprise. First hand holding and now this. It was unexpected, but she wasn't objecting. She wanted to reach up and touch the spot but Parris was watching.

"We're still on for our date, right?" Cecilia asked. "You look gorgeous, by the way."

"Uh...thanks?" Mia stared at her in confusion. They were supposed to go on a date but not until that evening.

Parris cleared his throat. He ran a hand over the ugly red and mustard tie he wore, looking uncomfortable. With a dismissive nod, he said, "If you'll excuse me, ladies."

He walked away without a backward glance. As he moved, another man ran up to him and said something low in his ear. Parris stiffened before hurrying away. He and the other man headed in the direction of the Salem Maritime National Site.

"Sorry about that," Cecilia said. Mia glanced at her and the other girl gave a sheepish smile. "He seemed like he was creeping you out. I figured a public display of affection might make him get lost."

"It worked."

Cecilia's mouth went tight as she stared at Parris's retreating form.

Mia's eyebrow cocked. "Do you know him or something?"

"Hmm?" She looked at her, her face softening. "Nah. He looked like the type of man who wouldn't support this." Cecilia waved a hand between the two of them. "And I can't stand bigots."

"I hear you," Mia said. "And you were right. I didn't want to talk to him."

Cecilia peeked over her shoulder at a row of shops behind her. "I was actually on my way to work when I saw you. Do you want to walk with me?"

"Sure."

A Common police officer walked by them to stand over the thief who was still passed out a few feet away. Another officer directed the still lingering crowd to move on and they began to disperse. Cecilia grabbed her hand so that they didn't get separated. Mia tried to ignore how good the contact felt.

"This town always gets so crazy this time of year," Cecilia said, "though nothing compared to Halloween. Have you ever experienced Salem around that time of year? You can barely move due to all the tourists. But it gives me the opportunity to get some overtime, which I like..."

She continued to talk animatedly as they made their way over to one of the stores. Mia was quiet. The dark energy that she took from the man was still inside her, but she was slowly sweating it away. As it left her, she began to feel the melancholy that always came after encountering the darkness. She tried to pull up a happy memory, but her mind drew a blank.

Cecilia let go of her hand as they entered a shop, her long, braided hair swishing back and forth as she walked. The memory of her coming to Mia's defense moments ago made her smile. She could still feel the warmth of Cecilia's lips on her cheek. Mia's spirit lifted and the sadness evaporated as though it had never been inside her. She let out a quiet sigh of relief.

How about that? Grandma was right.

She glanced around the store. Racks of shirts and sweatshirts with the word *Salem* written across them hung from every available space. There were visors on a stand next to the window, which also had the city's name imprinted across the front. It didn't look like there was anything in the shop that didn't have *Salem* or something witch-related all over it. Music from the overhead speakers blasted out a sugary pop song, the keyboard's repetitive melody making Mia cringe.

"You're late, Cecilia," a voice said from the back storage room.

"Sorry, Candy." She moved next to the sales counter and said in a quiet voice to Mia, "You're welcome to stay. I don't mind."

She was about to respond when she got distracted by the music, the song's keyboard continuing to clank on relentlessly. "What *is* this song?"

Cecilia gave her a funny look. "Do you live under a rock? It's 'Baby, Baby,' by Amy Grant. It's literally on every radio station."

"I, um, only listen to Classic Rock," Mia replied. Most of the members of the bands she did love, like Hazy Dawn, weren't even born yet. She pointed at the sunglasses Cecilia still wore. "Sunglasses inside?"

She laughed, the sound almost forced. "What can I say, I'm trying to start a new trend."

Mia took a few steps closer to the other girl, frowning. Now that the dark energy wasn't distracting her, she realized something was off. Cecilia's bright behavior since running into her was perhaps a little *too* bright. As she peered at the other girl, she noticed a small black smudge peeking out from underneath one of the lenses of her sunglasses. Sucking in a breath, Mia removed the frames.

Cecilia didn't meet her gaze as she reached out to touch the large bruise around her left eye. She flinched away a second before Mia could actually make contact.

Protectiveness surged through her. "Who did this?"

"It doesn't matter." The other girl still wouldn't look at her.

Had the Originals come back to hurt her again? "Was it the two from the other night?"

"No." Cecilia took the sunglasses from her and put them back on.

"You can tell me the truth. If it wasn't them, who was it?" Maybe some Unmentionable had gone after her—like the warlock who'd left the pentagram in the alley. Though she was still really confused why they'd go after Cecilia if they were the one behind her attack.

"I don't want to talk about it." She turned her cheek so Mia could only see the undamaged side of her profile. "Maybe you should go."

She didn't move as her mind raced. If Cecilia didn't know the person who gave her the black eye, why wouldn't she say something? Unless she did know the person. And she wanted to protect them. She had mentioned that her mom was an alcoholic the other night. Could she be abusive too?

"Was it your mother?" she whispered.

Cecilia's chin trembled. "Please don't say anything."

Fury erupted inside Mia. She clenched her fists to prevent any of her energy from escaping, though a rack of clothes behind Cecilia tremored slightly. "S-she shouldn't touch you." She tried to rein in her anger. She was going to lose it if she didn't calm down.

"It doesn't matter."

"How can you say that?"

"I turn eighteen next week and then I'm leaving Salem. So, like I said, it doesn't matter."

Mia paled, her anger evaporating instantly. "You're leaving next week?"

"I'm sorry I didn't say anything. I was afraid it would ruin things between us, and I still really want to go on our date, but yeah, I plan on leaving Sunday."

Thanks to the stories Mia heard about Cecilia's murder growing up, she knew she was seventeen when she died. Which meant someone would kill her sometime within the next few days.

Mia could stop it. Didn't she just discover that she could take dark energy from someone? Sure it had been a Common but who was to say she couldn't take on a warlock. Cecilia would have a chance to escape.

Tilly's voice popped into her head. *You can't stop what's supposed to take place.*

Mia wanted to beat her fists against the wall in frustration. Cecilia suffered so much already. Her mother was a monster. Her father wasn't in the picture. All she wanted was to escape her life and find something better. She didn't deserve any of what was about to happen.

She thought back to that moment in her timeline when the dark energy at Cecilia's house had touched her hand and shown her in vivid detail the brutal way she was going to die. It made Mia want to throw up.

Cecilia took hold of her clenched hand, and she relaxed her grip so that their fingers could lace together.

"Thank you," Cecilia said. "For caring about me."

"I wish I could help you."

"You've said that before." She let out a sad laugh. "My own personal hero."

Mia took a half step closer. "I mean it."

Her eyes drifted to Cecilia's perfectly shaped lips. They were so close, Mia could smell the honeysuckle perfume on her skin. Cecilia's eyelids fluttered down, her long lashes fanning her high cheeks. Mia's heart raced. What would it be like to kiss her, and not just a chaste kiss on the cheek? But to actually feel those soft looking lips against her own. She'd never kissed anyone before. She didn't know how to start the process, but she was very tempted to try it now.

Cecilia's hand tightened on hers before she let go and took a step back, breaking the spell over them. "I, um, I should get to work before my boss comes out and sees me standing around."

"Yeah, sure."

Mia turned to leave before she remembered something. She swung back and hugged Cecilia. Her energy rose inside her, flowing outward until it surrounded the other girl. Her blood sizzled with the power she was emanating as she focused on what she was doing.

Your mom will never touch you again.

Her energy grew stronger and for one second Mia felt invincible. Then it was over. Her energy returned to its normal hum inside her.

She bit back a smile. Like that time Tilly made her practice with the Aster flowers, her protection spell worked. Cecilia's mom would never be able to lift a finger against her again.

"Woah," Cecilia said, still in Mia's embrace. "That was weird."

"What was?"

"I don't know, static electricity or something."

Mia let her go and took a step back. "Sorry about that. I must have dragged my feet across the carpet. Built up a charge."

"It's fine." Cecilia stared at her, her expression soft and hopeful. "So, we're still on for tonight, right?"

"Absolutely," she said. "I'll see you at seven."

With a wave, Mia walked outside, breathing in the fresh air for rejuvenation. She'd done a minor protection spell, but at least it ensured that Cecilia would spend the last few days of her life free of her mother's abuse.

Mia wasn't worried that she just messed up the other girl's fate.

Her mom wasn't the one who killed her. The woman was a Common. If Cecilia's death was connected to Susan Flightfast's disappearance, only someone from the Other community could be responsible. It wasn't easy to kidnap a harpy. They were too quick for the Common eye. Not to mention Cecilia had crossed paths with two Originals and possibly a warlock, according to the evidence the Examiners found in the alley. If Mia had to point a finger at someone for her murder, it was one of them.

As she began to walk home, she noticed several people gathered at the Maritime National Historic Site. They stood at the end of the wharf staring at something.

Tilly appeared at her side and grabbed her arm, ushering her toward the family shop.

"What's going on?" Mia asked.

"Examiners." Her aunt nodded toward the crowd. "A mermaid was found on the shore. His heart's been cut out."

"What?" Mia tried to get a glimpse.

A large dolphin lay at the end of the dock. As her eyes pushed past the glamor the Assembly placed around the scene, she drew in a stunned breath. It was the mermaid she'd seen meeting with Parris.

She covered her mouth with her hand as she stared at him. His eyes had rolled toward the sky. His mouth hung open unnaturally wide as though his killer had caught him by surprise. There looked to be a hole in the area where his heart should have been.

Parris stood next to the mermaid while another Examiner spoke to him. He looked relaxed with his hands buried deep in his pockets. His lips shot up at whatever the other man said.

They reached their property and Tilly tugged her inside the house. "Come on."

They went upstairs to the living quarters and hurried into the kitchen where her grandparents waited.

Grandma Eabha hugged her as soon as she saw her. "Thanks be to Hecate."

Her grandpa stood behind his wife, gripping the back of a chair so tight his knuckles were white.

"I shouldn't have let you leave," her grandma said. "Did an Examiner see you? You didn't get too close to the body, did you?"

"No, of course not."

Grandma Eabha let her go before pointing to several crates of books on the kitchen table. "I had those sent from a coven I know in Greece. They arrived while you were out. It's more important than ever that we find the book you used to get here so we can figure out how to get you home. We can't risk the Assembly finding you, especially if they realize you were involved with the hex on the Originals. The black moon is this Sunday. It'll give us enough power to get you home if we can figure out the spell that got you here in the first place."

Mia's cheeks flushed with guilt at the memory of hexing the Originals. She walked over to the table. She didn't bother to tell her family about her run-in with Parris. Hopefully, the mermaid's death would keep him too distracted to give her another thought.

After several days without her A.D.H.D. medicine, Mia's memory of the book was a jumbled mess inside her head. She picked up a large heavy book, feeling the power of it thrum in her grasp. Nothing was remotely familiar about it. Same with several more that she looked at. She still opened them, hoping that she'd recognize *something*.

She and her family sat around the table for the next hour going through the different texts and pages. She was starting to feel defeated when her hand brushed against the second from last book in the remaining crate they were finishing. The book came alive under her touch, warming against her fingertips. Mia gasped.

"What is it?" Grandma Eabha asked.

"I... I think this is it," she said. "It feels like I know this book."

Tilly looked over her shoulder and whistled. "The Book of Aradia. That's some serious level witchcraft. Where did you get that?"

"Birthday present." Mia had already slipped up once and told her aunt it was a gift from her. If Tilly didn't remember her mentioning it, Mia wasn't going to remind her, especially given her aunt's earlier concern about knowing too much about the future.

With a swipe of her grandma's hand, the rest of the books flew through the air, piling neatly inside an empty crate underneath the kitchen window. Mia set the book on the table and shifted through the pages until she found the spell she'd done.

Tilly squinted at it. "This doesn't seem overly complicated. But it also shouldn't have made you time travel. This spell is more about a state of mind. It gets you in touch with your spirit and lets you travel the cosmos, but it's a mental state. There's nothing in these steps that should have made you physically go back in time."

"I might have screwed up the sequence," Mia admitted, not meeting any of her relatives' eyes.

"Which step?" Grandma Eabha asked.

"Uh...all of it."

Her grandma closed her eyes briefly before she turned toward her husband. "Can you put on a fresh cup of coffee? We're in for quite the afternoon."

CHAPTER 11

By the time evening rolled around, they weren't any closer to discovering what sequence Mia used to time travel. Her grandpa made them a cheese-less pizza for lunch, which they'd devoured while working, but that had been hours ago.

Tilly got up from the table and stretched. "Bathroom break."

Grandma Eabha rubbed at her eyes tiredly as her daughter left the room. "We should probably stop and get dinner started."

"I think I'll step out for some fresh air." Mia said, getting up from the table.

"That's not a good idea," her grandma replied.

Cecilia and her black eye had been on Mia's mind since they'd parted earlier. Colby had also been taking up headspace for most of the afternoon after seeing the mermaid's heart ripped out.

Was he still alive? Was Cecilia okay?

The thoughts kept playing on repeat in her head like an earworm she couldn't shake. Mia felt like she had an invisible clock hanging over her, counting down the minutes until there was no time left.

She needed to see Cecilia. *Now*. "I have to go."

Grandma Eabha narrowed her eyes. "Is this because of that girl?"

Mia looked at her hesitantly. "I don't want to lie to you."

"Then don't."

She lifted her chin. "Yes, I plan on seeing her tonight. She's the key to finding my friend, I know it."

Her grandma sighed before reaching out her hand for Mia to take. She did so, unsure what her grandma planned on doing as she turned her palm upward.

She touched the top of Mia's inner forearm with her index finger, moving it into the pattern of a star. The area lit up in a blueish hue, causing Mia's skin to tingle. As the light faded, a barely visible scar remained on her skin.

"A small protection spell," her grandma murmured. "If you get into any trouble, press that star, and it will let us know."

"Thank you," Mia said.

She all but ran out of the room to get ready. After changing into a fresh pair of jeans and a peasant top, the nicest thing Sadie had that wasn't overly dressy, she made her way into the hall. She could hear the soft theme of Colombo coming from the living room and her heart ached a little, knowing her grandpa was in there, watching reruns of his favorite show—though, maybe they were new episodes in this timeline.

Tilly was waiting for her by the stairs, her arms crossed over her chest. "This is a bad idea, but I understand why you're doing it. I just hope going out with this girl helps you figure who's behind your friend's disappearance. Because that's why you're doing this, right?"

"Of course," she said, avoiding looking at her.

Her aunt let out a sigh. "Here." She held out a scrunched up twenty-dollar bill.

When Mia looked at her questioningly, Tilly said, "I'm assuming you don't have any money for this date, right?"

Mia grinned. She leaned over and hugged her. "Thanks, Tilly."

"Yeah, yeah." Her aunt was dismissive but her arms tightened around her.

Cecilia was already waiting for her when Mia arrived at Pickney's. She wore a long, floral dress that had a tiny hole in the neckline, matched with a frayed straw crossbody purse and her family necklace. She wasn't wearing her sunglasses. The bruise around her eye wasn't as visible.

"The power of cover up," she joked when she noticed Mia staring. "Ready?"

"Yeah."

They walked down the street to a little hole-in-the-wall restaurant that served cheap Italian food. It was a Chinese takeout in Mia's timeline. As they sat down to eat, Cecilia began to talk a little more about going out to Seattle.

"I can't wait to start my life there," she said as she swirled some spaghetti on her fork.

Mia swallowed hard to stop the sudden plea from leaving her lips. She wanted to tell Cecilia to leave now. To go get her dream before it was too late.

"What, um..." Mia stumbled. "What will you do once you get there if you can't find your father?"

Cecilia's face turned thoughtful. She grabbed the necklace, rubbing the pendant with her thumb. "I want to start an assistance program for people who grew up like me. My mom and I have always financially struggled. It's a problem in this world—to try to break the cycle of poverty. So, that's what I want to do. I want to help people who've gone through similar tough times. My goal is to start a nonprofit that can offer assistance and advice to get people to their next potential."

Mia was hit with an acute sense of loss as she took in the animated excitement on Cecilia's face. She was already mourning this amazing girl, and Cecilia wasn't even dead yet.

She could have made such a positive difference in the world if she'd just been given the chance to live.

Changing the subject before she started crying, Mia said, "And the music scene in Seattle is unreal."

The other girl's nose scrunched adorably. "What? Like Nirvana? You can't understand what that guy is singing."

Mia's mouth dropped. "Smells Like Teen Spirit is a history changing song. I mean… I bet you anything it will be."

Cecilia tilted her head, causing her long hair to cascade over one shoulder. Mia watched it shimmer under the lights of the restaurant as it moved.

"Okay," Cecilia said. "What's your favorite band then?"

"My aunt told me that my dad used to sing Classic Rock to get me to go to sleep when I was a baby. So I guess I'd say bands from that era. It helps me feel close to my dad. I'm talking the Ramones, Led Zeppelin, Queen. Nothing can compare to them."

Cecilia laughed at her enthusiasm causing Mia's pulse to speed up. They continued to discuss favorite music until it was time to leave. Mia paid for their meals, and they made their way to Salem Willows Park. Galvanized portable barriers sectioned off the performance area. The girls waited in the entrance line before giving their tickets to an elderly woman.

"Are you a fan of Shakespeare?" Cecilia asked as they took their seats. They had a nice view, ten rows from the stage. Behind the stage was the harbor. The water was calm with barely a ripple across its smooth surface. Mia was surprised the mermaids weren't churning the waters, considering what happened to one of their kind earlier.

"I've never tried to watch it before," she admitted, "though my grandma loves West Side Story, and I heard that it was loosely based on Romeo and Juliet."

Cecilia gave her an understanding grin. As Mia took in her happiness, she started to understand why Tony and Maria fell so hard for each other at first sight. Cecilia could have been a miserable person given her lot in life, but she was filled with so much positivity. She could make anyone feel lightness just by her smile.

"It can be challenging at first to understand," Cecilia explained, nodding to the stage, "but once the story starts moving along, you get used to the dialogue. Macbeth is one of Shakespeare's most popular plays."

Mia observed the girl's excited expression. "You really like this stuff, huh?"

"What's not to like? Shakespeare really understood the world, you know?"

She didn't, but she nodded anyway as the lights on the stage came on.

As Cecilia predicted, she didn't understand half of what the actors were saying. Despite that, she found herself intrigued by the storyline mixed with the action on the stage. However, when the third act began, she found herself becoming distracted.

Cecilia leaned against her until their arms were pressed together. She was so close that Mia could smell the faint spritz of her perfume. It was nice. Feeling brave, she reached down and clasped her hand. Out of the corner of her eye, she saw a small smile appear on Cecilia's lips as she intertwined their fingers together. Mia let out a pleased breath, feeling some of her tension from everything going on ease slightly.

The feeling didn't last. Her skin prickled at the sense of someone watching them. Her eyes skimmed the crowd until she saw a guy, maybe a few years older than her, staring right at them from the other side of the audience. His face was mostly in shadow, hidden by a hood. She stiffened as she took in the black cloak he wore—from what she knew of Other history, that was the standard uniform of a warlock.

Mia jumped to her feet, not looking away from the figure.

"Sit down!" someone whispered angrily from the row behind her.

Cecilia tugged on her hand, saying in a quiet voice, "Mia, you're not supposed to stand in the middle of a performance."

The boy's lip curled into a sneer. He turned and disappeared into a patch of nearby trees. She wanted to go after him, but she hesitated. What if he wasn't alone and his friends were in the crowd, waiting to snatch Cecilia? She would be safer if she stayed with Mia.

"We have to go," she finally said. The person in front of her turned around to shush her.

Cecilia's eyebrows pulled down. "What? Now?"

"Yeah, now." She pulled on Cecilia's hand until the other girl grabbed her purse and got up, apologizing to the people around them. Mia practically dragged her as they headed toward the exit.

"Mia, wait!" Cecilia said in a hushed tone trying not to disturb the other patrons.

Once they left the seating area, Mia followed the path the warlock took through the park, looking around frantically. Where did he go?

They made their way to the street.

"What's going on?" Cecilia let go of her hand so she could move in front of her.

"Sorry," Mia said, scanning the area. "I thought I saw someone I knew."

"And that's why we had to leave like that?"

"Sorry," Mia repeated. "I haven't seen him in a while. I-I wanted to ask him something."

She glanced at Cecilia who looked upset, and she didn't blame her. Mia just messed up their date. She opened her mouth to explain, but what could she say that would make sense to a Common? *Sorry, but I just saw a warlock, and hey, he might try to murder you soon.* It sounded crazy even to someone who grew up in the Other world.

She lifted her hand and cupped Cecilia's cheek. The other girl's eyes widened, but Mia didn't miss how Cecilia's stature loosened at the contact. She leaned closer and whispered, "I'm really sorry."

Cecilia shrugged. "It's fine."

"It's not," Mia said. "Let me walk you home."

"Already? Why don't we go back to the play?"

"I'm sorry. I really need to find that guy."

Cecilia tugged lightly on the ruffle of Mia's peasant top. "Should I be jealous?"

She let out an awkward laugh as she looked around again for the warlock. The guy was clearly gone. "He's definitely not my type." She took in the beautiful girl in front of her, and despite everything that had just happened, she couldn't help but smile. "You are."

A blush formed on her delicate cheeks. Mia found herself getting a little dependent on that reaction.

She grabbed Cecilia's hand again, and they made their way down a narrow, quiet street. A lot of the shops were closed for the evening. As they reached one storefront, Cecilia paused. Mia gave her a questioning look and found the other girl staring up at a mannequin wearing a long, navy blue dress with spaghetti straps. It had white lace across the bodice. The store had paired it with long, silky, white gloves.

"Can you imagine owning something so nice?" she murmured, awestruck.

Mia glanced around for the warlock one more time before she leaned against the window so that she was facing her. "It's not really my type."

Cecilia copied her pose, leaning her head against the glass. "What's your type?"

"Avoiding dancing in public."

She laughed, the sound musical to Mia's ears. As Mia viewed her, she wondered how she ever confused Cecilia with Ella. Ella had changed since they entered high school. It wasn't just about Kurt. She had become guarded, more concerned with how others viewed her. Cecilia seemed warmer, more of a free spirit, not afraid to put herself out there, no matter what people thought.

As the two gazed at one another, the atmosphere around them changed, becoming charged. Cecilia tentatively reached out and gently drew her fingers down Mia's cheek. Heat sparked through her at the contact. She leaned closer to Cecilia, her heart flying into hyper speed as she did so.

"Mia…" Cecilia whispered.

"Hmm?"

"I-I'd really like to kiss you."

Butterflies started beating wildly inside her. "Yeah?"

"Yeah," Cecilia replied, her expression tender "Would that be okay?"

She licked her lips in preparation. "Yes."

Cecilia grinned before moving closer. She closed her eyes as she drew nearer to Mia's mouth. Was that what she was supposed to do too? Other than a chaste kiss during a game of spin the bottle when she was younger, she'd never kissed someone where it meant something. She wasn't sure how she was supposed to proceed.

Their noses were within touching distance. Cecilia turned her head slightly. Mia's eyes fluttered close.

The sound of someone coughing made the girls jump apart. Mia turned, ready to hex the person. A man stood in front of an open door frame across the street. As Mia glared at him, an upside down pentagram appeared on his neck, the color of it a blazing green. Another warlock.

This man appeared to be in his seventies. He was bald and had hunched shoulders. A wide, creepy grin appeared on his face. Even from a distance, Mia could count on one hand the number of teeth he had. She stepped protectively in front of Cecilia.

"Well, well, well..." The man's voice was rough, like he'd smoked ten packs of cigarettes a day his entire life. "What's a witch like you doin' in this neck of the woods?"

"What do you want?" Mia said. Her hand bunched into a fist, ready to unleash her energy if she needed to. She'd probably get excommunicated by the Assembly for performing hexes in front of a Common, but she didn't care.

The man held up his hands. "I ain't here to cause trouble."

"What do you want?" Mia repeated.

The warlock nodded at Cecilia. "There's a great evil that follows you." Cecilia sucked in a nervous breath. She grabbed Mia's hand, the one that wasn't in a fist.

Mia could feel her trembling.

The warlock's eyes shifted back to her. "But I don't want any part of this. I told the others and I'm tellin' you. This ain't my fight. You tell the Assembly that." He crept back inside his building and shut the metal door with a loud clang. The noise reverberated through the air.

Mia felt the vibrations deep in her bones. Her breathing became shallow as she stared at the rusted, red door he disappeared behind.

"Mia." Cecilia's face had gone pale. "What's he talking about? What's the Assembly?"

"No idea." She forced her lips into a shallow grin. "Let's get out of here. No need to hang out where the weirdos are."

They began walking. Fast. Despite Cecilia being the taller of the two, she could barely keep up with Mia.

"What did he mean when he called you a witch?" she asked as they turned onto her street.

"I assume he was being polite instead of calling me a bitch."

"Calling you a witch is polite?"

Mia shrugged as they stopped in front of Cecilia's home. "Here we are."

Cecilia looked at the house, her shoulders sagging. "Yeah, here we are."

As Mia looked at her, her stance on not saving her waivered. She wanted to stop her murder. Badly. All she had to do was place a ward around the house, and she'd be able to protect her. No warlock would be able to cross it.

But there were two problems with that. One, she didn't know how to do a ward that big.

And two... Tilly's voice popped into her head.

You can't stop what's supposed to take place.

Mia felt like a boulder was forming inside her stomach. As much as she wanted to protect Cecilia, she'd already interfered enough with the girl's fate. For what felt like the millionth time, she reminded herself that she couldn't stop what was supposed to happen.

She raised a hand to stroke Cecilia's face, but she grabbed one of the wood pickets that bordered the property instead. "I'm sorry I ruined our date."

"You didn't," she assured her before grinning. "At least it was memorable."

Mia laughed at that before saying, "I should go."

The other girl nodded before blurting out, "Can I see you again?"

The whole point of the date was to collect information, and now that she encountered the warlocks, she had two leads to follow up on. There really was no reason to see Cecilia anymore, but she selfishly wanted to spend a little more time with her.

"I'd like that," she said.

"The school is having a carnival on Saturday. Can you go?"

That was the day before the black moon. The day before Mia's family planned to send her home. "Definitely."

"I'll meet you at the school then. Around five?"

"Sounds good."

Cecilia leaned over and kissed Mia on the cheek before hurrying inside. Mia blinked back tears as she watched her go.

Please stay safe tonight.

She ran a finger over the spot on her cheek that Cecilia's lips had touched before remembering there was something more pressing to do. Spinning on her feet, she sprinted for home.

She had an old warlock to confront.

But first, she needed backup.

CHAPTER 12

"Grandma! Tilly!" Mia yelled as she flew up the stairs to the living quarters of their house. She passed her grandpa who was snoring in his recliner, undisturbed by her shouting.

"What's up?" her aunt asked, poking her head out of the bathroom. "Is your date over alrea—"

"Where ..." Mia tried to catch her breath from her sprint. "Where's Grandma?"

"She's working on your spell, trying to recreate the sequence."

"I-I need h-help," she said, panting so hard her speech was barely audible.

Tilly hurried over to her and put a calming hand on her arm. "Slow down and breathe for a second. Tell me what happened."

Mia inhaled deeply several times before trying to explain what she'd witnessed. "I saw two warlocks tonight. One disappeared. The other gave a cryptic message about how he didn't want to be a part of something, and he wanted me to tell the Assembly that. I need to talk to him."

"Okay." Tilly nodded. "You're not going alone."

She grinned at her. "Why do you think I'm talking to you?"

Her aunt snorted before hurrying into her room. Mia peeked in and saw Grandma Eabha sitting inside the pentagram, her legs crossed as her closed eyelids flickered back and forth.

Tilly came back out after putting on her shoes. She closed the door quietly behind her. "Ready?"

Mia nodded. "Yeah."

They snuck past Grandpa Ray and hurried outside. They began running in the direction Mia had seen the old man. By the time they arrived on his street, her sides hurt. She squinted at the shop across the road before glancing back at the brick wall in front of her.

"What is it?" Tilly asked.

"I swear this is where I saw him, but there was a door here before."

"Are you sure we're on the right street?"

"I-I thought so ..." Mia looked across the street again. She had a tendency to get things mixed up sometimes, but inside the store's window was the prom dress Cecilia had admired. This was the right place.

"Mia." Her aunt sounded alarmed. She glanced over and saw Tilly staring at the ground, her hand held to her mouth.

She followed her gaze to a large, dark puddle on the sidewalk a few feet away from them.

Blood.

As she took a step toward it, she felt a familiar presence press itself against her. The smell of something rotten reached her nose.

"Stay here," she warned. "There's dark energy."

The blood formed into a trail which Mia began to follow. As she reached a curve in the road, she heard a moan behind her.

She looked over her shoulder and saw that Tilly followed despite her warning. Tears ran down her cheeks.

"Too m-much d-dark energy." She could barely speak. "It's get-getting worse. Making me think b-bad things."

"I told you to stay," Mia said. She touched Tilly's arm, sensing the darkness trying to attach itself to her aunt. Picturing Cecilia's happy face from earlier, she drew the dark energy from her. As soon as it hit her system, she felt a surge of power. Tilly's tears stopped, though her body still shook.

"Thanks," her aunt said before letting out a gasp.

Mia swung around to see what she was looking at. Across the street from them was a parking lot, barely lit by a nearby streetlight. On the ground lay a man. Given the blood pooling around him and his lack of movement, Mia guessed he was dead. She took several steps toward him only to freeze. It was the old warlock.

And he wasn't alone.

A figure stood a few feet from him, barely noticeable in the blackness of the night. The creature had a human-like form but lacked any defining features or substance. It was like looking at a three-dimensional shadow.

Mia could feel the dark energy pouring off it.

Tilly's shaking grew worse. She began to grip her head, shaking it back and forth.

Mia grabbed her aunt's wrist again to drain the darkness before it consumed her, while not taking her eyes off the scene in front of her.

The shadow figure held something near its face and began chewing. As Mia watched, she realized with a sickening twist of her stomach what it was.

The warlock's heart.

"No!" she screamed, letting go of Tilly and raising both hands. Using the dark energy boost she'd received from draining her aunt, she blasted the creature, the energy releasing from her in a bright bluish black light.

The monster flew backwards, skidding across the parking lot before turning to face Mia. It opened its mouth revealing teeth—

human teeth—covered in blood. The monster let out a high-pitched screech before turning and hopping over the fence.

"Tilly, come on!" she yelled as she hurried after the creature.

Her aunt stumbled behind her.

As Mia ran by the corpse and half-eaten heart, she drew in the dark energy from the scene, gaining more strength. The boost helped her move with a burst of speed as she jumped over the fence.

Tilly started falling behind.

The shadow figure headed toward the Salem Harbor.

Mia pushed more of the dark energy toward her legs and felt herself go faster than what should have been possible.

"Stop!" she shouted just as the creature made it to the shoreline and came to an abrupt halt. "You have nowhere to go."

The monster cocked its head. It seemed to be analyzing her. Goosebumps broke out onto Mia's skin. So this was what it was like to look into the face of pure evil. The creature was the embodiment of everything twisted in the world, and Mia felt the unease of being so close to it run up and down her spine, making her insides clench in fear. She raised hands that shook, ready to release all her energy.

Tilly stumbled up to them, out of breath.

The creature smiled, cold and sinister, and raised its own hands. Even in the distance between them, Mia could see the old warlock's blood drip from the creature's claws. There was still so much blood.

Black hue blasted from monster, hitting Tilly. She screamed as she went skywards, flailing straight up into air at an alarming speed until she was nothing but a small dot in the night sky.

"NO!" Mia shouted. Her brain scrambled as she tried to think of a way to get the creature to release its grip on her aunt without killing her, but fear paralyzed her. Only one thought dominated.

She couldn't lose Tilly.

The monster threw its hands toward the harbor and her aunt went flying over the water. It turned and smiled at Mia, dropping its arms before diving into the lapping waves. Mia didn't notice. The only thing she could focus on was Tilly.

She fell from the sky, cartwheeling in circles, with nothing but the turbulent water far below to break her fall.

A memory snapped inside Mia's head. Of Aunt Tilly showing her how to move things with her mind. Mia could turn off TVs and draw her car keys to her hand on a whim. But she'd never tried to move something like a human before.

Her fear evaporated as she kept her laser focus on Tilly until she was all she could see. Pushing out her hands, Mia drew in all of the darkness the monster left behind. Power surged within her as she absorbed it. With everything she had in her, Mia pushed out her energy in a bright blue light. It launched from her so hard she stumbled slightly. It hit Tilly midair and wrapped around her like an invisible lasso. Mia drew it back into herself, pulling her aunt to the safety of the shoreline.

Tilly hit the solid ground with a loud thud before going into seizures. Her eyes rolled inside her head and foamy black spit spilled from her mouth. Mia dropped next to her on weakened limbs. She felt completely drained, but she didn't have time to worry about herself as she placed her hands above Tilly.

Dark energy soaked her aunt's skin. Using every bit of remaining strength she had, she drew the darkness from Tilly who went still, her breathing labored before she came back to consciousness with a gasp.

Mia glanced over to where the creature had disappeared into the water. There was no sign of it. The darkness began to play with her head.

It's your fault he's dead.

You almost got your aunt killed.

And yet, Mia just saved her. She used her magical energy in a way she didn't know she was capable of. She hyper focused on Tilly and managed to not screw up when it mattered most. Relief and pride resonated within her, and in an instant, the darkness left as though it had never been there.

"What..." Tilly sputtered. "What w-was that?"

"I don't know," Mia said, her own chest heaving.

But she had an idea.

She just met Cecilia's killer.

Chapter 13

Tilly had her arm slung over Mia's shoulder as they careened toward their house. She kept her own arm wrapped firmly around Tilly's waist, hoping her aunt wouldn't collapse until they were safely inside. The protection star her grandma placed on her skin earlier brushed against the belt Tilly wore, sensitizing the skin.

Crap! Mia had forgotten about it. Reaching across her aunt's stomach, she pressed her thumb against it.

Grandma, I could use your help.

The boost of dark energy had long left, leaving her with the remaining emotion of the tortured and suffering. She couldn't conjure up another happy thought for anything. As her mind grew sadder, her body felt weighed down, her legs becoming heavier and heavier.

One more step. Almost there.

Just as they stumbled onto the property, the door to the family's home entrance swung open. Her grandparents came rushing out, her grandma looking frantic.

Her grandpa looked relieved. "There they are. They're fine, Eabha."

"The protection spell I placed on Mia says otherwise," Grandma Eabha said before running over to the girls.

Exhaustion overwhelmed Mia. Unable to hold Tilly up anymore, she fell to her knees, her aunt falling beside her. Tilly let out a groan as she face-planted into the grass.

"Tilly!" Grandma Eabha yelled.

The world began to swerve before Mia's eyes and she fell the rest of the way to the ground, her cheek plastering against a bubble gum wrapper that had blown into the yard. Someone turned her over and the paper flew off into the wind. She met her grandpa's worried stare.

"You all right, Mia?" he asked. She nodded as she tried to weakly pat his hand to reassure him.

"Tilly?" her grandma said. Mia tilted her head to see her aunt cradled in Grandma Eabha's arms, unconscious.

"She'll be okay," Mia said. "The shadow figure attacked her, but I saved her."

"What are you talking about?" her grandma asked. "What shadow figure?"

"The heart stealer," she mumbled.

"Eabha," Grandpa Ray said. "We should get the girls inside before continuing this conversation."

Grandma Eabha gave a short nod and lifted her hands. A blue hue draped over the family, masking their presence from any nosy neighbors staring in their direction. With a wave of her hands, Mia and Tilly floated up from the ground and into the house.

As Mia drifted by Tilly's room, she saw her aunt land gently on her bed. The spell started to take her to Sadie's room, but she used what little energy she'd regained to sever the connection. She fell to the ground with a loud bang, crying out as pain ripped through her, but she forced herself to her knees.

Her grandpa crouched next to her. "Mia, you should really rest."

"No." She crawled into her aunt's room, bypassing her grandma who was sitting next to her daughter, checking her vitals. Mia climbed into the bed to lay next to her aunt on her other side, too terrified to let her out of her sight.

Grandma Eabha leaned over and pushed back Mia's hair in even, comforting strokes.

"Can you tell us what happened?"

Tears formed in her eyes as she thought about earlier—the young warlock she'd encountered, the shadow figure eating the older warlock's heart, Tilly dangling above the harbor, so close to being another victim of unforgiving waters—just like her dad.

A sob broke from Mia, and she buried her face against her aunt's neck. She'd come so close to losing her.

"Honey, talk to us," her grandpa said at the foot of the bed.

"C-Cecilia and I went to the park to see *Macbeth*. I saw a warlock and we followed him—"

"He didn't use magic in front of Cecilia, did he?" her grandma asked, clearly worried.

Mia shook her head. "Like I said, we tried following him. I... I don't know where he went, but we ran into another warlock. He was older. He told me he didn't want to get involved and he wanted me to tell the Assembly that."

"Involved with what?" Grandma Eabha asked.

"I don't know. I came back here to get help, but you were working on that astral projection spell. Tilly and I decided to go ask the guy some questions but—"

She began to shake all over.

Her grandma stopped stroking her hair so she could clasp her arm. A calming warmth spread through Mia and her shaking stopped.

"What happened next?" her grandma asked in a steady voice.

"We came across something. I don't know what it was. A creature or shadow or something. It gave off so much dark energy, it was as if it was created from the darkness itself. It... It was eating the warlock's heart."

Her grandpa's eyes widened with shock.

Her grandma didn't say anything, but her grip tightened on her.

"I... I told it to stop and hit it with a hex. It bared its teeth at me." She shuddered. "It had human teeth."

Grandma Eabha let go of Mia. She stood and walked over to the window, her posture stiff.

"What happened after it showed you the teeth?"

"It ran and I chased it. Tilly followed. It... It hit her with dark energy. I drained the darkness from her, but by the time I was done, the thing was long gone into the harbor."

Her grandma turned to face her. "Can you remember any other detail? Did it have a human shape? Was the creature tall, short? Did you see what color eyes it had?"

"It had a human shape, but I honestly can't tell you much about it. Looking at it was like staring into a dark void. It was just there."

Her grandma's look of concern grew, her features turning somber.

"What?" Mia asked. "Do you know what it is?"

Grandma Eabha shook her head. "I can't be certain."

"But you know something."

Lines formed on her grandma's forehead. "I've heard stories, though I've never seen it in person. There was once a rumor that certain Unmentionables could cloak themselves in dark energy. They wear it like a mask to hide their true selves."

"So, you think the creature I fought tonight could be an Unmentionable?" And not a freaking monster from her nightmares.

"It sounds like something a powerful warlock could do."

"Oh!" Mia thought back. "Maybe it was the other warlock. The one I saw earlier."

Her grandma nodded. "It's possible."

"I need to find him then before he kills anyone else."

Like Cecilia.

She tried to get up.

Her grandpa came over and put a gentle but firm hand on her shoulder. She tried not to flinch away. "You need to rest."

"I agree," Grandma Eabha said. "You should recuperate. The last thing you need to do right now is confront a warlock of this magnitude when you're drained." She turned back to look out the window. "If it's still in the harbor, hopefully, the merfolk will kill it."

Mia paled. "The mermaid that was killed. There was a hole where his heart should have been. Like someone had removed it. What if this creature is going around eating the hearts of Others?"

Her grandma's jaw tightened. "Then I'd say the missing harpy is in a lot of danger if she's not dead already."

Mia's anxiety shot up until she almost choked on air. "M-my friend. From my timeline. What if this thing is what kidnapped—"

Her grandma hurried back over to her and touched her arm again. Another wave of calmness flooded her.

"We don't know if this creature is alive in your timeline. Let's worry about one thing at a time. Mainly how to get you home so you can see for yourself how your friend is doing."

"But what are we going to do right *now*?" Mia whispered.

"At the moment? I'm going to put strong wards around the house," her grandma said. "I should have done that years ago, but it'll block some of our customers from coming inside. We'll worry about that later though. In the morning, I'm going to show you how to put wards around yourself. In the meantime, rest. Why don't you head for Sadie's room."

"I'm staying here," Mia said, grabbing Tilly's arm. Her aunt's skin was warm with life, giving her further reassurance that she would recover.

Her grandma nodded before looking at her husband. He left the room, returning shortly with a blanket in his hand, which he placed over both girls.

"We'll talk more in the morning," Grandma Eabha said.

Mia closed her eyes. She was so tired, she fell asleep before they left the room.

A sharp jab to her stomach made Mia bolt upward.

"Ow." She looked at Tilly who was rubbing her elbow, her hair sticking up on one end. Dark circles rested under her eyes. She looked like hell but at least she was alive.

"What are you doing in here?" Tilly croaked.

"I was...err...protecting you?"

She lifted an eyebrow. "I don't think you're supposed to fall asleep on protection duty."

Mia grinned sheepishly. Tilly threw the extra blanket at her face and got out of bed. Stretching, her back gave a satisfying crack. "I feel like I've been hit with a hundred sledgehammers." She walked slowly, shuffling her feet along the floor, until she reached her closet where she pulled out a grey jogging suit. It was nothing like her usual flannel and concert t-shirt combo.

"Are you okay?" Mia asked.

"Aside from being thrown hundreds of feet in the air and almost tossed in the harbor, yep, I'm doing great." Her grip tightened on the outfit she held. "Do you think it'll be back?"

"Yeah," Mia said. She got out of bed and went over to her aunt, wrapping her in a hug. "I won't ever let it get near you again. I promise."

Tilly hugged her back before pulling away to give her a sad look. "Mia, you might be a Desolate, but this thing is strong. Stronger than anything I've ever encountered, and trust me, I've seen some things in the shop. Please don't do anything crazy."

"I won't." She gave her a half smile. "If I die, who will keep you in line when I get home?"

Tilly made a "pfft" noise, though her eyes wandered over Mia's face in concern. She opened her mouth as if to say something else but shook her head and left the room.

Mia headed toward the kitchen. Her grandparents were at the table, pouring over piles of books.

"How do you expect me to find it?" her grandpa grumbled. "I have no idea what we're looking for."

"Any spells that mention defeating great evil." Her grandma sounded exasperated.

"Morning," Mia said, grabbing a coffee mug from the cupboard.

"Good morning, honey." Grandma Eabha stood to give her a hug. "How are you feeling today?"

"Fine." Aside from having nonstop nightmares all night about a faceless monster ripping out her heart and eating it while she watched. At least the depressive thoughts were gone. She poured herself a cup of coffee, blowing on it before taking a sip. Nodding at the table, Mia asked, "What's going on?"

"Research," her grandma said, going back to her seat. "I'm trying to find historical documents from the Other community that discusses defeating dark entities like the one you described last night. There has to be a way to win against this thing."

Grandma Eabha stared sightlessly at the pages in front of her. Something else seemed to be bothering her.

"Is there something you're not telling me?" Mia asked.

Her grandma sighed. She looked older in that moment, more like how Mia was used to seeing her in her timeline. "I'm concerned. Though Desolates are rare, their powers are well known. If a dark energy user comes across one, they typically don't try to challenge someone like you because you have the ability to drain them of their power. This monster didn't back down."

Mia shrugged. "Maybe it knew I was new to my gift."

"Maybe. That makes them all the more dangerous." Her grandma pressed the bridge of her nose with her fingers. "Can you do me a favor?"

She nodded.

"Can you just...please stay inside today until I can make sure you're safe?"

"Okay," Mia said. It wouldn't be a bad idea to spend time learning as much as she could from Tilly and her grandma. Plus after last night, she seriously had to work on balancing her spirit so that the dark energy didn't hit her so hard again.

As if reading her mind, Grandma Eabha said, "Thank you. After you finish breakfast, I want to work with you on creating wards."

She nodded as she sat down at the table. Tilly stumbled into the room. Her hair was wet from her shower and lay in limp strands against her shoulders. She took a seat next to Mia in an exhausted heap.

"How are you feeling today, honey?" Grandma Eabha asked, pressing a palm to her daughter's cheek.

"I feel awful."

"You look awful," Mia's grandpa replied as he pushed aside the book he'd been reading.

"Thanks, Dad."

"Tilly, I don't think you should work in the store today," Grandma Eabha said as she grabbed a glass of orange juice and handed it to her daughter. "You need to recover."

She responded by putting her head on the table as if she were too tired to hold it up any longer.

Mia looked at her aunt in sympathy before saying, "I can do it."

All three of her family members stopped what they were doing to stare at her.

"What?" she said defensively. "I work in the store all the time. I know what I'm doing."

"What if one of the Assembly members stops by?" her grandpa said. "They might suspect—"

"Summer is coming up. Tell them I'm temporary help for the season."

"It's too risky," Tilly said. She started to stand up, but her face went ghostly white. She swayed on her feet before slumping back in her chair.

"I'll do it," Mia's grandpa said. He clasped a comforting hand on his daughter's shoulder.

"You can't," Grandma Eabha replied. "You have a meeting with the bank and then another meeting with that new supplier."

"Oh, right."

"And I," her grandma said, "need to continue working on Mia's astral projection spell." She let out a weary breath. "That leaves Mia." She nodded to the protection spell still visible on her arm. "If you need anything, remember to press the star on your arm and I'll come to you."

"Okay, thanks," she replied.

"But the store can stay closed for the next few hours," her grandma said as she handed her husband his morning pills. "Because Mia and I have some wards to work on."

Mia finished her coffee and stood up. "I... I guess I should go get dressed."

With that, she got up and left the room. After last night, she was ready for a little normalcy.

Mia settled behind the store's counter with a couple of her grandma's books about defeating dark energy users. Since it was a Thursday midmorning, there wasn't a lot of business.

She stretched her back and heard a satisfying crack. Her grandma had put her through the wringer earlier, teaching Mia how to create a ward. From what she learned, it was a glorified protection spell, but instead of focusing on transferring her energy to another object, she'd had to transfer it around herself. It had taken three hours before she managed a weak ring of white around her. Her grandma was begrudgingly satisfied but told Mia to keep practicing when she could.

A few customers came into the store and went. Mia passed the time in between helping them by trying to focus on her reading. She was now on day four without her Adderall. Between blowing her date with Cecilia, Tilly almost dying, and her encounter with the monster, she was having a hard time concentrating. But most importantly, her worry for Colby was becoming all consuming. Whenever she tried to picture him, she saw the old warlock with his heart ripped out. What if that thing was around in her time and had Colby. Would it try to eat his heart? Mia couldn't handle that.

The sound of the shop's bell ringing above the entrance was a welcome distraction.

She closed the book and bent down to hide it somewhere under the counter. Commons didn't need to see what she was reading.

"Excuse me, is Sadie here?"

"I'm sorry, she'll be gone until Monday." Mia shoved the book next to the trash bin. She started to straighten. "Is there anything I can help you w—"

Her voice trailed off. Her heart spiraled as she stared at the guy in front of her. He was younger looking than in the one picture she had of him. His eyes were wide, his nose straight. His top lip had a bow to it that Mia knew well—she had the same shaped mouth. He wore a Queen t-shirt. Which wasn't surprising.

From what she'd been told, it was her dad's favorite band.

CHAPTER 14

"Hello." Her dad gave a half smile—so eerily similar to her own. "I haven't seen you before. Are you new?"

Mia tried to speak, but the emotion crushing her vocal chords made it impossible so she gave a tight nod.

His eyes scanned her face. "Are you related to Sadie?"

Mia opened her mouth. Closed it. Finally managed, "C-cousin."

"Ah, I see the family resemblance. Though you must be part Greek."

She swallowed hard before whispering, "My dad's Greek."

"I knew it." His expression turned awkward. "This is going to sound funny, but you remind me of my mom when she was younger. Weird, huh?"

"Weird," Mia repeated. She gripped the counter until her knuckles turned white.

"Well," he said. "It was nice meeting you. Could you let Sadie know that Jason stopped by?"

Mia nodded again. As he turned to leave, she shouted, "Wait!"

He looked at her with raised eyebrows.

"Um." She frantically looked around trying to figure out what else to say. "Did you... Did you want to buy anything while you're here? M-Maybe a present for your mom? We have some nice dolls." She waved to the nearby shelf that displayed a group of cheesy plastic witches.

Her dad laughed, and Mia's heart *hurt.* The sound was like something right out of a dream. Maybe he laughed a lot around her when she was a baby.

He picked up one of the dolls to examine it before placing it back in its spot. "That's not really my mom's style."

Mia knew absolutely nothing about her paternal grandparents, other than they had the good taste to instantly dislike her mom.

"What's your mom's style?" Her voice was hoarse as she spoke.

He gave a considering look. "Anything to do with Ancient Greece. She still prays to the gods and goddesses just like our ancestors did, if you can believe that."

Mia's eyebrows shot up. How funny that a guy whose family worshipped Originals, eventually fell in love with one of their creations.

Her dad glanced at his watch. "I should get going. It was nice to meet you."

"Yeah," Mia whispered. "See you around."

He left the store with a wave of his hand.

She struggled to breathe as she watched him go. A sob escaped her followed by another. Before she could stop herself, she was crying hysterically.

Why did she let him leave? Why hadn't she found another excuse—any excuse—to keep him with her. Just a little bit longer.

It's your fault he's dead.

"Mia?" Tilly stood in the doorframe that led to the back office. She was pale but steady on her feet. "Did I hear Jason Walker's voice?"

Mia ran over and flung her arms around her.

Tilly held her tight while making shh'ing noises.

"Seriously," her aunt said in a concerned tone. "You're going to make yourself sick. What's got you so upset?"

"M-my f-father," She tried to say.

"You have to calm down." Tilly cupped her face. She felt a rush of calmness wash over her, allowing her to catch her breath. "Tell me what happened."

"My dad. He was here. He was looking for Sadie."

"Your dad is Jason?" Tilly seemed surprised. When Mia affirmed that he was, a pleased expression appeared on her aunt's face. "Maybe Sadie's taste doesn't suck after all."

Mia sniffed loudly.

"You didn't tell him who you were, did you?" Tilly asked.

"Of course not."

"Okay, then there's nothing to get upset about. You'll see him when you get home."

She shook her head. "He's dead."

"What?"

"He dies when I'm three. I never got to know him."

"Mia …" Her aunt's face was a mix of emotions as she pulled away from her. "You shouldn't be telling me this."

Mia didn't care. She pleaded, "I need you to save him."

Tilly shook her head, her expression etched in sympathy. "If he's meant to die, I can't do anything about it."

"You can." She gripped Tilly's hands so tight her aunt winced. "He dies on June 16, 2000. He gets on a boat—"

"Mia, seriously, stop it. I—"

"A freak storm comes in. His boat capsizes. He drowns. Stop him from getting on the boat."

"I can't."

"Tilly, please. *Please* save my dad."

Her aunt walked over to a cabinet that held stuffed toys resembling purple-faced vampires. They were marked half off.

Her body sagged as she swayed on her feet. "I could seriously mess up the future by saving him."

"You'll be saving *my* future." Desperation choked Mia's voice. "Please."

Tilly sighed before turning to face her. "I can't promise anything. But I'll try."

Mia let out a breath she wasn't aware she was holding.

"Thank you," she whispered.

Tilly nodded before shooing her away with her hand. "You can't greet customers with a blotchy face like that. I'll take over."

"But you're ill."

"I'm feeling better. Besides, Dad should be back soon. Go get some fresh air, okay? But stay on the property. You'll be protected inside Mom's wards."

Mia nodded and headed outside to the patio. She sat down in her grandma's chaise lounge, the bright floral pad cushioning her from the frame's uncomfortable metal. She stared sightlessly at the harbor, mourning the loss of her father in a way she'd never experienced before. What was even more dangerous was the sliver of hope she now had.

What if Tilly was able to save her dad? What if he was waiting for her when she got back home?

Mia spent hours lying on the chaise, unwilling to move as she relived that precious moment with her dad over and over. The sun soon began to set.

"Mind if I join you?"

She looked up to see her grandpa standing next to her. She quickly looked away but motioned at the space beside her. He grabbed a lounge chair and sat down. They stared at the water in silence for a few moments. A truck rumbled past their shop, disrupting the quiet.

"Tilly filled me in," Grandpa Ray finally said. "So, that Jason kid. That's the one Sadie marries, huh?" Mia nodded and he shook his head, even as his eyes lightened. "You know, I never did like him. He's always lingering around the shop, though he never buys anything. Now I understand why. Trying to steal my Sadie, that's what he's doing. I knew he was nothing but trouble."

Mia let out a small laugh. "That's not what you told me. You always said what a great man my dad was."

Her grandpa grinned at her. "Maybe he grew up then."

She looked back at the water, biting her lip. She'd spoken to the two most important men in her life within the span of a few hours, and they were both gone in her timeline. It hurt so much.

Grandpa Ray let out a soft sigh. "It's okay, you know."

Mia cleared her throat before asking, "What is?"

"I might not be magical like you and the rest of the women in this family, but I'm not blind either. The first time you saw me after you arrived, you looked at me like I was a ghost. You sure hugged me like I was."

She ran her finger down the smooth metal of the chair's arm, unable to say anything.

"I also couldn't help but notice," he continued, "how you've been avoiding me ever since." Her grandpa scratched at the five o'clock shadow running along his jawline, the dark bristles speckled with gray. "I get it. It's a defense mechanism. You get that from me. When things got too painful for me when I was in Nam, I pretended I wasn't there anymore. You can block out anything if you try hard enough." He gave her a pointed look. "Not that that's a healthy lifestyle to live."

"I..." Mia couldn't think of what to say.

Her grandpa looked at her gently as though he understood anyway.

"I'm glad I know," he said. "It'll give me more time to cherish those around me. Including you." He brushed a gentle hand over her head. "I'm sure as hell proud to have a granddaughter like you."

Tears filled her eyes but she still couldn't speak. She grabbed his hand, holding it tightly in hers. They sat in silence, watching the boats sail across the harbor in the setting sun. Although it wasn't exactly a happy memory, Mia knew that moment with her grandpa would bring her back from the darkness whenever she needed a little light.

CHAPTER 15

Mia woke the next day feeling like she had a heavy weight in her stomach. The black moon was in two days, and she was no closer to finding solutions to any of her problems. Her family still hadn't figured out how to get her home, a shadow freak was eating the hearts out of Others, she still had no idea how to help Colby once she got back to her own timeline. And then there was Cecilia.

Mia was finding it harder to justify leaving her to die. Cecilia had such a shitty life. Why shouldn't she be able to escape it and start over? She was good and kind. And yeah, Mia liked her. Way more than she should. Despite all the warnings her family had given her; despite the talks she'd given herself. All of that seemed to matter less and less. Cecilia gave her hope. More so than she'd ever experienced with Ella. That maybe someday, someone would look at her like Cecilia did. Mia was becoming addicted to those looks. Needed them like she needed the elements to restore her.

How could she leave her to her grisly fate?

Shoving back the bed sheets in frustration, Mia got up to take a shower and get dressed. She threw on the first thing she saw in Sadie's closet—some frilly dumpster fire of a blouse—with jean shorts before heading to the kitchen and slumping down at the kitchen table, opposite her grandpa.

He folded down the corner of his newspaper to look at her. "Now, there's my little lump of sunshine."

She rolled her eyes before grabbing a bowl of oatmeal that was waiting for her, moving it a little closer. It was still warm, the steam rising from the oats as she stirred it.

"Thanks for this," she mumbled, knowing he made the vegan meal especially for her.

"You're welcome," he replied before returning his attention to his newspaper.

"Where are Tilly and Grandma?"

"After Doyle Parris stopped by this morning—"

Mia went rigid. "He was here?"

Her grandpa nodded. "He wanted to inform your grandma that the Examiners returned to Assembly Headquarters earlier today to do some research. From what Eabha told me once, there's no better place to look up supernatural information than the Assembly's library. Parris asked your grandma to keep an eye out for any unusual activity. After he left, she went back to working on your spell. As for Tilly, she wanted to keep her mind off recent events, so she's working in the store today."

"How's she doing?" Mia asked.

"She's not at a hundred percent. She's still really tired, but she'll get back on her feet soon enough. School's been out this week for the Wolf Trials, but the girls are supposed to return to class next week. If she's feeling up to it, Tilly just has to get through the next few weeks of her senior year, and then she can fully recuperate over the summer." Her grandpa picked up his glass of juice and took a swallow before placing it back down with a quiet clink. "What are your plans today?"

"I, um, I kind of wanted to go see my friend."

"The girl you like?"

Mia flushed. "We didn't exactly leave things off on the best note."

"Then you should go see her."

She perked up. "Yeah?"

"According to a coven your grandma consulted, shadow figures only move around in settings that let them blend in naturally, such as nighttime. You should be fine if you want to make up with your friend. I think it's important that you make peace with everything before you head back to your timeline. Because that's still the game plan, Mia. As much as we love you, you need to go home."

She forced herself to nod. Right. She had to leave. She had a whole life waiting for her. Colby needed her.

"I think I will go see her." She pushed her chair back and went over to her grandpa. She threw her arms around his shoulders and gave him a kiss on his temple.

He squeezed her arm. "Don't get mushy on me, kid."

A laugh escaped her as she let him go. She took in her grandpa, noticing the healthy color of his skin. She felt sad yet happy all over again for this time with him. "I love you."

"Love you, too. Now get out of here and be back before it gets dark."

Mia headed to Cecilia's house, not sure if she would find her there. If she wasn't there, she'd check the store she worked at. As she walked down the sidewalk, her skin began to prickle, and her feet slowed. She turned her head, trying to get a sense for what was off. Her eyes lowered to the ground. Dark lines jutted underneath the surface of sidewalk like varicose veins running under a person's skin.

What the serious hell?

She took a step to follow their path, and the cement under her feet buzzed.

Dark energy recognized that a Desolate was near.

Mia's mood grew solemn as the lines grew thicker, more powerful, the darkness affecting her like it always did. She headed westward until they disappeared beneath a large patch of dead grass. A wood picket fence prevented her from going any further. She stared at it, confused as to where it had come from before her head jerked up.

Cecilia's house stood in front of her. It seemed to pulse when Mia looked at it, a black shimmering hue momentarily appearing around the entire structure before disappearing. The darkness was stirring in the house, calling to her, wanting to draw her inside.

Mia's breathing became erratic.

Why was it appearing now? She hadn't sensed it the night she'd met Cecilia. What had changed?

A creaking sound came from the yard at the side of the house. She cautiously peeked around the corner and saw Cecilia sitting on the tire swing, pushing herself back and forth. One bare foot dragged in the dirt as she moved. She wore a long, white, maxi dress that looked like it had seen better days. The pendant necklace that meant so much to her rested below her collarbone.

Mia took a step forward, worry twisting her stomach. Even if Cecilia's clothes usually looked ragged, she always came across stylish and well kept. In that moment though, she was a mess.

Her long, caramel brown hair lay in snags and tangled curls down her back. There were dark circles under her large, unfocused eyes. The bruise around her one eye stood out prominently against the paleness of her skin. She stared vacantly at the house as she moved. Other than the motion of the swing, it was as if she'd turned into a zombie—and Mia had been unfortunate enough to see one when she was younger. The comparison was fair.

She walked slowly through the gate and felt the hum of dark energy surge underneath her feet. She focused on the conversation she'd had with her grandpa the night before. He had made her feel loved and she latched onto that feeling now. The darkness stirred angrily beneath her shoes, but it stayed at bay, unable to touch her.

"Cecilia?"

The other girl continued to push herself back and forth on the tire. There was no reaction from her. It was as though Mia hadn't spoken. She wondered if Cecilia knew she was there.

As she stepped closer, she noticed the tips of Cecilia's toes were raw. There were tracks of blood in the dirt underneath her foot. She didn't stop pushing herself in the swing.

What the holy hell?

"Cecilia," Mia repeated more firmly, her heart racing with nerves.

She leaned against the tree, trying to appear casual instead of worried. An electrical zap shot through her. Mia's vision zigzagged before everything went multicolored—as though she were staring through a kaleidoscope featuring a million different rainbows. She tried not to freak out as she gripped the tree with her hand, the firm bark centering her as the prisms in her eyes began to spin. Motion sickness pummeled her, and she thought she was going to throw up when her vision suddenly cleared. When she was able to focus, she saw that the scenery around her had changed.

She stood in front of a crowd, though no one seemed to notice her. The men wore breeches, the women wore long, black Puritan dresses. People gathered around a group of women standing on a platform with nooses around their necks, the ropes hung precariously around the thick branch of the oak tree.

A sinister looking man wearing a reverend's collar stood next to one woman, sneering at her. "This is your last chance to repent for your sins, Sarah Good. What do you have to confess?"

The woman glared at him, her expression filled with rage. "I am no more a witch than you are a wizard, and if you take away my life, God will give you blood to drink."

A gasp trickled through the crowd. The reverend stepped away from her and gave a sharp nod to a man wearing a black hood over his head. He reached for a lever and the floor of the platform opened. Sarah dropped through. The sound of her neck snapping ricocheted through the air.

"NO!" Mia screamed.

"Mia?"

She blinked and found Cecilia staring at her with bemusement. She jerked away from the tree.

What was that?

"Are you okay?" Cecilia asked.

"Yeah," Mia said. She shoved her trembling hands inside the pockets of her jeans. Did she really just watch Sarah Good's hanging? Or had it been her crazy imagination? She swallowed down bile as it rose in her throat.

"I'm sorry. I didn't hear you approach," Cecilia said. "I must have been daydreaming." She glanced nervously at the house. "What are you doing here?"

Mia remembered Cecilia's strange behavior before she touched the tree.

Though shaken, she forced herself to concentrate. She pointed at Cecilia's toes. "Your foot is bleeding."

She lifted it, staring at the bruised and broken skin as though it belonged to someone else. "Huh, I must have stubbed it and not realized."

"Are, um, are you feeling all right?"

"Yeah." Cecilia gave another quick glance toward the house. "You didn't answer my question. What are you doing here?"

Mia's eyes went back to the tree. "I... I wanted to see if you could hang out. I'm l-leaving in a couple days."

"CECILIA!" A woman yelled from one of the home's windows. Mia jumped as though someone slapped her.

Cecilia wiggled her way out of the tire quickly. Her hands clenched and unclenched as she stared at the house, her face a mix of humiliation and embarrassment. Mia reached out to touch her shoulder, hoping for...she didn't know exactly. Maybe to comfort her? Maybe to grab her so they could run away from all the darkness?

The same darkness that had taken advantage of Mia's moment of vulnerability had crept into her shoes. She quickly drew up the image of saving Tilly and the exhilaration of doing a spell right. The dark energy rippled around her feet but receded from her body.

"Cecilia!" the woman screamed again.

"I have to go." She began limping toward the house, saying over her shoulder as she went, "Are we still on for the carnival?"

"Yeah, but..." Mia took a step after her. "Cecilia—"

"I'll see you then, okay?" She entered the house and shut the door behind her.

Mia stood there for a moment, feeling confused and helpless, when she got the sense someone was watching her. She looked up at the window and saw a person standing in the shadows of the house. The figure disappeared from view.

It was too reminiscent of another shadow figure and Mia hurried off the property, shivering as she went. Her unease didn't let up until she was a safe distance away. She gnawed on her lip, worried about Cecilia and that weird vision she'd had, but comforted in knowing Cecilia's mom couldn't hurt her thanks to Mia's protection spell.

The dark energy at the house was another concern. Why was it there in the first place? Why had it started to become active now?

She answered her own question a few seconds later. Over the past few days, the shadow figure had murdered a mermaid and a warlock. Mia bet that the missing harpy was also dead. Their deaths were so heinous it must have awoken the dark energy that was accumulating at the house. But again, why there?

She had never given much thought about how dark energy could affect a Common. Cecilia's vacantness on the swing was something she'd never seen. It freaked her out. She had been a shell of herself. Mia could only hope that the darkness didn't get any worse while she was alive.

Because if it left Cecilia like that, she didn't stand a chance at fighting what was coming her way.

CHAPTER 16

The further she walked away from the house, the more the tension left her. Mia found herself at her high school. Carnival workers were busy setting up the rides. A Ferris wheel was already assembled and standing in one corner of the parking lot, while the crew worked on a pirate ship next to it. There was a spaceship-looking thing set up on the other side of the grounds, the name, *The Gravitron*, blinking in colorful lights above it.

She wandered over to the fun house where a line of mirrors leaned against the structure, waiting in the shadows to be installed. Some made her look tall and thin as a rail, others made her appear squat and wide. Just as she turned to leave, something in one of the mirrors caught her eye.

A small upside-down pentagram appeared inside it. She was so busy looking at it, trying to figure out why it was there, that she didn't notice her reflection changed. When she finally glanced at it, the shadow figure from the other night stared back. Mia took a hurried step backwards and tripped over a cable. She fell to the ground, scooting away from the mirror. Her heart sped as the creature grinned its human teeth at her before disappearing from view.

Jumping to her feet, she ran from the carnival until she reached the shoreline. The wind picked up, swirling around her to the point where it stung her eyes. She tried to move but the wind got stronger, whipping her black hair into her face. People walked by, not noticing the small non-moving tornado she was stuck inside.

The monster must have put some kind of hex on her!

"What do you want?" she screamed.

"Mia," a voice called out. It sounded far away.

Her entire body trembled with terror, but she lifted her chin in defiance. She wasn't going to go down without a fight.

"Show yourself, you piece of shit." Mia moved energy to her hands, ready for battle.

"Mia!" the voice said, firmer this time.

She paused, body relaxing slightly. That voice! It was familiar. It was *home*.

"A-Ailsa?" she whispered.

"Thanks be to Áine," the other girl said.

"Ailsa." A few tears slipped down Mia's cheeks. "Is … is it really you?"

"Yes..."

Mia tried to peer through the spinning tunnel of wind, but she didn't see her. "How are you doing this? Are you in 1992 as well?"

"No. I'll explain later." Ailsa's voice grew muffled for a second as though she was speaking to someone else before she said, "Mia, I can't hold our connection much longer. There's a black moon on Sunday and—"

"I know," she interrupted.

"Be inside a pentagram when the moon comes into its power. Whatever you do. Get inside a pent—"

The wind tunnel evaporated.

"Ailsa?" Mia was alone again. A feeling of homesickness saturated her, so powerful it took her breath away, and in that second, she wanted nothing more than to be home. She wanted to see Tilly, the aunt who always gave the best advice and knew her inside and out, not the teenaged version she was with now. She wanted to snuggle her dog, Winnie. She wanted to see Ailsa and find out how she was able to keep connecting to Mia. She wanted to talk to Ella and Colby—despite how she'd left things with both of her friends. She wanted to see Colby in person, to make sure he was okay.

Pushing her windblown hair from her face, Mia began walking again, keeping her head down so people wouldn't see the tears streaming down her cheeks. As she turned down a busy street, her sense of unease returned. She glanced frantically around, expecting to see the shadow figure. Instead, she saw a person walking away from her wearing the long, black cloak of a warlock.

Darkness radiated off him, which was what triggered Mia's unease. As he turned his head to the side, she realized it was the younger warlock she'd seen at the park. The boy weaved through the crowd of Commons, going unnoticed despite being out of place.

He disappeared around a corner. Against her better judgement, she followed. The warlock hurried down a street where some of Salem's older, more rundown houses were located. He stopped in front of what looked to be an abandoned red brick house. Boards covered the windows and doors. Grass and shrubbery grew out of control. This house hadn't seen anyone in years.

So, what was the guy doing there?

As he stared at the base of the house, an upside-down pentagram appeared in front of him on the structure. The brick melted away, revealing an opening. The warlock stepped through, hitting his wide shoulder against the narrow entryway.

Mia glanced around before creeping toward the building, her steps urgent in case the opening closed. Although the newly formed entrance was dark, there was just enough light inside to pick out old, wooden steps leading downward to a basement. Brighter light flickered below. The place reeked of dark energy.

Mia wished she knew a spell that could make herself invisible.

Lifting a hand, she pressed it against the spot on the doorframe where the warlock hit his shoulder. The dark energy he'd left behind overwhelmed her and she pulled her hand away. As she looked at her fingers, they flickered translucent before returning to their normal state.

It was as if the dark energy had heard Mia's wish and wanted to give her what she most desired. It made her feel powerful. It made her crave more.

She pressed her hand against the doorframe again. As the darkness entered her once more, slower this time, she gave it an order.

Make me invisible.

She held her breath, not expecting anything to really happen, and then she looked down at her hands. They disappeared from view. The rest of her body soon followed. Feeling confident that the glamor had worked, she inched down the steps, pausing before she reached the final one to peer inside the room.

She covered her mouth to hold back a gasp. Five Unmentionables stood around an enormous, round wood table. Hanging like a chandelier above it was a large upside-down pentagram. On top of the table lay the deceased warlock who'd had his heart eaten. He was spread eagle, naked with only a black sheet covering his groin area. Dry blood caked the hole in his chest where his heart should have been.

The warlock she'd followed threw back his hood and the others did the same. Mia's jaw dropped in surprise. They were young. Each one had to be only a few years older than Mia. They looked like a bunch of frat boys. They weren't just warlocks either. One had the pointy ears of an elf, and another's face was contorted into a partially shifted werewolf.

She could see that the boy she followed had dirty blond hair, long enough to touch his ears. His chiseled face had high cheekbones. He looked like an All-American football player. He would have been handsome, except for the coldness in his eyes distorting his face into something twisted and ugly.

"We need to be careful, McConnell," one of the other warlocks said, his voice cracking as he spoke. "There have been too many mistakes already."

"Don't be stupid," McConnell replied, pushing his blond hair away from his eyes. "The Commander doesn't make mistakes. You better hope your doubt is never known. There could be consequences."

He waved his hand toward the dead warlock.

"But what about—"

"We *will* get the girl. Do you need to be reminded that her heart is exactly what the Commander needs for our plans to fall into place? Her house is collecting dark energy as we speak."

Mia's fist curled as energy sizzled at her fingertips, ready for release.

"The vortex of dark energy *will* be opened soon. As soon as she's sacrificed," McConnell assured the group.

"Why don't we grab her now?" one of the older boys asked. "Then we will all be blessed in the darkness."

"As I've explained *many* times before," McConnell sounded impatient, "we have to wait until the appropriate moment for the dark energy to be unleashed. It will make us stronger if we wait until the black moon. Then we'll sacrifice her, feast on her flesh, and the darkness will bless us all with undefeatable power." McConnell glared at the dead body in front of him. "For now, we dine on the traitor. The Commander enjoyed eating his heart, but we get the rest. He may have been useless to our cause, but his power will become our strength."

The warlock sliced his hand through the air over the corpse and flesh ripped from bone, piling in front of each warlock. Mia didn't stick around to see what happened next. She ran outside and made it several blocks before she stopped to throw up on a rosebush. As she lost focus, the glamor left her, leaving her visible to anyone who wanted to watch her upchuck. Thankfully, no one was on this part of the street.

As she pulled her hand up to wipe at her mouth, Mia froze as she stared at her fingernails. Usually when she used magic, her fingers glowed with a blue hue. But now...the hue was black. The dark energy was still inside her, testing her soul for weaknesses. She could feel it, wanting to keep her under its influence.

Mia closed her eyes and thought of the hug Aunt Tilly had given her after she told her she was a lesbian. Her heart warmed and the grip the darkness had on her disappeared, pouring out of her in streams of grimy sweat.

Mia took several deep breaths as she remembered what the warlocks said. They were going to kill Cecilia for the dark energy inside her house. They were going to rip her skin from her so that they could...

She heaved into the bushes again. As she stood on wobbly legs, a black car passed by. The man behind the wheel was so intent on the road in front of him, he didn't notice Mia standing there. She recognized him instantly.

Doyle Parris.

What was he doing here? Wasn't he supposed to be heading back to the Assembly? Mia sent a silent prayer to Hecate that he wouldn't notice her and breathed a sigh of relief when the car continued on its way.

They're going to eat Cecilia.

With that urgent reminder popping in her head, Mia started to run back to her family's store. Her mind raced with too many thoughts as she went.

There was a Commander that led the warlocks. That had to be the shadow figure Mia had seen twice. She also had an idea of why they wanted to kill Cecilia now. She lived in a house that was the epicenter of dark energy.

She frowned and she came to a halt. According to what she just learned, Cecilia's death opened the vortex, but the darkness was still contained to only the property, though it had been steadily gaining strength in Mia's timeline. Why though? That's what she couldn't figure out.

She forced herself to start running again, her shoulders tense as she arrived at her home. She could only hope that Parris was following up on a lead and he was on his way to catch the warlocks. Because if he failed and didn't stop Others from getting killed, it was becoming clear to Mia what she needed to do.

If Cecilia's death caused a ripple effect that endangered Colby down the road, Mia only had one option to stop it.

She had to save Cecilia. If she stopped her murder, then maybe—just maybe—her interference with the timeline could save Colby, too.

CHAPTER 17

"Grandma! Tilly!" Mia yelled, running inside the house.

"In here," her grandma called from the store's office. "Tilly and your grandpa went out for groce—"

She stopped speaking as Mia hurried into the room, looking pale and wide-eyed.

She immediately got up from the desk. "What is it? What happened?"

"They're going to eat her and the house...the house is waking up...and..."

Grandma Eabha hurried over to her. "Honey, you're not making any sense."

"I saw that warlock again. The one I ran into at the park. I followed him." She ignored her grandma's dismayed gasp. "He met with some other warlocks—"

"Mia, they could have killed you."

"I was fine. I used a glamor to make myself invisible."

Grandma Eabha paused, looking momentarily impressed. "That's pretty advanced magic for someone your age."

Mia didn't meet her eyes, not wanting to admit she used dark energy to achieve it. That the energy was so powerful, even the werewolf didn't sense her, and he should have. They were known for their keen sense of smell. "I overheard them. They said they have a Commander. That has to be the one who attacked Tilly. It wants to eat Cecilia's heart—"

"The girl you've been meeting."

She nodded. "They said they needed her heart to complete their plan and that her house is starting to collect dark energy. Then...they had the body of the warlock who died. T-they ripped his flesh off. Said eating it would help give them his power."

Grandma Eabha gripped her arm. "Thank Hecate they didn't realize you were there. Is there anything else?

Mia tried to organize her thoughts but they were all over the place. She frowned. "I saw Parris driving around that same area."

Her grandma paused. "He was supposed to be leaving town but good. Hopefully, he'll bring the entire Examiner department with him and arrest those Unmentionables before any damage is done."

"Yeah..." Mia thought back to his strange interaction with the mermaid. She chewed on her inner cheek. "I saw him the other day speaking to a mermaid. Parris took something from him in exchange for money."

The older woman's eyes narrowed. "It may have been Assembly business."

"They found the mermaid dead the next day," Mia said. "I saw Parris at the crime scene speaking with another Examiner. He looked relaxed, happy even." She looked down at her hands and saw that they were shaking. She clasped them together tightly. She finally said, "Are we sure Parris is on our side? It wouldn't be the first time someone in our family went bad, after all."

"He's not a warlock if that's what you're thinking," Grandma Eabha said. "If he were, there'd be no way in this realm that the Other world would let him be an Examiner, let alone a part of the Assembly."

"I guess..." Mia still wasn't convinced.

"Besides, Doyle has always been a rather ambitious boy. I can't see him risking his position with the Assembly by becoming associated with murderers." Her grandma began to pace around the small area. "Can you think of any other details?"

Mia thought of the black lines leading to Cecilia's house and the dark energy that had begun to make its presence known. "For years in my timeline, dark energy has been inside Cecilia's house. It's pretty bad but it's always been contained to the property. No one has lived there for years. I didn't feel it when I first arrived in this timeline, but I felt it for the first time today when I went to talk to Cecilia. When I got there, she was sitting in her tire swing, looking like a ..." she paused, unsure of the best way to describe what she had seen before finally settling on her earlier thought, "she looked like a zombie. When I tried to get her attention, I touched the tree she was swinging from, and I saw something—a vision. It showed me..."

"What?"

"I think I saw them murder Sarah Good. They had her on a platform, and a man in a black hood pulled a lever. I saw her drop through. The sound was...it was..."

Mia swayed on her feet, feeling suddenly lightheaded at what she'd seen. Grandma Eabha wrapped her into a comforting hug, murmuring, "Shh, you're okay. You're safe now." As Mia's head cleared, her grandma asked, "Where does this girl live?" When she told her, her grandma nodded. "Come with me."

They walked up to the main living quarters and continued up a set of narrow, dusty stairs that led to the attic.

"What are we doing?" Mia asked as they passed through a doorway. Her grandma flipped on a light and walked around a stack of rusty cauldrons. She made her way toward a pile of boxes near one of the windows.

Mia looked around. She hadn't been in this part of the house in years. The attic had a steepled roof, wide wooden floorboards, and exposed beams. Dust-covered objects lay everywhere. Over in one section of the attic were shelves containing layers of dirty glass jars. Some had spices in them, while others had different types of sand. A few had mysterious liquids inside. As Mia walked over to look at one, whatever was in the jar began to swirl in bluish silvery light. She felt the urge to grab it and never let go. Mia lifted her hand.

Grandma Eabha said, "Don't touch that."

"I wasn't going to," Mia lied, but her grandma was no longer paying attention to her. Mia stepped away from the hypnotizing jar and made her way to where the older woman was.

"I don't know why I didn't think of this before." Her grandma was kneeling on the floor, looking at the cover of a box. Mia didn't recognize the writing on it. Grandma Eabha ripped open the lid while muttering to herself, "I must be getting forgetful in my old age."

Mia's stomach knotted at that, but she didn't say anything. Her grandma's Alzheimer's wouldn't start for another fifteen years. She was still so alert in 1992 that she sometimes forgot the state her grandma would be in when she got home. She fought back tears before Grandma Eabha could see them.

Clearing her throat, she asked again, "What are we doing?"

"We're looking for documents. Our family has lived in Salem for centuries. If there's anything off about the area where Cecilia lives, it's sure to be mentioned in this paperwork somewhere."

She grabbed another box and pushed it Mia's way, who sat on the floor and started looking through the papers inside. Some of them were so old, she was afraid they would disintegrate in her hands. There were dates scrawled across several documents going back to the 1600s. When she got toward the bottom of the box, she stiffened when she saw a frail book that had a dull blue cover. In faded writing across the front were the words, *Property of Elizabeth Parris.*

Mia pulled it out of the box and began skimming the pages, though she struggled to comprehend anything. She really wished she had her Adderall as she began to read. Elizabeth mostly lamented about her daughter, Betty's, terrible behavior. Considering Betty was the reason the Salem Witch Trials started, that didn't surprise her. As she delved deeper into the diary, Elizabeth's concern turned toward her husband and his obsession with persecuting people for witchcraft. Mia froze when she came across one entry. She reread it three times, trying to comprehend it before she realized what it was.

"Grandma, I think I found something."

Her grandma looked at what she was holding. Her face turned jubilant.

"Of course!" She took the diary from Mia's proffered hand and began to read. "Sarah Good was hanged today along with four others, but not before she cursed the reverend who sentenced her to die. Her hex will cause him to suffer a terrible death. I know I should lift it, but it seems to be equal justice. The man has darkness in his heart for what he is doing to these unfortunate people. As Sarah's body hung, the ground beneath her turned black. I do not think the Commons noticed, but I did. Each innocent life hanged during this travesty has met their end on this land. Their deaths have created dark energy. It has saturated the ground. I tried to rid us of it before the darkness could spread, but I was unsuccessful. The most I have been able to do is put it to sleep. I can only hope people do not disturb the ground and leave it as a place of honor for the poor souls who have lost their lives..."

Mia stared at her grandma in dread. "Do you think...?"

"Yes," Grandma Eabha was grim. "I believe your friend's house was built on the spot where they hung people. The tree you touched was probably the same one they used to murder the innocent. Elizabeth made the darkness go dormant, but from what you said, it's somehow waking back up."

"Between the Others who've been killed and Cecilia's death, the vortex *will* open," Mia said, "but in my timeline, it's still contained to just the home's property." She stared at the diary in thought. "Grandma, I told you about my friend who disappeared. The darkness has been getting stronger in my timeline. What if the shadow figure is in Salem again and it kidnapped…" Mia's throat choked with fear. "If it kills someone good and innocent like the people who were hung—"

Her grandma stared at her with a horrified expression. "Then the vortex could crack wide open, spreading darkness throughout Salem. Every Unmentionable who wants to use dark energy as a weapon will have an unlimited supply." She put the diary back in its box and carefully closed the lid. Her eyes scanned over the different objects around the attic before she randomly said, "I should really come up here and get rid of this stuff. Some of it's been up here for generations." She stood and walked over to a table that had several pieces of jewelry on it, picking up an old locket held by a busted chain. "Do you know that when something is in your possession for so long, it becomes a part of you? You see it and it triggers a memory. It can lift your spirit and give you energy. In exchange, it develops its own energy from you. You are a part of its history and it's a part of yours."

Mia tilted her head as she thought about what her grandma was saying. She sucked in a breath. "The house has a connection to Cecilia because she lives there. It's become a part of her." Mia stilled. "She's the key. All this time, I thought they had chosen to murder her because it was convenient, but that's not it at all. They're targeting her because she has a connection with the house. They share energy."

Her grandma nodded. "The ultimate sacrifice. She's young and pure. Her death would be a tribute to those grounds. And with the black moon coming on Sunday, it would make sense for the warlocks to want to kill her when the moon comes into its power."

Grandma Eabha stared at Mia, her look thoughtful. "Mia, what are you going to do with this information?"

She looked down at the box that held the diary and began tracing her finger through the dust.

"Nothing," she said before flat-out lying, "the warlocks aren't going to try anything during the black moon. I overheard them say they wanted to kill Cecilia during an eclipse. Said it would give them more power."

Her grandma looked tired, worry lines etched on her forehead. "There is a solar eclipse expected next month."

Mia let out a pent-up breath she didn't realize she was holding as her stomach went taut with guilt. Her grandma believed her. She hated lying but she had to do what she could to save Cecilia. "Well, I'll be gone by then so there's nothing to worry about."

Grandma Eabha looked at her sympathetically. "I'm sorry about your friend. I know how much this hurts you. You're a good person." She walked over to her and patted her cheek. "You remind me so much of Sadie."

Mia's expression turned brittle. Yeah, she was just like Sadie. Great at betraying her family and leaving them behind to deal with the mess.

Mia walked outside for some fresh air an hour later. She thought of Cecilia and all the things that could go wrong with her plan to save the other girl. If she thought about it too much, she worried she might change her mind. But saving Cecilia meant she was possibly saving Colby as well. She couldn't save her father, grandma, or grandpa, but at least she could do this. She thought back to her friend, the worry on his face before she walked away from him. She had to make this right somehow. He'd do the same for her. Despite the distance between them these days, she knew Colby would do everything in his power to help her if the circumstances were flipped. That was the kind of person he was.

Mia screamed as she fell from the tree she'd been climbing. Colby and Ella rushed over to her.

"I told you not to climb it," Ella said, even as worry etched into her seven-year-old face.

"Ella, go get her Aunt Tilly," Colby ordered, and she hurried away.

"You should go, you're faster," Mia grunted, clutching her arm which tingled painfully.

"No, I'm not leaving you," Colby insisted, his little chest pushing out proudly. "What if an Unmentionable shows up? Ella can't protect you like I can."

Mia pressed her hand to her head, trying to resist giving into the emotion pouring through her. Closing her eyes, she used her energy to seek out the protection spell she had placed on Cecilia. She knew it was possible for witches to sense where they had left traces of their own magic. It was how her grandma could tell if Mia needed her if she was ever in danger. But Mia had never attempted the spell herself. She sat in the patio chair for a half hour trying to push her energy outside of the wards her grandma had placed around the property. Once she managed it, Mia used her energy to search for the piece of her magic she'd left on Cecilia. It took another frustrating half hour before she finally felt the faint ping of her energy bounce back to her. Her eyes flew open. Running back inside the house, she headed to where her family kept a supply of chicory cookies.

Cecilia was across town and Mia needed to speak with her fast. She reached into a cupboard and thanked whatever deity was listening that her family still stored them in the same place as they did in her timeline. Taking one, she thought of Cecilia's location and popped the cookie in her mouth.

Mia took a step forward. The cells in her body cracked apart until she was nothing but particles. She catapulted forward and was at her destination in the blink of an eye.

Cecilia stood outside the bus station in the same white, flowing dress she'd been wearing earlier. She must've run a brush through her hair at some point because it now lay in organized waves around her shoulders. She held a ticket in her hand.

She looked at peace. Content.

The turbulence inside Mia calmed as she stared at her. "Hey."

Cecilia turned to see who was speaking to her. Joy lit her face when she noticed Mia. "It's kind of funny. Anytime I think of you, you suddenly appear right in front of me like magic."

She let out an awkward laugh. "Yeah, funny." She nodded toward Cecilia's hand. "What's that?"

Cecilia showed her the ticket. The destination was for Seattle. The bus was leaving at seven on Sunday night—the night she was supposed to die.

"This is my ticket to freedom," Cecilia said. "I'm done with this town, with my mom, all of it."

She looked at Mia indecisively before she grabbed her hand and led her to an outside courtyard. There were several tall bushes next to a metal-rod bench. The girls sat on it, hiding them from view of the people milling around the station.

Cecilia let go of her to clutch her necklace. "Mia, I've been giving this a lot of thought, and...why don't you come with me?"

Her stomach dropped. "What?"

"Come with me."

"I-I can't. I have to go home."

Cecilia leaned toward her, her face eager. "Why? You said yourself you feel like a burden to your aunt. Let her live her life and you can live yours." She bit her lip nervously, before she added, "With me."

"I…" She didn't know what to say. "My friend, Colby, he's went missing. I shouldn't have even made this trip. I need to get home and make sure he's okay."

"Oh." Cecilia looked crushed. "I get it, and I know it seems silly to ask you to come with me. We've only known each other a few days, right? And obviously, you should get back to help look for your friend. But…I can't explain it." She picked up Mia's hand and began to trace the lines of her skin with the tip of her finger. Goosebumps popped up on Mia's arms at the touch. Cecilia continued, "There's something about you that makes me feel safe. I like you. A lot. And I hope you like me."

"I do," Mia whispered.

"This is going to sound so weird, but when I woke up in that alley and saw you standing over me—protecting me—I knew you were going to be important." She laced their fingers together before giving her a cheeky grin. "You said you've watched *West Side Story*. I always thought Maria and Tony falling for each other at first sight was lame."

Mia snorted. "Same."

She gave her a sweet smile. "From the moment I saw you, my world went away."

Mia melted. She still tried to play it off. "Are you seriously quoting a line from 'Tonight?'"

Cecilia's face turned serious. "This may be crazy, but I feel like we were destined to meet, you know?"

She did know. She'd felt anchored to her in a way she couldn't explain. "Yeah."

"Mia, you're my future. I *know* it." Cecilia leaned forward and brushed her lips against hers.

Mia's heart flew into her throat. She'd only kissed one other person, Mark Ethos, during a game of spin the bottle in seventh grade. Mark's lips had been dry and chapped.

Cecilia's mouth was soft. Her lips fit perfectly against Mia's, like they'd been created just for hers. She opened her mouth slightly, wanting more. Cecilia's tongue slipped in, brushing against hers, and Mia saw stars.

She let out a soft groan and reached around Cecilia's back, pulling her in until their chests pressed hard against each other. Cecilia cupped the back of her neck, holding her in place. Mia's hands went to her waist and tightened.

The moment broke when something sharp stabbed into Mia's skin. She pulled back in confusion then glanced down. Cecilia's necklace glinted in the sun. The raised bracket that held the jewel in place must have poked Mia.

"Sorry," Cecilia said, taking hold of the necklace. "I keep meaning to get that fixed. The one edge is a bit sharper."

Her cheeks had a delicate flush to them and Mia reached up, running her thumb across the color in fascination.

"You're beautiful," she said so quietly she wasn't sure if she'd spoken aloud.

Cecilia held her hand to her cheek. "I know you want to get back to your friend, and it's not fair of me to ask you this, but please come to Seattle with me. Once we get there, we can work together to find your friend."

She knew that it was impossible. She had to get home. Colby needed her, not to mention that by saving Cecilia, she was about to create a domino effect that she'd need to clean up. That didn't stop her from fantasizing for a moment.

"I'll think about it."

Cecilia gave her a gentle smile. "Okay, think about it overnight. If you decide you want to go, we'll come here after our date tomorrow and get your ticket. I've got some money saved."

Mia forced herself to smile. "I'll let you know."

The other girl stood. "I need to start my shift at work soon. I'll see you tomorrow. I'll be waiting for you at the carnival by the ticket booth stand."

"See you tomorrow."

Cecilia leaned over and brushed her mouth once more over Mia's.

After she left, Mia continued to sit there, enjoying the tingling sensation on her lips. The skin on her chest throbbed and she frowned. She pulled her shirt away and saw that a little trickle of blood had gathered where the necklace had gouged her. It was slowly dripping down her chest. Her mouth quirked into a smile. If Mia was going to kiss her again—and she really hoped she would—Cecilia was going to need to do something about that necklace.

CHAPTER 18

Mia stared at Sadie's bedroom ceiling as she lay in bed. She was exhausted, but that was nothing new. She hadn't slept well all week. Cecilia's proposal had been on her mind throughout the night, causing her to wake up every few hours.

She still didn't know what she was going to do. Her brain told her she had to go home. Her heart told her she wanted to stay.

In the back of her mind, she wondered if traveling to 1992 was always what was meant to be. Maybe it was her fate to meet Cecilia and save her so that they could live happily ever after. And if she stayed, she could come back to Salem the day Colby gets kidnapped and stop his attacker since she already knew it was coming.

Mia shot up in bed at that realization.

She could save Colby!

Why hadn't she thought of that plan before?

But she knew why. She'd been distracted by Cecilia.

From the moment they met, she'd felt drawn to her. She never felt this way about anyone, not even Ella. Something had always been missing in Mia's life. Though she had the love of her family, she still felt so lonely sometimes. Like she didn't fit in.

Whenever she was around Cecilia, she didn't feel like that. She felt lighthearted...like she found her person. Being around Cecilia was like finding a part of herself that was missing.

Mia's desire to protect her was so strong, she knew she would do anything for her. Even mess up the timeline. But did that really include Mia leaving her life behind to be with her?

Sighing, she pushed back the sheets and went over to Sadie's closet, pulling the sliding doors open. She wanted to look good for their date, but she also wanted to be comfortable since they were going to the carnival. If they went on a ride like *The Gravitron*, she didn't want to wear anything that would result in her flashing the citizens of Salem. She pulled out a simple lacy periwinkle tank top and a pair of Guess jeans.

After finishing her morning routine, she headed for the kitchen. Her grandma and Tilly were speaking excitedly at the table while her grandpa read the newspaper. Tilly still had an air of frailty to her, but she didn't look as pale as she had the day before.

"Good news!" her aunt said as soon as she saw her. "Mom figured out the sequence you used to travel back in time."

Mia sat in the spare kitchen chair with a thump. "You did?"

"Yes." Her grandma looked tired but pleased. "You'll be able to head home tomorrow. The best time to do the spell will be during the black moon's rise in power at nine. Make sure you're in the house before it gets dark. We can't risk you running into that creature again."

Mia nodded, not meeting Grandma Eabha's stare. From what she saw of Cecilia's bus ticket, she was supposed to leave Salem a couple hours before the moon hit its stride. Mia had to make sure she got on that bus and out of harm's way.

She glanced around the table, noting her aunt's happy face, the healthiness of her grandpa, before her gaze finally settled on her grandma. Grandma Eabha gave her a considering look. Mia shifted her eyes to the table.

"Aren't you excited?" Tilly said.

"Yeah." She tried to inject some enthusiasm into her tone. "How'd you figure it out?"

"Trial and error," her grandma said. "But when I physically travelled back to the early 1900s last night, I knew I had it. I wasn't able to stay long. We'll need the energy of the black moon to give us the boost we need to send you home permanently."

"Sounds good." Her voice was flat.

"One day left with us," Tilly said. "What are you going to do when you get back?"

Mia thought about one of the changes she would make if she did go back. "Talk to you about enrolling me into Cunningham instead of public school."

Tilly snorted but her grandma frowned. "That's Sadie's decision, isn't it?"

Mia reached for the bowl of oatmeal that her grandpa made her. "I guess."

"Your mom must be so worried about you."

Mia looked at her aunt, the only mom she'd ever known. "I know she is."

Tilly was fighting for her even now, working with Ailsa to bring her home. She would be heartbroken if Mia didn't return. Then again, maybe she could get back to her own life instead of having to worry about Mia all the time or the stupid things she did.

"I have a little over twenty-four hours left with you," she said in an effort to lighten her mood. "What should we do?"

"You want to help me in the shop today?" her grandpa asked.

She smiled at him. "Yeah. I'd love to."

No matter what happened, whether she returned to her timeline or ran away with Cecilia, she was going to lose her grandpa. She wished she hadn't avoided him so much while she was there.

They spent the rest of the morning helping customers and talking. Her grandpa told her about some of his lighter experiences in Vietnam, and she told him all about her friends, though she didn't mention her former crush on her best friend. She'd only been in 1992 for a week, but her feelings for Ella seemed so distant now. It made her wonder if she actually ever was in love with her, or if she'd confused her feelings for loneliness.

When it was time to meet Cecilia at the carnival, Mia left the house and headed toward the school. The smell of cotton candy and popcorn blending with the scent of the distant harbor greeted her when she arrived. Every resident in Salem seemed to be there. Parents stood around talking to their neighbors while children screamed as they were tossed around on the different rides. Mia found Cecilia waiting for her by the ticket stand. She had on frayed white shorts that showed off her shapely legs and a stretched out blue t-shirt that had *Save the Earth* written on it. Her ever-present necklace glinted in the sun.

Cecilia walked over to her, her expression eager and excited. Mia wanted to remember how she looked in that moment, storing the memory away in case she needed something happy to focus on when dealing with the darkness.

"Hi," Cecilia greeted. "I already bought tickets. We have enough to go on at least five rides."

"Thanks." She wanted to kiss her but there were too many people around. She didn't need to deal with any potential bigoted remarks. Not right then.

"What should we do first?" Cecilia asked.

"Ferris Wheel?" She suggested the one ride where they could be together and get away from the crowd.

As if reading her mind, the other girl's eyes softened. "Yeah, let's do that."

They waited in line talking about nothing serious. When it was finally their turn, they climbed into the carriage car and the worker secured them in. The wheel began to move, the car swinging back and forth gently until they were at the top. It came to a halt, giving them a view of the harbor in the distance. The cloudless sky allowed the sun to shine brightly on the water, turning the surface into shimmering jewels. The sounds of the carnival below seemed muted. It felt as though they were the only two people in the world.

"Listen," Cecilia said. "I wasn't going to bring this up until you said something first, but did you think any more on what we talked about yesterday?"

Mia grabbed the bar in front of her in a tight grip. She had to give an answer, despite how conflicted she was. Her thoughts drifted to Ailsa and her aunt working to bring her home. She thought about teenaged Tilly and her grandma staying up late to figure out the sequence of the spell she used. Her mind shifted to Colby, who was probably terrified right now.

Once Cecilia was safe in this timeline, she could only hope that her friend would be safe, too. But who knew what else lay ahead for her, especially considering how much she was about to mess things up by saving Cecilia. She let out an unsettled breath. There was only one thing to do.

"I have to go home," she whispered. "I have responsibilities there that I need to see through."

"Your friend, Colby?"

"Yes, him. But I've got my family, too." She saw the disappointment on her face, and it crushed her.

Cecilia nodded wearily in acceptance. "Fine. I won't leave then."

"What?" Her heart sank. Cecilia had to go. If she stayed, the warlocks would kill her.

"I won't leave," she repeated. "If there's a chance you'll come visit your family here, then we'll still be able to see each other."

"Cecilia." She let go of the bar to grab the girl's chin, turning her to face Mia. "I'm not coming back. I live too far away, and it was too hard to get here in the first place."

Cecilia pulled away, her face stubborn. "You could."

"Why would you put your dreams on hold for me?"

"Because I love you!" she shouted. "I've loved you since the first second I saw you, and I—"

She didn't finish what else she was going to say. Cecilia pressed their mouths insistently together. Sparks raced over Mia's entire body as those determined soft lips held hers captive. She wished time could stop and freeze them like that forever.

Cecilia broke contact and whispered something, just as the Ferris wheel began to move again, interrupting the moment. Mia pulled back, running her tongue over her lips and tasting the cherry lip-gloss Cecilia wore.

"What did you say?" she asked.

A faint blush broke over her cheeks. "Um, I called you, *my love.*"

Mia grinned so hard her cheeks hurt. "My love?"

The red on Cecilia's face grew deeper. "Too cheesy?"

"Absolutely," she said. "But you can call me that anyway."

As the Ferris wheel brought them toward the ground, Mia opened her mouth several times to say something—*anything*. Her emotions were all over the place. She knew that she should say, *I love you, too*. It was what Cecilia wanted to hear. She could tell by the way she stared at her hopefully. And didn't she deserve to hear those words? She was about to die, and the world had shown her so little kindness in her short life. Hecate knew her mom had never given her any love.

And it wouldn't exactly be a lie. It wasn't just the anxiety of Cecilia's impending death messing with Mia. She couldn't imagine a world where Cecilia's brightness wasn't a part of it. This beautiful, brave girl who made her heart soar just with a smile.

She opened her mouth to say, *I'm in love with you.* Instead, Mia found herself blurting, "Cecilia, you *have* to go."

"Why?"

They came to a halt and the operator released their lap bar. She eyed the different rides, looking for another place they could talk privately. Cecilia solved the issue by dragging Mia toward the only place that would offer them privacy...the funhouse. Mia reluctantly entered, checking the mirrors just inside the entrance for the shadow figure, but thankfully not seeing anything.

"Why do I have to leave?" Cecilia asked again as they entered a long hall lit with red lights. "Isn't it my decision?" A mechanical creature popped out of the wall and she jumped at Mia, burying her face into her neck with a shuddering breath. Mia wrapped her arms around her, holding her close.

"These aren't the monsters you need to be afraid of," Mia whispered into her ear, rejoicing in the feel of her, warm and safe in her arms. She was trying to tell the truth about their world without actually saying anything about Unmentionables. Cecilia didn't seem to understand though as she pulled out of her grasp.

"Whatever that means." She eyed the walls as if she expected something else to pop out. "Stop evading and answer my question."

Mia ran a hand over her eyes, wondering how much she should say. She settled on, "I had a dream you died."

Cecilia frowned. "Well, it was just a dream."

She stepped closer to Mia, looking as though she wanted to offer some kind of comfort. Her eyes drifted to her mouth. Yearning tugged at Mia as she wrapped a hand around Cecilia's neck, closing the distance between them. Their lips brushed once...twice...before Mia pulled back.

"No." Her voice ached. "It wasn't just a dream."

Cecilia stared at her in confusion. She started walking again and the other girl followed. They came to a stop when they reached a corner of the attraction lit in olive green light.

Cecilia crossed her arms over her chest. "What are you talking about?"

"Let's just say I have a gift," she said. "I can see into the future." She ran her hands over Cecilia's crossed arms, looking her straight in the eye. "Someone is going to murder you tomorrow."

"A gift? Really?" Her jaw tightened. "I don't think this is very funny."

"I'm not lying."

"Stop it, Mia."

"Look, I'm not saying this to upset you. I need to keep you safe."

Cecilia pulled away from her. "I'm going home."

Mia thought of something and hoped it would convince her. "You have a large table in your basement, right? It's made of some kind of granite and looks like something King Arthur and his knights would have used."

Cecilia stilled. "It's marble." Her eyes were huge as she stared at her. "How did you know about that? Have you been spying on me?"

"Of course not."

"Then how do you know about the table?"

Time seemed to slow as Mia opened and closed her mouth several times, trying to figure out how to explain everything without revealing too much about the Other world. Somewhere in another part of the funhouse, a couple of children screamed at whatever had frightened them.

It wouldn't just be Mia who suffered the consequences if the Assembly ever found out she told a Common about their world. They'd go after her whole family And Hecate knew what they'd do to Cecilia.

But the problem was quickly taken out of Mia's hands when she heard the sound of a footstep scuffing across the metal floor behind her.

"Because, dear girl," a deep, menacing voice said. "Our friend, Mia, is a witch."

Chapter 19

Mia swung around.

The blond warlock, McConnell, stood there with two of his cronies.

As her heart kicked with adrenaline, she stepped between Cecilia and the warlocks. "You're not going to hurt her."

"Pretty confident, huh?" McConnell sneered. "There's three of us and one of you."

Before she knew what she was doing, energy blasted from her, bright blue light flying toward the warlock. McConnell swept his hands out to either side of him, splitting her hex in two. It hit the other warlocks and threw them into the walls. They fell to the ground, both unconscious.

Cecilia screamed. She took off running. The loud sound of her shoes hitting the metal floor of the funhouse momentarily distracted Mia, giving McConnell the edge. He hit her with a hex and she collapsed to the ground, her body aching all over. The warlock lunged past her. She struggled to get to her feet before remembering her grandma's lesson about tapping into her spirit.

A vision of Cecilia popped into her head. She heard Cecilia calling her *my love* and Mia felt happiness flood through her, filling her with strength. She got to her feet and ran after them.

As she hurried outside, she blinked against the brightness of the sun. She tried to use her energy to figure out which direction Cecilia had gone, but the noise of the rides kept distracting her, making her lose focus.

Think. Think. Think.

The protective spell on the other girl pinged back that she had gone eastward toward the bus station. Mia shoved her way through the crowd until she was on a sidewalk.

What Mia needed in that moment was some dark energy to give her momentum. She cursed herself for not pulling it from the warlocks she'd left behind in the funhouse.

As she ran, she passed a guy with his arm wrapped around a younger woman's waist. She could sense the dark energy on him. The man had a wedding ring on his finger. The woman didn't.

Mia hated cheaters.

She zapped the ugliness from his heart as she went by and his arm dropped from the woman, his expression turning to one of deep remorse. The darkness gave Mia the boost she needed. The sounds of the carnival faded as she continued to run, heading deeper into a residential area. She turned onto a street where trees lined the sidewalk, casting it in shadow.

Mia soon saw the back of McConnell's blond head as he ran after Cecilia. She lifted her hands and threw out a hex. It hit him square in the shoulders and he stumbled to the ground. She watched in relief as Cecilia made it to the safety of the bus station, disappearing inside.

The warlock tried to stand up. Mia blasted him with another burst of energy. He fell into a spot of sunshine peeking between two trees.

"I told you," Mia said, her hands still raised. "You're not going to touch her."

"Not up to you, girly," he gritted.

"Oh, screw your 'girly' crap. You're barely older than me."

"But I am older than you, aren't I? By quite a lot."

Mia's arms slowly lowered.

McConnell sneered as he stood up. "This isn't your timeline."

"What do you know of it?" she said, her chin lifting defensively.

"I know all about the Desolate witch staying in Salem. There are eyes everywhere. But I think the Commander might be wrong about you not being a problem. You're just going to get in the way."

"Didn't I hear you say you shouldn't second guess your Commander unless you're prepared to face the consequences?" Mia watched a slight tick at the corner of his mouth go off, his only reaction. She grinned. "See, I know some stuff about you too, you sick cannibalistic prick."

"Clever girl." He clenched his fists. Flames formed around them. He raised one up, looking proud. "Like it?"

Mia felt her own energy sizzle underneath her skin, rushing toward her hands in readiness. "Not really."

She lifted her palm again and tried to pull the darkness from him. He countered before she could do anything, blasting fire at her. She jumped backwards, her spine hitting a tree on someone's property, causing her to wince as pain shot across her back. The fire missed her by mere inches before drawing back toward its caster.

McConnell nodded toward his fist, still in flames. "This right here is part of the Firestarter family legacy."

"Wait. Your last name is Firestarter?" Mia said drolly. "McConnell Firestarter. Did you get beat up a lot as a kid?"

McConnell took a menacing step toward her before he regained his composure. "After some great-grandma of mine accidentally set her barn on fire and burned Chicago to the ground, the Assembly excommunicated my family and made us warlocks." McConnell's face turned to rage. "We have to carry the name of our ancestor's crime for the rest of our existence. It used to piss me off.

To be treated like garbage for something I wasn't responsible for. But now..." The flames on his hand blazed brighter. "I embrace it."

He threw a fireball at her. The reddish orange ball rocketed toward her, the air heating in warning.

The dark energy, still simmering inside of Mia, responded to the challenge.

The fire hit her in the chest but she didn't feel it as it rebounded and flew back toward McConnell. The warlock's eyes widened right before his own hex hit him in the face. Flames raced down his cheek, and he screamed. He fell into a patch of sidewalk bathed in sunlight, withering on the ground as the fire began to spread down his left side.

Mia stood there, too stunned to move.

Something slammed into her, knocking her off her feet. Mia hit the ground hard and jerked her head to see what hit her. She tried to scramble back as she came face to face with the shadow figure.

It was out during *daytime*!

The creature roared at Mia before stepping into the spot of sun McConnell was lying in. The surface of its skin began to smoke, and the monster screeched in pain. It grabbed the warlock, pulling him quickly into another tree's shadow. It crouched over the still burning man, and black hue shot out from the creature, dousing the fire.

Mia's stomach lurched at the damage to McConnell's face. Steam rose off the skin, singed black; the upper layers melted away like shrink-wrap. The monster latched onto McConnell's burned arm, ignoring his pained howl. It dragged him closer to the tree. They blended into the darkness cast by the trunk's shadow. Before Mia's eyes, they disappeared into the blackness.

She rose on unsteady feet, trying to ignore the stench of burning flesh that still lingered in the air. She stumbled her way to the tree to make sure they were gone. When she didn't see any trace of them, she looked around to make sure there weren't any witnesses. A tiny gasp escaped her as she realized she was standing in front of Colby's house, though he wasn't born yet.

She checked her internal senses and couldn't trace any dark energy lingering inside after whatever she had done to McConnell. Mia forced herself to run on weakened limbs, hurrying toward the bus station. Cecilia was in the courtyard, sitting on the bench where they'd exchanged their first kiss.

Her arms were around her knees, and she was rocking herself back and forth. She looked pale as a corpse.

Mia approached her slowly. "Cecilia?"

She jerked her head up. Tears streaked down her cheeks. Her body shook all over.

"Stop! Stay where you are," Cecilia said and Mia froze. "What are you?"

She raised her hands to show she meant no harm. When the other girl didn't look like she was about to bolt, Mia moved so that she could sit in the spot next to her. She made sure to leave plenty of space between them.

"I'm a witch."

"Are you... Are you going to hurt me?"

"I'd never hurt you." Mia wanted to touch her—to reassure her—but she kept her hands at her sides. "I want to protect you."

I love you.

McConnell had gotten so close to catching Cecilia. What if Mia had been too late and he'd succeeded. They'd be off with the shadow monster right now, possibly cutting her heart out. Mia couldn't breathe at the idea.

The intensity of her feelings didn't make any sense. She never believed in love at first sight. But she did now. From the first moment they met, she'd fallen hard. She couldn't stay away from her if she tried.

Cecilia tightened her grip on her legs. "Who was that man?"

Mia turned in her seat so she could stare at her profile. "He's the bad guy."

"He's the one who wants to k-kill me." When she nodded, Cecilia asked, "Why?"

"Your house. It was built on the spot where they hung people during the Salem Witch Trials. There's something there—something called dark energy—and that guy and his friends want access to it. For them to do that, they're looking to sacrifice someone with a pure heart. Because you live in the house and have a connection to it, you'd be the ultimate prize."

Cecilia shook even harder. "I tried to get another ticket so I could leave tonight. There aren't any more buses leaving until tomorrow."

Mia's heart ached. As she stared at her terrified face, her conscience tore into a million different pieces, before she finally settled on a decision. "I'll go with you. If you'll still have me."

"What?" Comprehension seemed to fail Cecilia.

"I can protect you. I'll go with you so you can have your dream. You can have your life."

And when the time came, Mia would return to Salem and stop Colby's kidnapper. She'd also find Tilly and explain—to beg her for forgiveness. If she played her timing right, her aunt wouldn't have a chance to miss her—though the future Mia she'd meet would be an adult instead of the girl she knew.

"B-But what about your family," Cecilia murmured. "Your own life?"

"They'll understand." It wasn't true. The decision would break her family's heart. "In the meantime, stay with me at my family's house. You shouldn't go back to your home."

Cecilia shook her head. "What about my mom?"

"What about her?" Mia didn't understand. "Your mom is abusive. You can be free of her now."

"I can't just leave her there," she argued. "I know she's horrible, but she's my mom. She shouldn't live in that house if some killer wants it."

"You still shouldn't stay there—"

"What time do they k-kill me?"

Mia gave her an unsure look, not fathoming why she was asking "At nine tomorrow night. That's when the black moon will come into its power."

Cecilia shook her head. "You really are a witch."

"Yep."

Her shoulders sagged. "My mom won't leave that house willingly. It's going to take a lot of convincing on my end, but I'll leave early in the morning with or without her. I was going to do one more shift at work tomorrow anyway to make some extra cash. I'll meet you here afterward. Let's say six thirty. Okay?"

Mia's stomach swiveled into knots. It was a bad idea leaving Cecilia, especially since McConnell had already tried to grab her once.

"It's not safe," she insisted. "We'll go to your house together, I'll knock your mom out with a spell, and we'll stay at my house." Or *sleep in a park.* Tilly and her grandma would be irate once they realized Mia planned to interfere with Cecilia's fate, not to mention that Mia used magic in front of a Common. She'd deal with all of that later.

Cecilia looked despondent, her eyes staring unseeingly at the ground. "My mom will just go back to the house the first moment she can. It's been in our family too many generations for her to give it up now."

"Then we'll burn it to the ground," Mia said desperately.

Cecilia laughed sadly. "You seriously don't understand my mom and how much that property means to her. She'll just pitch a tent and live there." She clasped Mia's cheek, her hand warm against Mia's face. "Let me do this. Please. I have to try."

As Mia stared into the honey color of Cecilia's eyes, she felt her panic subside slightly. It was still a bad idea, but she could tell she wasn't going to change her mind. She thought back to the protection spell she'd placed on Cecilia the other day. The intent of the spell had been to protect her against her mother. If Mia was going to let Cecilia out of her sight for the next twenty-four hours, she needed to do something broader.

She let out a sigh. "Give me your hand."

Cecilia gave her a questioning look but held it out. Mia turned it over so it was palm up. She placed an index finger on the girl's inner wrist and concentrated, pushing her energy into the spell as she traced a brand on her skin. It glowed briefly in bluish light.

"What did you do?" Cecilia whispered.

"A spell. It'll give you some protection from your enemies. If anyone tries to hurt you, I'll know and get to you in seconds."

Cecilia smiled. "You're truly magical."

She leaned over and kissed Mia. Mia savored the feel of Cecilia so close, relieved to know that for a moment she was safe.

As she pulled back, she tucked a strand of hair behind Cecilia's ears. "Hey, why don't we go get some dinner?"

Cecilia nodded. She tried to get up but fell back in her seat. She let out an embarrassed laugh. "I'm sorry. I can't seem to stop shaking. Can we sit here for a minute?"

"Yeah," Mia said, holding Cecilia's hand in hers. "We've got plenty of time."

Chapter 20

Mia allowed herself to take one final look around Sadie's room on the morning of the black moon—the day she was supposed to go back to her timeline. She'd made up her mind to stay and she didn't regret it. Mia was going to run away with Cecilia. It was the only way to keep her and Colby safe.

She would live out the remainder of her life from this point in time, but she vowed to fix any ripples she created in the universe. No one else would suffer because of her actions. She'd do her best to ensure the warlocks and their Commander didn't hurt anyone else. Once she knew Cecilia was out of harm, she'd track them down, one by one. Not that she relished the idea of facing that shadow figure anytime soon. She still had no idea how to defeat it.

The fact that the monster could transport itself and another person in and out of shadows terrified her. Mia had never heard of an Other or Unmentionable being able to do that, only Originals. But she knew the monster was from her realm thanks to its human teeth.

Mia hadn't ruled out Parris despite what her grandma said. Aunt Tilly always felt there was something sketchy about their cousin's quick rise to the top—he was one of the youngest people ever elected chancellor. Had Mia discovered the secret to his success?

Getting up from Sadie's bed, she paused in the doorway. Maybe she should leave her mom a note. Something that would explain Mia's anger toward her for leaving. Or maybe something simpler. A message that read, *screw you, you selfish piece of crap.*

She decided against it. Her grandma would have a lot of questions if she ever saw it, and Mia preferred that her family didn't realize how awful Sadie was until they found out as they were meant to. She could at least give them that.

She changed into the clothes she'd been wearing when she first arrived in 1992. The clothes she borrowed from Sadie all week were in a rumpled ball on the closet floor.

Mia made her way to the living room where Tilly was reading a spell book.

"Hey," she said, sitting in the chair next to her.

Her aunt closed the book. "Today's the big day, huh?"

"Yep."

"Are you excited?"

Mia shrugged. "It'll be good to get my life back on track."

"*Everything* will get back on track," Tilly said. "The murders and the disappearances will stop soon, right?"

"They're supposed to." She didn't meet her aunt's eyes. Who knew for sure how the warlocks would react once they realized Cecilia wasn't available to sacrifice, or who they might go after in her place.

Tilly put her book on a table between their two chairs. "I know this isn't easy for you, Mia. I'm just so sorry your friend has to die."

She swallowed painfully. "Yeah, me too."

"You care for her." her aunt said. "From what you told me, it doesn't sound like she's ever had that before. You showed her compassion, at least."

"I guess."

Tilly leaned over and squeezed her hand where it rested on her armchair. Mia finally lifted her eyes to meet her aunt's gaze. Tilly grinned at her. "For what it's worth? I can't wait to meet you."

Tears formed in her eyes. "You...you're the best person I know. I'm so thankful for you."

Tilly laughed. "It's not like we won't ever see each other again. We'll talk about this week twenty-one years from now."

"Yeah." She brushed a tear away with her fist.

"Well, what do you want to do for the rest of your time in 1992? We could dye your hair. Have you ever considered going red?"

Mia snorted. "You'd kill me if I came back with dyed hair."

"Yeah, but I'm sure Sadie would like it. She was always one for the dramatic."

"You're worth ten of Sadie. Don't ever let anyone in this family make you feel otherwise."

Tilly reached for her book again, placing it in her lap. "Yeah...sure."

Mia shook her head. Her aunt was the most brilliant witch Mia knew. She never realized the other woman struggled with so much self-doubt. They had that in common.

"Tilly, if things don't go as expected today, don't blame yourself, okay?"

"What are you talking about?"

"You've always been really awesome to me."

Her face softened. "Thanks, but if you're worried about the spell not working, there's no need. Mom worked on this until she knew it was safe. She's doing another test run right now to make sure there aren't any hiccups. You're going home tonight. Everything will be fine."

"Okay." Mia didn't know how to convey what she really wanted to say. She didn't want her aunt to blame herself for what Mia was about to do. She hoped she'd see Tilly again in the future so she could explain everything. She also wanted to ask what the hell her aunt had been thinking giving her the Book of Aradia in the first place.

"Listen," Mia said. "I think I'll go spend time with Grandpa before I leave." She turned her head so Tilly wouldn't see the remorse on her face.

"He's in the shop."

Mia nodded before making her way downstairs. She found her grandpa next to the store's register with a tape measure in his hand, doing measurements of the counter.

"What are you doing?" she asked.

"Oh, Tilly's been begging me to put in a tea station. Rename the shop *Fitzgerald's Tea & Gifts*. Seems like a waste of shelf space, but she thinks it'll be all the rage after the coffee shop craze dies down."

"She's right." Mia leaned against the counter to watch him work. "Not that tea shops pop up everywhere, but ours is pretty successful."

Grandpa Ray nodded. "You know, of my two girls, I've never worried about Tilly. She's always had a good head on her shoulders." Her grandpa looked around before he leaned in and whispered, "Your grandma had a bad miscarriage the year before Sadie was born. The Healers didn't think she'd ever be able to have kids again. She was devastated. When we found out she was pregnant with Sadie, well, I'm afraid we were just so relieved to have another baby, we spoiled her a bit too much once she got here. I love my youngest, but she doesn't have the commonsense her sister has."

"No," Mia agreed, deciding not to say what she really thought.

Her grandpa's face turned sad. "I've noticed you get either angry or quiet whenever Sadie's brought up. I take it you two aren't as close as Eabha probably hopes you are. You're mom's not a bad person. She's just very used to getting her own way."

"Yeah, okay. Thanks for explaining." She bit her tongue to not say anything further. She moved so she could give him a tight hug, breathing in that comforting orange scent he always had. "I'm going to miss you so much."

He held her close. "You too, kid. And you remember something." He patted her gently on the back. "I'm proud of you. Now, what do you say about helping me out a bit in the shop?"

Mia agreed. She worked with her grandpa until late afternoon. She finally pointed toward the backroom with her chin. "I think I'm going to take a walk before I have to leave. You know, say goodbye to 1992."

"Sure, just be back before it gets dark. Your grandma wants to make sure there aren't any issues."

Mia nodded before heading out to the Maritime National Historic Site around the corner. She walked down the wharf, stopping once she reached the edge. A gentle spray of mist crossed her face as she breathed in the fresh harbor air. Though the elements didn't give her the power that the darkness did, she needed as much energy as she could in case anything went wrong. Mia was pretty sure McConnell was out of commission—he had received some pretty bad burns— but his friends were still lurking around.

As it got closer to the time Mia was supposed to meet Cecilia, she looked at the back of her family's store in the distance, knowing she would probably never see it again. She was about to walk away when a hurricane strength wind surrounded her, creating a funnel. She stood calmly as she recognized what was happening.

"Mia?" a voice said.

"Ailsa," she replied.

"Everything is all set on our end. Just be inside the pentagram at nine."

"I'm not coming back."

Ailsa paused. "What?"

"I'm not coming back."

"You have to." The other girl sounded panicked.

"Please tell Tilly I love her and I'm sorry. And...thank you for trying to help."

"Mia—"

"This is the only way to save Colby."

She pushed out her energy and broke the spell. The wind immediately died down. With one last glance at the shop, she started walking toward the center of town. She headed toward the bus station, passing the residential area where she'd confronted McConnell. Once she arrived at her destination, the station's clock showed she had about a half hour before Cecilia was expected to arrive.

Going out to the courtyard, Mia sat on their bench and began tracing the faint outline of the protection spell her grandma had placed on her arm. Knowing that her family would come looking for her, she closed her eyes and focused on the symbol. She could see the blue hue imbedded in her skin. She could feel the pulse of the spell at work. Mia saw her energy responding to it, cutting through it until her grandma's brand dissolved.

Letting her energy intensify, Mia placed a glamor on herself. She knew that it wouldn't stop a family as powerful as hers from finding her if they wanted to, but she hoped it would slow them down long enough for her and Cecilia to get out of town. Now all that was left to do was wait.

The time for Cecilia to arrive, came and went. Mia watched the clock, her leg bouncing with nervous energy.

Five minutes late...ten minutes late...fifteen minutes late...

She started pacing as she thought about the last protection spell she'd placed on Cecilia. Had she messed it up? Surely, if she did it correctly and Cecilia had come into danger, she would have felt it.

When she was a half hour late and her bus began boarding, Mia knew something was horribly wrong. She left the station and headed for the shop Cecilia worked at. She entered, looking frantically around.

"Can I help you?"

Mia turned to see a woman in her late thirties standing there, her frizzy, dark blonde hair pulled into a bun on top of her head. She looked exhausted.

"Is Cecilia here?"

"No, she was supposed to come in earlier, but she never showed. I hope she doesn't expect me to give her a good reference once she gets to wherever she's going. And let me tell you another thing, if that stupid bl—"

"Don't ever call her stupid!" Mia snapped before slamming her way out of the shop.

She tried her best to push down her rising panic. Had the warlocks grabbed her? She started running in the direction of Cecilia's house.

She didn't get too far when suffocating pain slammed into her. She fell to the ground with a shout, shaking all over.

Dark energy was forming in Salem on a scale Mia had never felt before. As she looked up, she saw the darkness flying toward her like a missile, picking up speed the closer it got. It ignored a group of Commons walking nearby as though its objective was to reach Mia and only her. The Commons went on their way, completely unaffected by being near such pure evil. Mia didn't know that was possible.

It shot inside her, invading her system. She moaned and squeezed her eyes closed. It was too much. *Too much!*

She felt recklessly powerful. She felt like she could conquer the world. She would destroy everything that got in her way. It'd be so easy. Nothing could stop her.

A vision popped in her head, a conversation between her grandma and her.

"You need to find balance."

"How do I do that?"

"You do that by focusing on your spirit," her grandma replied. *"Tell me about something that makes you happy."*

Mia's eyes flew open.

Cecilia.

Cecilia made her happy.

She thought about Cecilia telling her that she loved her. Warmth spread through her chest, meeting the darkness within, greeting it like an old friend. The dark and light combined and the turmoil inside Mia calmed.

Power surged through her system. She got slowly to her feet. Her body hummed with energy at the slightest movement, strengthening her muscles until she felt invincible.

Tilting her head, Mia scanned the streets. Everything was in bright color. The aura of different objects and people shimmered before her eyes until everything stuck out in vivid clarity. She could see the freckles on someone's face across the street. But it wasn't just her eyes that enhanced. She could hear the steps of a squirrel walking across a tree branch. She could pick up the scent of cotton candy coming from the carnival a few miles away.

Mia looked in the distance. A black hue hovered over one location. As she hyperfocused on the spot, she could hear voices. A vision soon appeared in front of her. Of long, dark-robed figures.

The warlocks! They were celebrating. Something had happened that made them very happy.

Mia's breath caught in her throat as the scenery around them crystallized. They were at Cecilia's house. That's where the darkness was coming from. The warlocks must've done something to awaken it.

Like sacrifice someone.

Suddenly, as if a switch flipped on inside Mia's head, the scenery in front of her changed.

"No!" She covered her eyes with her palms trying to block out what the dark energy wanted to show her. She had already seen the vision in her timeline too many times, but the darkness wouldn't be denied.

A body lay on the large table in Cecilia's basement. Blood caked the girl's hair into matted strands. The warlocks had begun to dissect her for consumption. Her finger was gone. Her toe was next. But her heart still beat.

Mia's own heart sped up.

There was still time to save Cecilia.

"Excuse me, Miss. Are you okay?" A Common asked.

She removed her hands from her face and the man backed away. Mia angled her head and caught sight of her reflection in a shop window.

Her eyes were black. They had no other color. She turned toward the house. Rage raced inside her and the positivity she'd held onto wavered.

She began to run. Fast. So fast that the Assembly was probably going to receive concerns about a girl with black eyes running with inhuman speed. She didn't care.

Within seconds, she reached Cecilia's house. There was no sign that anyone was there, no lights on despite the sun growing lower in the sky. Mia wondered briefly if Cecilia had been successful in getting her mother to leave town.

Dark energy bubbled through the cracks of the home's foundation. For now, it was still contained to the interior of the house. It wasn't trying to reach out to Mia like it did in her timeline. No. The energy she'd felt earlier had come from too many warlocks gathering at the same time.

Mia burst through the front entrance, desperate to get to Cecelia. She quickly found the door leading to the basement. As she descended the stairs, she listened for signs of the warlocks. Eerie silence made her shiver.

Where *were* they?

It crossed her mind as she took the final step that she should have made herself invisible, but the thought quickly left as she entered the basement. On one side of the room was an empty fireplace, plaster peeling off it in some areas. In the middle of the room was the table from Mia's nightmares.

Cecilia lay in the middle of it, resting inside a large crude pentagram scratched onto the surface. Her head faced away from Mia, toward the basement windows where evening light filtered in.

Mia took a step closer.

A pained whimper escaped her.

There was a bloody hole in Cecilia's chest where her heart should've been.

She was too late.

The warlocks had killed her. They'd taken some of her body parts for consumption and left the rest of her to rot. Mia struggled to breathe as she slowly approached the table. With shaking hands, she reverently turned Cecilia's head.

She tore her hands away. An adult woman stared back at Mia with vacant, lifeless eyes. Her face was marred with deep, old scars as though someone or something had attacked her repeatedly over the course of her life.

Who the hell was that?

The back of Mia's head suddenly exploded in pain and the world went black.

Mia sluggishly opened her eyes, her head throbbing. She tried to move, but her arms and feet were bound to the table. The basement windows revealed that the sun was about to set. The main source of light in the room came from a crackling fire that now roared in the fireplace, drenching the area in yellow and red flickering colors.

She tried to think of a counter spell to loosen her bindings, but her mind raced in too many different directions to focus.

There was a scuffing noise and Mia turned her head. Eight robed figures stood before her. The warlocks began to spread out and surround the table.

One corner of the basement grew darker until something appeared. Mia began shaking with fear when she saw what it was.

The shadow figure approached her slowly. As it moved, the skin covering its head rippled and ripped open with a loud, wet squelch, revealing the face underneath.

Mia stared with disbelieving eyes at the girl in front of her.

"Hello, my love."

CHAPTER 21

Mia glared at the silent warlocks around the table, fury replacing her terror. "What did you do to her?"

Cecilia walked over to the front of the fireplace where the corpse of the older woman now lay. She held out her hand and a dark hue formed around her palm before it floated to the woman's face. The features on the woman began to change, the skin softening and becoming youthful. The face transformed into a copy of Cecilia's before blurring into someone else's—an old woman, a young boy. The glamour changed from one face to another, never settling on a particular one for too long.

Mia stared at Cecilia, sick realization hitting her. "You're a warlock."

"Finally, she gets it." Cecilia crouched down and grabbed the woman's face, jerking the head so that she could stare into those blank eyes. "She was such a useless person." She glared at the corpse with so much hatred her features were barely recognizable. "But my mother's death served its purpose. She was a weak warlock but one from a powerful bloodline. It should give me the strength I need."

"Your mother?" Mia swallowed the bile that rose in her throat. "You killed your own mother?"

Cecilia's face was absent of emotion. "She tried to get in some defensive hits before she died, but they never landed. I guess I should thank *you* for that. You put a protection spell on me the day we ran into Parris, didn't you? My mother couldn't protect herself from my hexes after that, not that she was ever good at defending herself to begin with."

Mia wanted to throw up. Was this really happening? Was Cecilia really the monster who tried to kill Tilly? The Commander the warlocks served? Had Mia left Cecilia's mom defenseless against her psychotic daughter?

Cecilia stood up and walked toward the table, pushing between two warlocks. She hopped onto it so that their hips were touching. Mia tried to squirm away, but the bindings were too tight.

"Calm down, Mia." Cecilia touched her face with her fingertips.

Her unease lessened at the contact. She stared at her with a horrifying sense of dawning. "You did that to me before. When I said I didn't want you to go home last night, you touched me, and I agreed to let you go."

Cecilia simply smiled.

"I don't understand," She finally said, humiliated. "Why?"

"Why did my mom die? Did you not hear the part where I said she was useless?"

Mia could only stare at her, her emotions fighting between heartache and rage. How the hell hadn't she seen the truth? Desolates were supposed to be able to detect warlocks.

"Why are you doing this?" she asked. "Why are you hurting people?"

"Do you know what it's like to grow up with absolutely nothing?" Cecilia turned her head slightly to stare at the fireplace, the flames framing her face in reddish light. "To be labeled in a way that no matter what you do in life—no matter how much you prove your worth to society—they still refuse to see you as anything but trash to disregard?" Her expression transformed into anger as she met her eyes. Mia flinched at the hatred she saw there. "No, of course you don't. The descendants of Elizabeth Parris have never had to pay for their sins like I have."

"What are you talking about?"

Cecilia started running her finger up and down Mia's arm until it irritated her skin. "What do you know about Sarah Good?"

She frowned. "Why?"

Cecilia swished a hand and the rope around Mia's left wrist tightened painfully for a second. "Answer the question."

"She ..." Mia said through clenched teeth. "She was a witch they hung during the Salem Witch Trials. She lied about a Common. Said she was a witch to save her own neck, though she knew the woman was innocent."

Cecilia stopped rubbing her arm only to dig her fingernails into her skin, breaking the flesh. Mia gasped at the sharp pain.

"Of course that's what a Parris descendant would say." Her lip curled. "Blame the victim. What about your precious ancestor, Elizabeth?"

"What about her?" Mia's head was aching from where the warlocks hit her, her arm was hurting now, and her patience was quickly dissolving. "What the hell does this have to do with anything?"

"Everything!" Cecilia grabbed her arm and pressed hard on the puncture wounds.

Mia cried out. Blood dripped down from the injury and landed on the table. The pentagram surrounding her heated as it came to life.

The warlocks around her shifted restlessly—their only sign of motion since taking their place around the table.

Cecilia increased her grip.

Mia's arm began to throb, but she clamped her mouth shut to keep from reacting anymore. She wouldn't give her the satisfaction.

Cecilia let go of her arm and leaned back. "Do you know what happened to Sarah Good's family?"

Her grandma told her about Sarah when they'd gone to the cemetery shortly after she found out she was a Desolate. But she really didn't feel like indulging in story time with Cecilia. When the other girl started to reach for her injured arm again, she begrudgingly said, "Sarah had a baby in prison but it died, and her other kid was thrown in prison with her."

"At just four years old. However, history doesn't tell the true story."

"And what's that?" Mia tried to act casual, but she was seriously starting to panic. She couldn't think of the spell to loosen her bindings. If only she hadn't gotten rid of her grandma's protection spell.

Cecilia reached out to straighten a nearby warlock's robe before her hand returned to her lap. "Sarah's youngest child, Thomas, didn't die as Commons were led to believe."

Mia tried to wiggle her foot as subtly as she could in an effort to loosen the rope there. "Okay?"

Cecilia yanked her face in a hard grip, forcing Mia to look at her. She winced as her skin bruised.

"You're not paying attention," Cecilia said. "And you need to. This is where you and I *really* begin." She sat back and started running her fingers up and down Mia's arm again, smearing blood that still dripped from her nail punctures. "As I was saying, Thomas didn't die. The Assembly came in on their white horses and took him away, but not before giving Sarah the ultimate dishonor. After she accused a Common of witchcraft—and who could blame her, she was trying to protect her children—she hoped she would spare her family—"

"An innocent person died because of her!" Mia snapped.

Cecilia's nails bit into her skin again and Mia shut up. "As I was saying, the Assembly branded Sarah with a new name. From that moment on, people would no longer recognize her descendants as Good. Their new last name would be Evil Liar to represent her alleged crime. It wasn't very inventive, but the Assembly always did have a flare for the melodramatic." Cecilia pulled her fingers back from Mia and folded her hands together. "The Assembly told Thomas's father that he died, then took Thomas and gave him to a warlock to raise. Sarah died knowing that instead of protecting her family, the Assembly destroyed it." Her eyes narrowed with contempt. "The warlock raising Thomas didn't want to be burdened with him. He kicked him out at just ten years old!" Cecilia's fingers turned white as she held them tighter together. "He eventually married and had children while continuing to be shunned by society and the family line limped on. They couldn't change their last name because—"

"It's the curse of the Assembly," Mia said, remembering what McConnell told her. "The family has to carry the name of their ancestor's crime for the rest of their existence."

Cecilia nodded. "The family was shunned by the Other community. Even Unmentionables wanted nothing to do with them since there's no honor among criminals that sell people out to save their own skin. Until one day, a descendant of Sarah's found a loophole around the curse. They couldn't get rid of the last name, but they could spell it differently."

Mia tried to picture the letters but her comprehension was at an all-time low.

"I can see that you're struggling," Cecilia said, her tone amused. "Evil Liar spelled backwards is—"

"Raillive." Mia whispered, finally putting it together.

Cecilia tapped the side of her temple. "Got it in one." Her face twisted with fury. "Meanwhile, as Sarah hung from a tree, Elizabeth Parris kept her mouth shut. She could have done something—stopped her worthless family with a simple hex before they could hurt anyone—but she protected herself. She was a coward! And how was she repaid? By receiving the gift of the Desolate. She went around helping people only after her husband hanged their loved ones. The community adored her, never understanding that *she* was the true Evil Liar."

Mia started to feel dizzy as her head throbbed. She blinked a couple of times before saying, "You don't understand. She could have exposed the Other community if she'd done something. More innocent Commons would have been accused of witchcraft and been hanged if people realized that witches were real."

"If she'd said anything," Cecilia countered. "She and Sarah could have worked together and stopped the trials before people lost their lives in the first place. Your family carried on like they didn't have blood on their hands. You prospered while my family had to wear secondhand clothes and eat scraps out of dumpsters! Even Commons stayed away from us, only giving us minimal paying jobs that barely kept us alive. The Assembly's curse is quite effective, after all."

Somewhere in the house, a clock chimed, indicating that it was a quarter to nine. It was almost the time Mia's family told her the black moon would come into its full mystical power. Perfect for sacrificing someone. She tried to move her energy to the ropes in earnest to cut them loose.

Cecilia watched her struggle. "It's cute that you think you can get out of those ropes. But they have magic in them that even a Desolate like you can't escape from."

Mia stopped moving.

"That's right. I know." Cecilia hopped off the table and walked over to the fireplace mantle. She pulled a silver knife down, the sharp edge glinting in the flames. She stared at it, transfixed. "All my life, I wanted nothing more than to make your family pay for what it did to mine. It's only been recently that I realized there was a much bigger picture that needed to be addressed."

Mia eyed the knife nervously. "And what's that?"

"Do you have any clue what's going on in the Other community, or are you too protected in your safe little bubble?" She came back, knife in hand. "Of course you are. Others have been disappearing for years; unicorns sold on the black market, pixies enslaved to do the bidding of the powerful."

"If that's true." Mia's eyes began to blur as another wave of pain slammed into her head. "The Assembly should be notified. They can stop it."

Cecilia laughed, cold and cruel. "God, you really are naïve. The Assembly is the one behind the disappearances. How do you think ranking members have been in power for so long? They sell us off to the highest bidder and use the money to buy their positions."

"You're lying."

Cecilia's hand tightened on the knife. "Contrary to the name, I'm not a liar."

Mia scoffed. "Our whole relationship has been a lie."

The other girl seemed to waver briefly. "I do like you. I wasn't expecting that, but you have something I need."

"What's that?" She began to writher against the ropes again.

"Your heart." Cecilia drew the knife to Mia's chest, and she stilled as it pressed against her skin. "You have no idea how powerful you are, do you?"

"I'm not," she said, though it was weak. A week ago, she honestly thought she was useless and pathetic, not a good enough witch to be in the Fitzgerald coven. Now, she was starting to believe differently.

"You think any witch can go back in time?" Cecilia asked. "Do you know how difficult that is to do?"

"It was an accident."

"There are no accidents. There are only fated occurrences."

Mia stared at her, realizing something. "How do you know I traveled back in time?"

She grinned, pulling the knife back slightly. "Given how powerful your family is, I'm surprised dear sweet Eabha didn't put much stronger wards around the house until the other day. Though she's probably arrogant enough to think no one would dare bother the Fitzgeralds." Mia was about to tell her to piss off, but Cecilia kept speaking, "To answer your question, I was standing outside your shop a few nights ago, thinking how lovely it would be to watch McConnell burn it to the ground—he's alive by the way, thanks for asking."

"Like I give a sh—"

"He's bedridden at the moment, so unfortunately, he wasn't able to join us tonight. He wasn't happy about it. He really wanted to see you suffer after what you put him through."

"I didn't—"

Cecilia continued as if Mia hadn't spoken. "We were going to take you yesterday, but then you had to go and use magic in public. We tried to get away from you in case the Assembly showed up, but of course, they wouldn't go after a Parris descendant. Still, I want you to know I wasn't happy that McConnell tried to kill you. He knew how important you were, so ... he's healing without magic." Cecilia moved the blade in her hand, tilting it back and forth. "Luckily, you agreed to run off with me. Your family will think you're a runaway instead of a kidnap victim. At least, you better hope they think that. I'm not quite ready to destroy such a prominent family. Not yet anyway."

She grinned at Mia. "But as I was saying ... I was standing outside your family shop, longing for everyone inside to die an excruciating death, when who should stumble out the front door, but you. At first, I thought I was looking at Sadie herself, and figured *how convenient, I can kill the little princess right here and now.* But then I realized you were someone else entirely. When you went back inside, I used my dark energy to listen as you told your grandparents you were from the future." Cecilia tried to touch

Mia's cheek but she turned her face away. Cecilia snorted. "I waited for an opportunity to meet you. I saw you sneak out of your house that night ,so I followed you. As luck would have it, I came across a harpy and cut out her heart." She looked proud of herself. "Do you know that by eating the heart of a magical creature, you can absorb their power? Hers was the first heart I ever ate and look what I was able to do. I conjured two Originals. It was a fun experiment."

Mia's breathing intensified. "The Originals said a girl hexed them. They were talking about you, not me."

Cecilia's smile grew. "Isn't that great? When I heard you enter the alley to come check on me, I stunned the Originals and pretended to be unconscious. And then ..." She stared at Mia with a greedy expression. "You drew in the dark energy created by the harpy's murder and obliterated those Originals. I realized in that moment you weren't just a time traveler, but a Desolate, and what a gift it would be to have your power."

Mia swallowed painfully. "So, that's been your plan the whole time. To cut out my heart for my power?"

Cecilia lifted a shoulder. "I have to. I'll be able to wield dark energy and not have it affect me."

Mia thought about when she saw Cecilia on the tire swing. The girl had already killed several people and turned herself into the shadow figure by then. She'd been using so much dark energy, it had started to consume her, which explained why she'd been so out of it that day.

Cecilia watched the flickering emotions cross her face. "Absorbing your power will be the beginning of the Assembly's end. Once I collect all five hearts, they won't be able to stop me.

Mia stiffened. "What five hearts?"

Cecilia looked at her like she was dumb. "The hearts of the Assembly. As much as I hate to admit it, Mia, you come from a very powerful line of witches—a direct descendant of Hecate herself."

She squinted as another throb hit her head. "What are you talking about?"

Cecilia raised her eyebrows, amusement filling her features. "Is it possible that the Fitzgerald family doesn't know they're directly related to the Original who created the witch race? Oh, that's hilarious."

A couple of the warlocks began whispering to each other, but cut their speech when Cecilia gave them a sharp look.

She turned back to Mia. "The Other community respects the Fitzgeralds. They're loyal to you and their loyalty gives you power. I'm not talking money or a strong reputation. I'm talking actual, tangible power. Between you being a Desolate and a descendant of Hecate, your death would be on par with killing the chancellor herself. Even more so.

"And to answer your question, if I have your heart, I'll need to eat four equally powerful hearts from the other branches of the Assembly. But not just anyone will do, you understand. I thought by eating the heart of the warlock, harpy, and mermaid, it would give me the strength I needed, but they weren't powerful enough, though the mermaid put up quite a fight." She pointed to her black eye. Cecilia had told her that her mom caused the injury.

Mia let out a pained breath. God, she really *was* naïve.

"It has to be someone powerful," Cecilia reiterated. "And there are no Others more powerful than the Representatives of the Assembly or their family members. Once I have their hearts, I'll be impossible to stop."

Mia thought of the top officials who governed the Assembly. The Wolf King wouldn't be easy for Cecilia to kill. He was the most powerful Other in the world. He didn't have any heirs though so the king would be her main target. The Vampire Queen didn't have a living heart, but her daughter did and would continue to have one until she gave birth, and her life-energy passed to her child. The

Fae Queen and Queen of the Mermaids would be hard to reach, but if Cecilia stole Mia's power, who knew what she'd be able to do.

Mia looked at her in disgust. "And then what? World domination?"

"Of course."

Her eyes widened at how casual and serious Cecilia's response was.

"What?" she said. "You think Commons deserve to be in charge? Look what they've done to the planet so far. They continuously attack the five elements. Our waters are so toxic, people can't swim in them. They treat Earth like it's their personal trash bin. People can't breathe the air in some cities, and they're so casual with the use of fire that they burn our forests down to ash. Not to mention, that after they do all that, it destroys their spirit and they're too stupid to realize it. Look at how many of them complain about being stressed and having anxiety."

"You won't succeed." Mia began to feel genuine fear.

"You don't think? Look around you." Cecilia nodded at the warlocks. As if that was their cue, they lifted their hands in eerie unison and drew down the hoods that covered their faces. Mia let out a strangled breath.

Most of them were barely older than her. They began to chant, and a dark purplish light formed around the table. Cecilia waved at them. "This is just the beginning of my army. There are many Unmentionables out there who've been cast out unjustly by the Assembly and Other society. It's our time to right all that's wrong." She picked up the knife again, raising it so that it was above Mia's heart.

"Why didn't you kill me earlier this week? You could have done it any time."

"My love, one doesn't become Commander by simply taking what they want. If I wanted to understand your Desolate heart, I had to study you first. See how you work; how your powers work."

She closed her eyes. And here she thought she'd found someone who loved her.

"Answer one more question for me," she said. "How come I didn't sense you were a warlock using dark energy?"

Cecilia lifted the necklace she always wore and pulled it over her head. Her face transformed. Instead of having long, caramel colored curls, her hair turned the color of mud, the locks becoming short and stringy. Her nose narrowed and her eyes went from soft brown to icy blue. An upside -down pentagram appeared on her neck.

But the change in her appearance wasn't the only difference. The constant pull Mia felt towards Cecilia since first meeting her fractured and dimmed. She'd never believed in love at first sight, so it hadn't made sense why she'd fallen so quickly for Cecilia. Now, she wondered if her feelings had ever been real in the first place.

"What the hell is that?" she asked, her eyes burning.

Cecilia caressed the pendant with a finger. "The white in the necklace is the crushed bone of Sarah Good. Since she specialized in deceit according to your people, her power transferred into the pendant, giving me the same abilities. It allows me to change my appearance into whoever or whatever you crave the most. I look different to everyone who sees me. A friend. A family member. Someone you can't live without." She gave Mia a knowing look and laughed when she glared back. She put the necklace back on and her face changed so it looked more like Ella again. And with it, the pull returned as well, stronger than ever, making Mia momentarily want to believe this was all a big misunderstanding, and Cecilia was still the girl she adored.

Her rage began to boil. She thought she'd found someone who cared about her. Instead, Cecilia had been busy learning her vulnerabilities so she could prey on them. The dark energy saturating the basement responded to her anger and started rushing toward her. The room shook as the darkness hit the barrier the warlocks created. It didn't matter. Mia still had enough dark energy from earlier and she let it spread through her body.

"Commander ..." one of the warlocks finally spoke. He sounded scared. He should be. Mia turned her head to look at him with eyes that were now black.

"Don't break the barrier!" Cecilia ordered. "She can't use the darkness against us with the barrier in place."

Mia continued to stare at the guy. His expression turned to terror as he gazed into her Desolate eyes. The barrier faltered for only a second.

That was all she needed.

One by one, Mia drew the dark energy from the warlocks, bringing it inside her. She continued to take their energy until they were left whimpering like small children. One turned and threw up on the floor next to him. Others covered their ears as if the darkness taunted them as it exited their bodies. The smell of urine filled the air. The purplish line that trapped Mia wobbled before fizzling out completely as she drew in darkness from the last warlock.

It was unfortunate that her emotions were all over the place. The last thing on her mind was a happy thought. The anguish of the suffering created from the darkness consumed her.

It began its usual taunts ... telling her she was a failure ... telling her that no one would ever fall in love with her.

She did her best to pull up something uplifting so that she could cleanse the dark energy like she had at the cemetery. It was impossible. Her heart felt too destroyed.

To Mia's dismay, she could sense the darkness refilling inside the warlocks' hearts—too far gone to ever see the light again. They lifted their hands and began chanting, ready to trap Mia inside the circle once more.

Nothing happened.

"She's done something to us," one boy said.

"I'd say so," Cecilia replied, her voice a cross between humor and annoyance.

"Then we'll do this the old fashion way," one of the older boys yelled. He took a step toward Mia with his hands raised toward her neck, intent on strangling her.

"Stop!" Cecilia yelled but it was too late.

The darkness pulsed inside her as the remaining dark energy in the room came rushing into her all at once. It was too much. She threw back her head and screamed. Bright blackish blue light exploded from her and hit the warlocks, their agonized shouts of pain filling the air. Mia didn't stop screaming, even as each boy vaporized into a cloud of dust. With each death, the structure of the house shook.

And then it was over.

The dark energy left Mia, its work finished. Her breathing turned ragged at the realization of what she'd done. She killed those warlocks. Tears rolled down from the corners of her eyes and her stomach turned to acid.

Buried deep in the ground, she could sense the darkness Elizabeth Parris put to sleep so long ago slowly rumbling awake. It wasn't Cecilia's supposed death that opened the vortex in the house. Mia's actions were what caused it.

"Well …" Cecilia said. "That was impressive. Again, I thank you for putting a protection spell on me. Otherwise, you might have hurt me. But as for my warriors, that was uncalled for."

Cecilia walked toward her, knife still in hand. The clock in the house began to chime again, nine times. If Mia had listened to her grandma, she would be on her way back to her timeline. She'd be on her way to Aunt Tilly instead of with her psycho ex-girlfriend who was about to murder her.

Grandma, I'm so sorry.

"Goodbye, my love." Cecilia raised the knife, pointing the blade toward her heart.

Mia closed her eyes, thinking of her aunt and Ailsa.

I want to go home.

A strange sensation trickled over Mia. At first it was just a small heat, but it grew hotter until Mia felt like she was on fire. The sudden sensation of being ripped from her body overtook her senses.

"No!" Cecilia shouted.

Mia's eyes flew open. She was in her celestial form, floating above the table and her body, which lay inside the pentagram. The star glowed fiery blue. Her body began to tremor, the skin turning into bubbles. In a flash, light shot out from inside the pentagram, filling the room with blinding brightness.

Cecilia slashed the knife downward. It hit the now empty table with a loud clang. Mia's body had already dissolved inside the star and disappeared. Cecilia's head jerked up, her eyes widening in surprise when she saw Mia still floating above the table. Outrage twisted her face into something inhumane.

Mia smiled and gave her the finger.

The sound of Cecilia cursing was music to her ears as she began to fly upward, going through the house and skyward until she was shooting into the atmosphere. She was soon in outer space. She hovered for a moment, the earth below her in all its glory, before she hurtled back down. A familiar building grew larger and larger until Mia descended straight into the roof of her house and into her room. Her body was waiting for her inside the pentagram. She slammed back into it. Hard.

Everything went black.

CHAPTER 22

"Cecilia!" Mia jolted into a sitting position as she came to.

"Mia, thank Hecate." Someone tried to pull her into a hug, but she flinched away.

She put her trembling hands up to her head, which felt like it was about to explode. Her body ached all over. She took several shaky breaths as her mind caught up to what just happened.

She wasn't tied to the table anymore. She'd escaped Cecilia and time travelled again.

As she took an unsteady breath, she picked up the familiar scent of her aunt's perfume.

She was home.

Mia pulled her hand away and looked at her aunt's strained face. It was the Tilly who'd raised her instead of the teenage version.

"Aunt Tilly?" Mia let out a sob as she threw her arms around her. "You brought me back?"

Tilly's embrace tightened before she let go. "I had some help."

She turned to see Ailsa on her other side. She wore a huge, relieved smile that emphasized her unnatural beauty.

"You're a fae," Mia blurted.

Ailsa's face turned shy. "Half fae. Half Common."

"You helped bring me back?"

She blushed but nodded. Mia leaned over and hugged her, too. Ailsa hesitated for a second before she returned the embrace.

"We were worried that you weren't going to return." The girl reluctantly pulled away. "When you told me you weren't planning on coming back..."

Mia stared at her. "So...it was real and not some horrible nightmare."

"Yes," Aunt Tilly confirmed. "You traveled back to 1992."

She frowned. "You've known all these years that I was going to go back in time, didn't you? That's why you've been so tense lately."

"To be honest," her aunt said. "I kept debating whether I should interfere or not—"

"You probably shouldn't have given me the Book of Aradia then."

Aunt Tilly's forehead wrinkled. "What are you talking about? I never gave you that book. The magic is too advanced."

"Yes, you did. It was included in the books you gave me for my birthday."

Tilly's face became increasingly concerned. "Mia, I never gave you that book. I was never sure how you got it."

"Then who..." Vomit rose in Mia's throat. "Cecilia. It had to be Cecilia."

"Who?" Ailsa asked.

"Cecilia Raillive," Mia told them.

"Honey." Her aunt brushed a sweaty strand of her raven black hair away from her face. "Cecilia Raillive died years ago. Her body was found in the basement of her house."

"No. It wasn't her. Cecilia's a warlock. She killed her mom and put a glamor on her so everyone would think she was dead."

Mia proceeded to tell her aunt and Ailsa about her final confrontation with Cecilia. She left out the details of how Mia had been dumb enough to develop feelings for her. It hurt too much to think about. When she got to the part where she found herself tied to the table in the basement, Aunt Tilly pulled her into another hug, her hold so tight it hurt. Mia leaned away, knowing her aunt would hate her when she admitted the next part.

"And then I..." She stopped, unable to continue as she remembered her slip of control, which resulted in killing the warlocks. Her breathing grew shallower as an impending anxiety attack loomed.

Sensing it, Tilly cupped her cheeks in both of her hands and a rush of calming warmth loosened up her lungs so she could take a breath.

Her aunt gave her a reassuring look. "It's okay, honey."

Mia shook her head. "No. It's not. I... I k-killed them."

"What? Who?"

"The w-w-warlocks. I tried to cleanse them, but the darkness kept refilling in their hearts. And then..." She twisted her hands. "One tried to attack me and I-I lost control."

"It's not your fault," Tilly insisted. "If they attempted to hurt you, even after you tried to help them, then you acted in defense."

"But why?" she whispered. "Why couldn't I save them?"

"Because some people don't want to be saved," her aunt replied simply. She gave Mia's shoulder a comforting squeeze. "Unmentionables who play with darkness get addicted to it. They don't always want to let it go."

Mia didn't look at her aunt. She understood only too well how good the darkness felt. How much of a rush it was to have that kind of power.

"I still shouldn't have lost control," she finally said. "I should have tried again and again with them. Instead, I automatically went into defense mode, and they paid the price. I didn't even consciously make the decision. It just happened. If I use my power again, I could hurt someone. I'm dangerous."

"That's not true," Ailsa spoke up.

"She's right," Tilly said. "Mia, you have a gift that was designed to protect people. In this case, you were the one who needed protecting and the Desolate power responded." Her aunt carefully tilted Mia's chin until she was looking at her. "Don't you dare beat yourself up over this. If they'd won, Cecilia would've eaten your heart, and Hecate knows where we'd be. If anyone's to blame, it's your grandma and me. We should have done more to prepare you. She was so upset when she realized you'd removed her protection tracker. And you must have put some kind of glamor on yourself because we had trouble locating you." Tilly gave her a watery smile. "She planned on giving you a stern lecture about everything when you got back to this timeline. She talked about it for years, even when you were toddling around the house. But then..."

Mia's sadness shifted into something unbearable. It felt like her heart was in a vice as she remembered what else she'd lost by returning home. Her grandma was bedridden, and her grandpa was dead.

Looking at her aunt, she asked, "How'd you know I'd make it back?"

"Well, you had to *want* to come back," she answered. Mia thought about the moment right before Cecilia tried to stab her, how she'd just wished she could go home. "But I knew you made the right decision despite what you told Ailsa about staying. Granted, at the time, your grandma and I were worried when you went missing. We were just about to go searching for you when the pentagram in your room began to sizzle, and we saw an image of you inside another pentagram. Since all we needed was for you to be inside one to complete the spell, we got to work." Tilly smiled. "We knew when you left your body to travel into the cosmos. It showed us you landing safely home, before the connection went blank."

Mia stiffened as she remembered something. "You promised to save my dad." She tried not to feel too eager. "Did you? Is he here?"

Aunt Tilly's shoulders slumped. She traced the edge of the pentagram with her finger. "I tried. Your grandma and I both tried so hard to save him. We put every protection spell on him we could think of. Sadie even offered to take him out of town that day so he wouldn't get onto his boat. I could never figure out how he ended up on the water. Your mom was inconsolable. All she could tell me was that he'd been with her when they went to sleep that night. When she woke up, he was gone."

Mia buried her face in her hands. She'd hoped so much that they would be able to save him. That one brief meeting with her dad in the store was all she would ever have with him.

"I'm so sorry, sweetie," Tilly said, touching her arm.

Mia blanched at the contact, causing her aunt to look down. She let out an alarmed gasp. Cecilia's nail marks were still visible on Mia's skin, the imprints outlined in a sickening black color. The blood Cecilia had smeared all over her arm had dried and turned crusty.

The dark energy Mia had been exposed to was now embedded in her flesh, filling the broken skin like a tattoo. Ailsa reached over and ran her fingers across it. A golden hue encircled the injured area and warmed the mark. The pain in Mia's arm and the dried blood disappeared. The black marks remained.

Lines of frustration formed around the lovely fae's mouth. "I can't get the marks out."

"It's okay, it's dark energy." Mia closed her eyes and tried to use her Desolate power to remove the tattoo. When she opened them again, the nail prints were still there. She stared at the five marks in dismay. "I can't get rid of them."

She felt queasy. Was she permanently branded by Cecilia?

"We'll figure it out," Tilly assured her.

"No!" Panic was making her feel on edge. "Cecilia was only eighteen when I met her, and she knew magic that I had no idea how to fight. She tied me to a table with ropes I couldn't break. She wore a necklace that was so powerful, I couldn't see the warlock mark on her. I can't beat her, and if she's still out there... she now has twenty more years of knowledge. I don't know how to stop her. She wants my heart, not to mention four other hearts connected to the Assembly representatives."

Tilly got up from the floor. "I have a friend who works at the Assembly. I'll call him and see if there's anything he can do to help."

"Aunt Tilly..." Mia looked hesitantly at Ailsa who also stood.

"Excuse me, I need to go wash my hands," Ailsa said, understanding that Mia needed to speak with her aunt in private.

As soon as Ailsa left, Mia asked, "Why didn't you tell me any of this was going to happen?"

Her aunt's face filled with remorse. "One should never know too much about their destiny. We messed with time once. I wasn't going to do it again." She locked eyes with Mia. "Besides, you needed your grandma. She was always able to get through to you better than me."

"But you said you didn't want me to work on astral projection spells. I saw you before I went back in time. You busted into my room like you were going to try and stop me."

Aunt Tilly smiled sadly. "Mia, I love you like you're my own daughter. Just because I knew you had to go back in time didn't mean I didn't feel conflicted about it. Your reaction to seeing my dad made so much more sense to me after he died. I knew it broke your heart to spend time with him, not to mention getting that brief moment with your dad. You mourned them once. No one should have to say goodbye twice to the people we love and lose."

Mia got up on legs that shook, her body exhausted from time travelling, her head still aching. Staggering over to her aunt, she wrapped an arm around her waist. She could read between the lines. Mia saw firsthand how her grandparents, particularly her grandma, had always made Tilly feel like she was second best. It was no wonder Tilly didn't think she could teach Mia how to use her Desolate power.

"It wasn't fair," Mia said as she laid her cheek on her aunt's shoulder.

"What wasn't?" Tilly asked.

"How Grandma treated you. She acted like Sadie could do no wrong, and we both know that wasn't the case at all. You were and are the best witch to teach me everything I need to know. She shouldn't have made you doubt your abilities."

Tilly squeezed Mia's waist. "Thank you for choosing to come back."

Mia nodded before moving to open the bedroom window. She ran her fingers along the windowsill as she breathed in the fresh night air.

"Cecilia said we're direct descendants of Hecate."

"The Original who started our race?" When Mia nodded, Tilly sighed. "Who knows. It's not impossible."

"She said that's why we're so powerful."

"We're an old family for sure. But there are only two confirmed Other families related to the Originals who started everything. And that's only because the Wolf King and Vampire Queen are hundreds and hundreds of years old. Their grandparents were *literally* the Originals who started their species."

"But is there a chance that we descended from Hecate?" she asked.

"Mia, how many people do you know who can trace their family back over two thousand years?" Tilly sat on Mia's bed. "As far as I know, Hecate never had children in this world. She simply went up to a bunch of Commons, blessed them with some of her power, and bam... The world had witches."

The night air from the window continued to soothe Mia. She asked another question that was bothering her. "Why didn't you ever leave Salem? I overheard you talking to Grandma and Grandpa when I first arrived in 1992. You said you wanted to go to the Assembly."

"Oh, that." She looked amused. "I was young and impulsive. I had a crush on a guy who was at the Assembly."

"Gavin Alexander," Mia said, and her aunt nodded.

"We attended high school together though he was a grade ahead of me. We dated briefly, but after he graduated, he said he wanted to go to the Assembly and make a career out of it. He didn't want to be distracted from his apprenticeship, so he broke up with me."

"What a jerk," Mia said, angry on her aunt's behalf.

Aunt Tilly laughed. "We were just kids, Mia. We've both moved on."

Mia looked at her aunt thoughtfully. "It's interesting."

"What is?"

"That he didn't let Parris get away with accusing you of hexing those Originals."

"Oh, stop." Tilly shook her head. "Though I should contact him. He'll need to know about Cecilia Raillive." She walked over and kissed Mia's temple before turning to leave.

"Aunt Tilly?"

"Yeah?"

"Why aren't you a Desolate? You've been through just as much as I have in life."

Her aunt looked thoughtful. "No one knows why some people have the power and others don't. Maybe I watched how you interacted with my parents—how you always seemed so sad around them—and realized the future wasn't so bright for them. I think subconsciously I'd been preparing for the inevitable for years, so I wasn't as traumatized when life finally happened. Or, maybe there was a powerful witch on your dad's side of the family at some point. Maybe the gene only awakens when a Desolate is truly needed. It's anyone's guess." Tilly gave Mia a gentle smile before walking toward the bedroom door.

"Are you coming back after your call?" Mia didn't want to be alone just yet.

Tilly pushed her shoulders back as though trying to relieve some tension. "After I call Gavin, I want to make sure the wards around the house are still good. I don't like the idea that the Book of Aradia just popped into your room without explanation."

Mia nodded. "Thank you again. For everything."

"I'll always be watching out for you, you know that."

"I was wrong for what I said, you know." When Tilly gave her a bemused look, Mia said, "You're the best mom I could have ever asked for."

Her aunt's eyes turned misty. "I'll be back in a few minutes."

After she left, Mia went over to her bed and sat down. Despite trying to put on a brave front, she began shaking all over as shock flooded her system.

There was something else she was becoming aware of. Aside from what happened to her, something felt really off, and she couldn't pinpoint what. Restless, she got up and walked back over to the window, staring out at the night.

"Hey."

Mia spun around and found Ailsa standing in the doorway. The quick movement made her slightly dizzy, and her head throbbed.

"Hey," she replied. She gestured for her to enter.

Ailsa did so, her expression shy and unsure.

"Thank you again for helping bring me back," Mia said. She wasn't sure how to act around her, knowing the other girl was aware of what she had done.

"Sure ..." Ailsa smiled but she seemed unhappy. "You loved her. Didn't you?"

The shaking inside Mia stopped as she froze in place. "What?"

"I have a sensitivity to people's emotions. You feel heartbroken. Like people do after a bad break up."

"I..." It wasn't the conversation she was expecting. She didn't know what to say. She felt too messed up inside. Too raw.

Mia rubbed at her temple. "She wasn't real. She showed me what she wanted me to see so she could manipulate me."

Ailsa gave her a sad smile before walking over to Mia. Lifting a tentative hand, she placed it against the back of her head. The area still aching from where the warlocks hit her began to warm. It felt like the softest caress moving over her skin. As Ailsa pulled away, the pain faded.

Mia reached up to touch the spot. It no longer hurt, the ache in her head gone. She gave Ailsa an unsure smile. "Thanks."

Mia started watching, thinking about everything she had done to help.

"Ailsa? Can I ask you something?"

She nodded.

"How did you speak to me through the wind?"

Ailsa smiled, the expression lighting up her entire face. "Fae trick. You have to manipulate the elements just right."

"Can you show me?"

"Maybe. I'm studying at the Assembly this summer, but perhaps when I get back."

"You're leaving?" Mia wasn't sure how to feel about that other than a strange sense of loss. After everything they'd just been through, she hoped they could grow as friends.

"Just for the summer," Ailsa assured her. "I want to be a Healer someday, and they accepted me into their apprenticeship program."

"You'll be great at it."

"Thanks."

The girls stared awkwardly at each other before Ailsa said, "I should let you rest."

Mia nodded absently before staring out the window again. She could see the other girl frowning at her in the glass's reflection. "Are you okay? Other than the obvious?"

"I just can't shake the feeling that something is off," she admitted. She gazed at the water, observing the choppiness of the harbor in the moonlight. Her unease continued to grow until realization hit her. "There's dark energy in Salem." She swung around to look at Ailsa. "Something's wrong. The last time I felt it this bad, Cecilia and her warlocks had just killed her mother." She took an urgent step toward the other girl. "Did something happen while I was gone?"

Aunt Tilly entered the room, carrying a mug of tea in her hand. "We didn't want to tell you so soon after you returned."

Mia's stomach coiled with dread. "What?"

Tilly placed the tea on Mia's bedside table with a sigh. "They found Colby Mond this morning."

"Is he okay?" Mia asked but she knew. Oh god, she knew.

"He was found in the basement of the Raillive estate."

"How?" Mia whispered.

Regret formed heavily on her aunt's face. "His heart was cut out. I'm so sorry, sweetheart. When you told me your friend had been kidnapped back then, I thought you were referring to Ella. I put protection spells around her. I never imagined it'd be Colby—"

The floor beneath Mia's feet began to shake before she realized it wasn't the floor. It was her. She trembled so hard, her vision blurred. Colby was dead. And it was all her fault. She'd told Cecilia about him.

It's your fault he's dead. It's your fault he's dead.

"Ailsa, get back!" Tilly shouted.

Mia screamed as she lost control. The dark energy embedded in her skin acted like a trigger. It shot out from her, hitting her closet door and splintering the wood into pieces. Tilly threw her hands out and a white ward flew around Mia as she screamed out her anguish and pain. The darkness swirled around Mia like a tornado.

Ailsa walked slowly toward her and lifted her hand.

"Don't! You'll get hurt," Tilly warned.

Ailsa didn't listen. She pushed her hand through Tilly's ward. Her skin began to scrape and bruise as the darkness attacked her, but she continued to move forward until she could clasp Mia on the shoulder. As soon as she touched her, a golden hue encompassed Mia, calming the chaos inside. She collapsed to the floor and Ailsa dropped next to her, hugging her close.

"How did you ...?" Tilly said, as she hurried over to them. "That could have killed you." She paused before she looked at the two girls huddled closely together. Her face relaxed slightly. "Oh. I see..."

Mia didn't notice any of this.

She'd tried to help Colby. She'd originally sought Cecilia out because of him. She failed him.

"Do you think Others will ever accept us?" Mia asked Colby when they were eleven.

"Who cares if they do," he responded. "We have each other and that's all that matters."

She let out a sob, and Ailsa's arms tightened around her.

It's your fault he's dead.

But it wasn't just her fault. Cecilia was behind this.

Mia had hoped she'd left her behind in 1992, at least for a little while. But the way Colby died was the exact same way she had killed her mom, and she knew Mia was aware of that.

There was only one explanation.

Cecilia was in Salem. Colby's murder was her way of sending Mia a message. And she understood it, loud and clear.

Time may have changed, but the hunt was still on.

CHAPTER 23

Mia lay in bed for hours, staring at the ceiling. Every time she closed her eyes, she saw Cecilia standing over her with a knife, heard the screams of the warlocks she'd killed, or pictured Colby lying dead on that table.

As the night wore on, Salem slowly turned into bedlam as the dark energy spread. Cop cars and fire trucks raced down neighboring streets. People kept yelling and screaming.

At one point, Aunt Tilly poked her head into Mia's room to check on her. Her aunt assured her that the Assembly was working on containing the situation.

Mia had no idea how they would accomplish that. It wasn't like they could get near the source of the darkness without losing their minds.

And no one was to blame but Mia. She cracked open the vortex in Cecilia's house when she killed those warlocks. But they had darkness in their hearts, and the dark energy needed a pure sacrifice to escape its prison.

Colby's death gave it that. He was a good soul. His murder freed the darkness to spread throughout the city like a plague. The thought destroyed Mia's heart.

When it grew close to five in the morning, she threw back her bed sheets. She grabbed her phone for something to do. She had a missed text from Ella that was sent the night she went back in time, stating that Kurt was feeling better and that they were going to prom without her. She briefly wondered if Ella knew she had disappeared for a week. Did she care? Did Ella know about Colby yet?

Winnie lay in her own bed, next to Mia, snoring softly. Not wanting to disturb the senior dog, she exited her room as quietly as she could. She tiptoed into her grandma's room and sat beside Grandma Eabha's bed.

"I really wish I could talk to you right now," she whispered to the quiet form. She rubbed at the empty spot on her arm where her grandma's protection spell once marked her. She brushed her thumb against it, hoping that some part of it still lingered on her, and it would wake her grandma up. Nothing happened. Even if Mia hadn't destroyed the connection, it would have disappeared once she reached her timeline since Grandma Eabha no longer had power.

Mia let out a sigh as she thought back to the different conversations she'd had with her grandma in 1992. There was one thing that Grandma Eabha never told her. "Why didn't you tell me how dangerous I was?"

Her grandma continued to lay motionless. Mia moved her head from side to side to relieve her tension. The dark energy was looking for her. It felt like an itch under her skin that she couldn't scratch. It was getting steadily worse, driving her slowly out of her mind. Unable to take it anymore, Mia left her grandma's room after kissing the elderly woman's forehead. She headed downstairs and outside before making her way toward the sidewalk.

As soon as she walked past the wards on their property line, the darkness came up to greet her. It grabbed onto her, dousing Mia in wave after wave of dark energy. She focused on the memory of Tilly's hug when she'd returned to the correct timeline. She felt her aunt's jubilation and relief in their embrace. She kept that memory at the forefront of her mind as she walked toward the dark energy's epicenter, feeling power surge through her with every step.

As she moved, she saw a guy from her history class run by with a gun in his hand. She reached out with her energy and took it from him, sending it toward the middle of the harbor. She passed a house where she could hear a man and woman yelling at each other while a baby screamed its head off.

"You're so dammed useless, look what you made me do!" the man said.

"It's not my fault you're an idiot."

"Idiot? I'll show you who the idiot is."

There was a tousling noise before the woman shouted, "Let go of me!"

Mia lifted her hand and drew the darkness coming from the home but kept walking. The occupants went silent for a second, and then started crying and apologizing to each other. She continued to draw dark energy from out-of-control Commons she passed until she came to a halt in front of the Raillive house. It looked even worse than it had before she time traveled. From what she could see of it from the light cast by streetlights, the grass and weeds that overtook the yard had all died. The tree that sat next to the house was missing all its leaves. If Mia closed her eyes, she could almost see Cecilia sitting on the tire swing, her foot bleeding as she swung back and forth.

The tree they'd used to hang people during the Salem Witch Trials was dead.

Good riddance.

The darkness had damaged the neighbors' properties as well. All the trees, shrubs, and flowers up and down the street were dry and brown. Her forehead furrowed as she realized there weren't any signs of life in the homes either. There were no lights on, no cars parked on the street. Even though most of the people who lived in the area were Commons, they must have noticed something wasn't right and packed up and left. Either that or the Assembly came into town and did some spell work to get the Commons away from the Raillive house. Maybe they had told them there was a gas leak or something.

Or maybe Cecilia's neighbors were out participating in the current chaos.

The niggling feeling under her skin grew worse. The longer Mia stood there, the more she wanted to claw her flesh off. Maybe if she entered the house, the dark energy would go with her and stop bothering Salem. It had been seeking her out all night, its true master. The picket fence that surrounded the property had yellow police tape across it, barring people from entering. Mia glanced around before hopping over the fence.

The darkness surged within her, approving of her actions. The crawling under her skin receded as her power magnified at the contact. While the dark energy had been seeping into Salem, it hadn't fully escaped yet. Most of it was still on the property and it entered Mia like the true vessel she was.

Mia closed her eyes briefly so she could picture Tilly's happy face again. With her spirit in balance, she entered the house. Her hands began to glow with a bluish hue. This time she wouldn't be caught off guard—she was ready for anything.

She crept down the basement stairs, half expecting to see a body on the large basement table. There was nothing—not a trace of blood from Colby or Mrs. Raillive. Even the table was gone.

Mia's breathing intensified as she looked around. *What am I doing here?*

As if awakening from a trance, she turned to leave.

"Hello, my love."

A chill shot down her spine. She slowly turned back toward the room. There was no one there.

"You haven't changed a bit since the last time I saw you," Cecilia's voice bounced around the room. "Of course, it was just yesterday that you saw me. For me, it's been, what? Twenty plus years?"

Mia scanned the room. "You're not really here."

"Got it in one," Cecilia said. "Oh, stop looking so scared. I'm only here to talk to you."

"Sorry for not appearing more relaxed, given that you tried to cut out my heart the last time we saw each other and you killed my friend."

"Yes, but you escaped before any real damage was done," Cecilia said, her tone casual while ignoring the reference to Colby.

Fury licked at Mia's spine. "Real damage? You tried to kill me, you psychotic bitch."

"Too soon," she whispered right next to Mia's ear. Mia whirled around. There was nothing but shadow. She thought back to when she'd faced McConnell. When Cecilia had shown up as the shadow figure, the sunlight had hurt her.

Mia stepped further into the room and lifted her arms. Using her energy, she formed a protective white ward around her, casting herself in light.

Cecilia laughed. "You weren't ready back then. I see that now. I got ahead of myself. You still have so much more to learn about your powers. Once you truly become the witch you're meant to be, then we'll see each other again."

"Is that why you planted the Book of Aradia in my room?" Mia asked, her eyes locking onto one corner of the basement where the voice was coming from. "So that I would go back in time and meet you?"

"Cute idea but you've got it wrong. Guess again." When she remained silent, Cecilia said, "Yes, it was important for you to travel back in time. It's where your journey to becoming a Desolate began. And it gave me the chance to learn all about you. For instance, I got to learn about your friend, Colby. And let's not forget about your dear sweet father's tragic death."

A sickening feeling twisted inside Mia. "What are you saying?"

"For you to become the witch you were meant to be someday, a door inside you had to be jarred opened. The earlier you began your path to your Desolate powers, the earlier you would be able to embrace them. You needed a trigger. He had to die."

It's your fault he's dead.

Mia shook her head, hoping Cecilia was lying. "You...you killed my father? Because of me?"

"I didn't kill him. Your aunt and grandmother placed so many wards and protective spells around your dad, there was no way I could get to him." A smile crept into her voice. "No, the only person who could get to your father was a family member. One whose blood matched the powers put into the spells protecting him."

The air in Mia's lungs felt like cement as she struggled to breathe. "That's bullshit. No one in my family would—"

"Not even your mother?"

Mia went rigid as shock rippled through her.

"You're an evil liar," she whispered.

The atmosphere in the basement turned icy at the mention of Cecilia's true last name.

"Ask your aunt if you don't believe me."

"My parents loved each other," she snapped.

"How would you know? You were a child when your dad died. Your mother was in love with a warlock—had been for years—but because of your grandparents' prejudices, the two weren't allowed to be together. Your mother married your father to get her parents off her back."

"Liar!" Mia screamed, the protective white line around her wavering as she lost focus.

"Ask your aunt if I'm lying," Cecilia repeated. She sighed before adding, "I wish it didn't have to be this way. I wish you hadn't had to suffer. You would have been a powerful ally if circumstances were different, and I didn't need your heart."

"I would never have joined you." She could barely speak past the emotion choking her.

Cecilia continued as if she hadn't spoken. "When you told me your dad died when you were three, I knew that was the trigger to open the Desolate power inside of you. And Sadie, so filled with injustice for the man she truly loved was only too willing to help. Unlike you, she understands my vision. She's willing to do anything to right the wrongs the Assembly has inflicted on Unmentionables since our creation. Sadie was the one who planted the Book of Aradia in your room. Only family could get around the wards your aunt and grandmother put around your house."

Mia couldn't comprehend it. Her mother had killed her father? Her voice shook as she asked, "And Colby? Why him?"

"Training. Every year I have more Unmentionables joining our revolution. They needed the experience of a sacrifice." Mia's hands balled into fists. Cecilia let out a light chuckle at her reaction before adding, "But his death was also for you. The more trauma you face, the stronger you'll become. He cried for you, you know? He was convinced you wouldn't let him down. It was all so sad and pathetic."

Mia's heart tightened painfully at that. Something black and small hit the barrier around her, testing it.

"The time is coming for the Assembly to end." Cecilia's voice grew distant as though she were walking away from Mia. "Your heart is almost ready. And then it'll be mine. Like it was always meant to be. See you soon, my love."

Some of the darkness in the room lessened. What Cecilia said couldn't be true. Her father loved Sadie. Mia only met him briefly but she could tell that.

But had Sadie ever loved her dad? She certainly hadn't loved his child enough to stick around.

Tears spilled down Mia's cheeks, slowly at first, and then steadily increased. She shook her head frantically as the truth slammed into her.

Sadie murdered her dad, and she got the idea because Mia told Cecilia about her father's boating accident.

It's your fault he's dead.

As she looked down at the dark object Cecilia had thrown at her, she saw the sunglasses Colby always wore to help with his colorblindness. Blood covered the frame.

Pain and rage decimated Mia. The white protective circle around her shattered. The darkness swarmed her as she threw her hands out, palms down, and began to absorb its energy. Centuries of pain, dating back to the deaths that took place during the Salem Witch Trials, entered Mia's system. She took it all in—all the darkness running rampant around Salem—everything, until she didn't know if she existed anymore or if she was death itself.

Her head flew back.

And Mia screamed.

CHAPTER 24

Bright blue energy burst from Mia and hit the house, making it shudder. She didn't stop releasing it, even as Cecilia's home began to cave in around her, encircling her in rubble. The crumbled remains started to vibrate, shaking hard until they turned to dust. The old tree and tire swing fell into the pit she was creating, turning into ash upon hitting the ground. The dirt pushed beneath her feet and thrust her upward until she was in the yard. Ash continued to fill the space until the basement was completely covered.

Mia didn't stop releasing the energy as the dust particles turned to mud. The mud transformed into rich, black earth. Seedlings sprouted from the ground and became grass. And still, she didn't stop until a single oak tree shot up from the grass, growing larger and taller. It formed a beautiful green canopy of leaves.

Where there was once a hideous house that symbolized pain and death, now stood a symbol of life.

Mia collapsed to the ground, crying as the dark energy dissipated completely. For the life of her, she couldn't pull up any happy memories. The depressive feeling she always got when she encountered dark energy along with a sense of mourning ate at her. A part of her wondered if she would be able to come back from this.

How could she ever find happiness again when she now had it confirmed she was responsible for her dad's death? That Colby had died because she'd been foolish enough to give her heart and secrets away to a girl who'd weaponize them.

"Mia?"

She jerked her head up, her hands ready to release whatever she had left inside. She blinked in confusion. A man in his early forties stood next to her. He was of Native American descent with black hair that was graying at the temples and dark brown eyes. It took her a second to realize she knew him. The man crouched down to her level, making sure not to touch her.

"I don't think we've ever met," the man said. "I'm—"

"Gavin Alexander," Mia said with a raw throat. "You're the Lead Examiner."

He nodded before resting his arms on his knees, taking in the tree. "That was quite some magic. Your aunt never told me you were a Desolate."

Mia tried to stand up but fell again. She wanted to throw up. Physically, she felt okay. Emotionally, she was dead inside.

"Take it easy," Gavin said. "You just cleansed the entire city."

Mia blinked at him in confusion. "I did what?"

"Look around you."

Her eyes wandered down the street. While she'd been in the house confronting Cecilia, the sun had begun to rise, bathing everything in soft morning light. The street looked lifeless when she'd entered the home, but now life had returned to the area. Grass grew in yards. Shrubs blossomed in abundance. Leaves had returned to their trees and birds chirped from their branches. The scent of flowers filled the air. It was beautiful. She turned to find Gavin staring at her.

"I've never heard of a Desolate who was able to do what you just did." He nodded toward the empty yard where the house once stood.

Mia forced herself to get up. Her legs wobbled in protest, unwilling to move. She wanted to lay down and cry. Now that it was clear Mia wasn't about to go on the defense, Gavin offered his arm, which she reluctantly took.

"Why are you here?" she asked, her throat still aching from the scream she'd released.

"Tilly told me you recently time travelled—which is highly impressive, by the way. We'll have to look into strengthening our wards in that regard. She explained that Cecilia Raillive was behind an attack that happened on some Originals in this area years ago." When Mia nodded, he said, "She also told me you had information about Ms. Raillive that I should know."

"Yeah," Mia replied.

As they walked slowly back to *Fitzgerald's Tea & Gifts*, she told him everything she knew about Cecilia. She left out some details, such as what Cecilia had said about the corruption at the Assembly. If the warlock actually had been telling the truth for once in her life, and higher ups in the government were capturing and selling off Others to the highest bidder, Mia needed to know that Gavin wasn't a part of it.

The Examiner's face was hard by the time they made it back to her house. They entered the kitchen to find Tilly at the stove with her back to them. She wore her favorite pink robe and a pair of bunny slippers. Mia had bought the slippers for her as a gift when she was a kid. They'd seen better days, but her aunt never had the heart to throw them out. Winnie lay on the large dog bed they kept in the kitchen, her tail wagging lazily when she saw them.

"Aunt Tilly?" she said.

Her aunt whirled around, spatula in hand.

"Mia, I thought you were in bed. I..." Her eyes grew wide as she noticed the Lead Examiner standing there. She reached up to pat her hair into something that didn't look like crazy bedhead. "Gavin, what... What are you doing here?"

"I got your message about Mia," he said, his mouth quirking as he took in her mortified expression.

"Does that mean—?"

"Aunt Tilly," Mia said in a rush, because she had to know. "How did my dad really die?"

Tilly frowned in confusion. "You know how. He died in a boating accident."

"But how did he get on the water? You said you put protection spells on him."

"We did. Your grandma and I both did."

"The only person who could get around those kinds of spells would need to be someone with the same blood inside them, right? Like another family member?"

"In theory but... Mia, where are you going with this?"

Mia walked over to a kitchen chair and clutched the back of it. "My mother could have broken the spells."

Tilly immediately shook her head. "Sadie would never do anything like that. My sister isn't perfect by any means, but she's not a killer."

Mia looked her dead in the eye. "Tell me the truth. Was my mother ever in love with a warlock?"

Her aunt's eyebrows shot up. "How do you know about that?"

"I ran into Cecilia this morning. She told me."

"You ran into..." She looked like she either wanted to throttle Mia for leaving the house or hug her close. "Sadie might be many things, but I can't believe she would have hurt your dad."

"Please tell me the truth," Mia repeated. "Was my mother in love with a warlock?"

Tilly's whole body seemed to tighten as she confessed, "There was this one boy around about the same time you showed up in 1992. I don't remember much about him except he had horrible burns on his skin."

Mia's breath caught. "McConnell."

"That's it." Tilly's eyes narrowed. "How do you know that name?"

"I'm the one who gave him those burns." She sat down in the chair, feeling numb. "My mother killed my father."

"No." Her aunt walked over and wrapped her arm around Mia's shoulder. A feeling of safety flowed over her. The remaining emotional suffering from the darkness abated a little and some of her strength returned.

Tilly still insisted, "Sadie wouldn't have done that."

"She was the one who planted the Book of Aradia in my room. They *wanted* me to go back in time. I met the younger version of Cecilia and told her all kinds of personal information about myself. I told her about Colby getting kidnapped. That's why she went after him. She knew I was a Desolate, and she wanted to keep stoking my power. She also knew that my dad's death started my Desolate powers because I told her he'd drowned in a boating accident when I was a kid. The only person who could have gotten around your wards to get to my dad and plant that book in my room was Sadie."

Tilly shook her head in denial, even as tears started to run down her cheeks.

Gavin cleared his throat "Tilly..."

Her aunt looked at him, her eyes becoming red-rimmed.

His face was full of remorse as he said, "This was going to come out soon anyway... I don't know how to tell you this, but we've been investigating Sadie for some time. She has repeatedly posted information on Common websites exposing our world, and we have proof that she's behind the kidnapping of Colby Mond." He hesitated. "The Assembly has begun formal proceedings to recognize Sadie Fitzgerald as a warlock."

"You can't do that." Tilly hurried over to Gavin and grabbed his arm, her face pleading. "If you do that, Mia will inherit the title and will also be considered a warlock."

Mia shot out of her chair, looking from Gavin to her aunt. She was about to formally become an outcast. If she became an Unmentionable, she wouldn't be able to stay with Tilly. Others would turn their back on her. She'd be easy pickings for Cecilia.

"You raised her, Tilly," Gavin said gently to her aunt before turning to her. "Mia, you can file paperwork with the Assembly asking for emancipation from Sadie."

"You know those cases are rarely recognized by the Assembly," Tilly argued.

"That's because most of those children have already been raised in a warlock household, subjected to the same corruption as their parents."

Mia stared unseeingly in front of her. No wonder Unmentionables were pissed off at the Assembly. If they were made to feel like outcasts all their lives because of their parents' mistakes... Mia started to reconsider the drive behind their motivation.

The Lead Examiner continued, "I'll offer myself as a witness to Mia's character. She'll be formerly recognized as your daughter."

Tilly walked over to him and pulled him into a hug. "Thank you, Gavin."

He hugged her back, regret and tenderness crossing his face. Mia looked away, giving them a moment. Gavin eventually stepped away from Tilly and turned to her. "The Assembly offers a summer apprenticeship program. We could really use someone with your talents on our team. You're welcome to join us over your break."

"You want Mia to join the Assembly?" her aunt repeated, her face draining of color.

"With your permission, of course." Gavin touched Tilly on the shoulder. "To be honest, I've never seen anyone with Mia's abilities before. The Raillive house has been a problem for the Assembly for years, and with a sweep of her hands, Mia cleansed dark energy from the entire city. The house is gone."

"She did what?" Tilly asked, looking at her niece. "Elizabeth Parris couldn't even do that."

Gavin nodded toward Mia. "We could really use her help." His face lost some of its seriousness as he looked at Tilly. "Does she have your permission?"

Her aunt eyed her, her features sad and proud. "Mia's one of the strongest people I know. It's her decision, not mine."

A slight smile tugged on his lips as he stared at her before he coughed and turned his attention back to Mia. "What do you say?"

"I don't have very good control of my powers yet. I could really hurt someone."

He nodded thoughtfully. "There's someone on my team I'd like you to meet. Her name's Tara. She's a Desolate about your age, but she's been dealing with dark energy for a while now. She's actually the one who found Mr. Mond and helped stem some of the dark energy from pouring into the city. She could teach you a thing or two."

Mia glanced from the Lead Examiner, trying not to get hopeful, and then back to her aunt. Reality crashed down on her. If she left Salem, her aunt would be all alone to take care of her grandma.

"I can see what you're thinking," Tilly said. "Don't even think about staying here because of me. If you want to go, it'll be a great opportunity for you."

"You can train with me," Gavin added.

That piqued Mia's interest. He was one of the most powerful witches known in the Other world. If anyone could teach Mia the skills she needed to defeat Cecilia, it was Gavin Alexander. Plus, she really wanted to meet the other Desolate, not to mention Ailsa would be at the Assembly for the summer. At least she would know someone there. But the idea of leaving Tilly and everything she knew to go study in New York made her nervous. She wanted to keep the people she cared about close in case Cecilia tried to take her away from them again.

Gavin reached inside his coat pocket and pulled out his phone. He pressed the home screen and scrolled until he found what he was looking for.

"Under Other law, you're considered an adult," Gavin said to Mia. "As such, I'm going to always respect and treat you like one. If you join my team, it won't be easy. Especially in my department. You'll see the very worst this world has to offer. Are you able to handle that?"

"I saw a bunch of warlocks eating a person," she said. "What do you think?"

Gavin's face was somber as he set the phone down.

Mia held her breath as she looked at the picture on display. It had been years since she'd seen her mother last. She barely remembered her. The woman in the picture bore little resemblance to the Sadie Mia knew. Her face was harder, the lines on her face, deeper. Her long red hair flew in every direction. A man stood at her side, his arm wrapped around her waist. Fury infused inside Mia as she recognized McConnell. He still bore the burn scars from their last encounter. They were both laughing in the picture as they spoke to another man wearing the standard warlock robe. The hooded figure had a pixie in his hand, squeezing her neck so hard that one of her eyes had popped out.

Tilly walked over to see what was in the picture and covered her mouth in shock.

"We could use your help finding dark energy users," Gavin told Mia. "As I mentioned, you have powers I've never quite seen before. Your abilities can help us stop them before they hurt anyone else."

She understood what the Lead Examiner was getting at. He wouldn't have showed her that particular picture for nothing. "You want my help hunting down my mother?"

He nodded. "We believe she's second in command to a person they call the Commander... Cecilia." He picked up his phone and looked at the picture, his expression turning sad. "This pixie did nothing wrong other than be in the wrong place at the wrong time. She died for no reason. Help us. Please. Before they can do any further damage."

Mia stared at the phone, unable to get the image of her mom's smiling face out of her head. She looked happy, living her life without a single concern.

Mia's dad died a horrible death, all so Sadie could help trigger her Desolate powers. She then ran off with the man who'd tried to kill her own daughter. Cecilia may have put the orders in place to destroy Mia's life, but Sadie... Sadie took everything from her.

"Mia, what do you say?" Gavin asked.

She looked up at the Lead Examiner, her decision made.

"When do I start?"

"Honey, are you sure about this?" Aunt Tilly asked.

"Grandma told me being a Desolate is a gift and responsibility." She remembered Grandma Eabha's confidence in her that day at the cemetery. The memory balanced her, helping calm some of the fury inside. She gave her aunt a grim smile. "I'm sure."

"Okay." Tilly looked at Gavin. "Stay for breakfast?"

Mia didn't listen to his reply. She walked over to the kitchen window and lifted the frame.

The future was uncertain, but she was eager to face it. She would learn everything she could to stop Cecilia and her mother. If they wanted to face a powerful Desolate, she'd make sure that's what happened.

But no matter what, Mia would use her Desolate power to become the protector she was meant to be. It was her responsibility, just like her grandma said.

She once wished that she had some life goals. Some type of purpose. Mia knew what her purpose was now. She would destroy Cecilia and her organization if it was the last thing she ever did.

The cool, rejuvenating air of the harbor brushed against her face.

And Mia breathed.

Acknowledgements

First, I need to thank Stephanie Winter, who was the first person in the publishing industry to not only believe in *Desolate*, but also to see potential in me as an author. I'd like to thank Natalie Day, whose suggestions and edits helped strengthen *Desolate* into a story that could be published (and thank you for being *Desolate*'s first fan). Thanks to Galen Surlak-Ramsey and the rest of the Tiny Fox team for giving *Desolate* a chance.

I need to thank and acknowledge my friend, Sarah Kaake. Sarah, I'm so glad a slow day in the office led to a conversation about your writing group. If you hadn't encouraged me to attend a meeting—and if you hadn't been willing to give me feedback on my drafts—none of this would have happened.

I want to thank my writing group for helping me become a writer capable of landing a publishing deal, and for teaching me the difference between "show, don't tell."

Finally, I want to thank my family. Thank you to my mom, who I miss every day. She typed up my first story when I was in second grade, and she not only encouraged me to read, but also took me on special trips to the bookstore so I could pick out another book. Thank you to my dad, who was a rock when I felt lost. And thanks to my brother and sister for their constant support.

About the Author

When the 2008 recession hit, Kelli Storm found herself without a job and with too much time on her hands. To fill the void, she began writing fan fiction. She soon developed a following, and her readers encouraged her to write an original story. Kelli's debut book, His Small-Town Challenge, is an ode to her love of boy bands.

Kelli graduated with a bachelor's from Grand Valley State University, and resides in the Great Lake State with her three rescue dogs and a fifteen-year-old fish named Henry O'Malley.

ABOUT THE PUBLISHER

Tiny Fox Press LLC
11782 Little River Way
Parrish, Fl 34219

www.ingramcontent.com/pod-product-compliance
Lightning Source LLC
Chambersburg PA
CBHW060705190726
48289CB00002B/553